T0314775

A Tale of Brittany

This tale of Breton peasant life, with its simple joys and sorrows, is beautifully told. There are grim and sordid scenes at Brest showing the temptations that lie in wait for the sailor as he comes ashore, and the sufferings of the wives living in the seaport, and of course there are characteristic description of the Breton country-side. Parallel with these there are descriptions of life in a warship during its cruise about the world.

Pierre Loti, perhaps the world's most prolific, romantic and exotic travel writer and novelist, was born as Julien Marie Viaud in Rochefort in Western France in 1850. A childhood fascination with exotic lands across the seas led him to embark on a naval career that enabled him to seek love and adventure in many latitudes. He drew on these real life experiences when writing the romantic novels and travel books that made him one of the most popular authors of his day. Although his prolific output brought him both fame and fortune he remained a romantic escapist and never gave up his beloved naval career. He retired from the French navy in 1910 and died in 1923.

The Pierre Loti Library

A Tale of

Brittany

Pierre Loti

Routledge
Taylor & Francis Group

LONDON AND NEW YORK

First published in 2002 by
Kegan Paul International

This edition first published in 2011 by
Routledge
2 Park Square, Milton Park, Abingdon, Oxon, OX14 4RN

Simultaneously published in the USA and Canada
by Routledge
711 Third Avenue, New York, NY 10017

Routledge is an imprint of the Taylor & Francis Group, an informa business

British Library Cataloguing in Publication Data
A catalogue record for this book is available from the British Library

ISBN 10: 0-7103-0863-9 (hbk)
ISBN 13: 978-0-7103-0863-4 (hbk)

Publisher's Note
The publisher has gone to great lengths to ensure the quality of this reprint
but points out that some imperfections in the original copies may be
apparent. The publisher has made every effort to contact original copyright
holders and would welcome correspondence from those they have been
unable to trace.

DEDICATION

To ALPHONSE DAUDET

Here is a little tale which I wish to dedicate to you. Accept it, I pray, with my affection.

It has been urged against my books that there is always in them too much of the trouble of love. This time there is only a little love and that an honest love and it comes only towards the end.

It was you who gave me the idea of writing the life story of a sailor and of putting into it the immense monotony of the sea.

It may be that this book will make me enemies, although I have touched as lightly as possible on the regulations of the service. But you who love everything connected with the sea, even the wind and the fog and the great waves—yes, and the brave and simple sailors—you, assuredly, will understand me. And in that I shall find my recompense.

PIERRE LOTI.

A TALE OF BRITTANY

CHAPTER I

THE pay-book of my brother Yves differs in no wise from the pay-book of all other sailors.

It is covered with a yellow-coloured parchment paper and, as it has travelled much about the sea, in many a ship's locker, it is absolutely wanting in freshness.

In large letters on the cover appears:

KERMADEC, 2091. P.

Kermadec is his family name; 2091, his number in the army of the sea; and P., the initial letter of Paimpol, the port at which he was enrolled.

Opening the book, one finds, on the first page, the following description:

"Kermadec (Yves-Marie), son of Yves-Marie and Jeanne Danveoch. Born 28 August, 1851, at Saint Pol-de-Léon (Finistère). Height 5 ft. 11 inches. Hair brown, eyebrows brown, eyes brown, nose ordinary, chin ordinary, forehead ordinary, face oval.

"Distinctive marks: tattooed on the left breast

with an anchor and, on the right **wrist**, with a bracelet in the form of a fish."

These tattooings were still the fashion, some ten years ago, for your true sailor.   Executed on board the *Flore* by a friend in an hour of idleness, they became an object of mortification for Yves, who many a time had tortured himself in an effort to obliterate them.   The idea that he was marked in this indelible manner, and that he might be recognized always and everywhere by these little blue designs was to him absolutely insupportable.

Turning over the page one comes across a series of printed leaves setting out, in a clear and concise form, all the shortcomings to which sailors are subject, with, opposite them, the tariff of the penalties incurred—from insignificant irregularities which may be expiated by a few nights in irons to the dire rebellions which are punished by death.

Unhappily this quotidian reading has never sufficed to inspire the salutary awe which it should, either in sailors in general, or in my poor Yves in particular.

Follow several pages of manuscript containing the names of ships, with blue stamp impressions, figures and dates.   The quartermasters, men of taste as they are, have decorated this part of the book with elegant flourishes.   It is here that particulars of his voyages are set out and details of the pay he has received.

The first years, in which he earned fifteen francs a month, ten of which he saved for his mother; years passed in the onrush of the wind, in which he lived half naked at the top of those great oscillating shafts which are the masts of ships; years in which he wandered without a care in the world over the changing desert of the sea; then the more troubled years in which love was born and took shape in the virgin and untutored heart—to be translated into brutal orgies or into dreams naïvely pure according to the hazard of the places to which the wind drove him, according to the hazard of the women thrown into his arms; terrible awakenings of the heart and senses, wild excesses, and then the return to the ascetic life of the ocean, to the sequestration on the floating monastery; all this may be divined behind these figures and these names and dates which accumulate, year by year, in the poor little pay-book of a sailor. A whole poem of strange adventures and sufferings lies within its yellow pages.

CHAPTER II

THE 28th of August, 1851, was, it seems, a fine summer's day at Saint Pol-de-Léon, in Finistère.

The pale sun of Brittany smiled and made festival for this little newcomer, who later on was to love the sun so much, and to love Brittany so much.

Yves made his entrance into the world in the form of a large baby, very round and very brown.

The good women present at his arrival gave him the name of *Bugel-Du*, which in English means: little black boy. This bronzed colouring was, for that matter, characteristic of the family, the Kermadecs from father to son, having been ocean-going sailors and men deeply bitten by the tan of the sea.

A fine summer's day in Saint Pol-de-Léon is a rare thing in this region of fogs: a kind of melancholy radiance is shed over everything; the old town of the Middle Ages is, as it were, awakened out of its mournful slumber in the mist and made young again; the old granite warms itself in the sun; the tower of Creizker, the giant of Breton towers, bathes in the blue sky, in the full light, its delicate grey fretwork marbled with yellow lichens. And all around is the wild moorland, with its pink heather, its golden gorse, exhaling a soft perfume of flowering broom.

At the baptism were a young girl, the godmother; a sailor, the godfather; and, behind, the two little brothers, Goulven and Gildas, holding by the hand the two little sisters, Yvonne and Marie, who carried flowers.

When the little company entered the old church of the bishops of Léon, the verger, hanging on the rope of a bell, made ready to start the joyous carillon called for by the occasion. But the Curé, coming on the scene, said to him harshly:

" Be quiet, Marie Bervrac'h, for the love of God! These Kermadecs are people who never give anything to the Church, and the father wastes all his substance in the tavern. We'll have no ringing, if you please, for people of that sort."

And that is how my brother Yves made his entrance into the world in the guise of poverty.

Jeanne Danveoch, from her bed, listened with uneasiness, waited with a foreboding of ill, for the vibrations of the bell which were so slow to begin. For a long time she listened and heard nothing. Then she understood the public affront and wept.

Her eyes were wet with tears when the party returned, crestfallen, to the house.

All his life this humiliation weighed upon the heart of Yves; he was never able to forgive this unkind reception at his entrance into the world, nor the cruel tears shed by his mother; and as a result he preserved for the Roman clergy an unforgetting rancour and closed his Breton heart to Our Mother the Church.

CHAPTER III

IT was twenty-four years later, on an evening of December, at Brest.

A fine rain was falling, cold, penetrating, continuous; it streamed down the walls, rendering deeper in colour the high-pitched roofs of slate, and the tall houses of granite; it watered with calm indifference the noisy crowd of the Sunday, which swarmed nevertheless, wet and bedraggled, in the narrow streets, beneath the mournful grey of the twilight.

This Sunday crowd consisted of inebriated sailors singing, of soldiers who stumbled, making with their sabres a clatter of steel, of people of the lower class adrift—workers of the town looking drawn and miserable; women in little merino shawls and pointed muslin head-dresses, who walked along with shining eyes and reddened cheek bones, exhaling an odour of brandy; of old men and old women in a disgusting state of drunkenness, who had fallen and been picked up, and were lurching forward, on their way, with backs covered with mud.

The rain continued to fall, wetting everything, the silver-buckled hats of the Bretons, the tilted bonnets of the sailors, the laced shakos and the white head-dresses, and the umbrellas.

There was something so wan, so dead, about the air, that it was difficult to imagine that there could be anywhere a sun . . . the notion of it had gone. There was a feeling that you were imprisoned under layers and thicknesses of dense, humid clouds which were deluging you. It did not seem that they would ever be able to break, or that behind them there could be a sky. You breathed water. You were no longer conscious of the hour, and knew not whether the darkness was the darkness of all this rain or whether the real winter's night was closing in.

The sailors brought into the streets a certain rather surprising note of gaiety and youth, with their cheery faces and their songs, with their large bright collars and their red pompoms standing out in sharp contrast with the navy blue of their uniform. They went and came from one tavern to another, jostling the crowd, saying things which had no sense but which made them laugh. And sometimes they stopped on the footpath, before the stalls of the shops where were retailed the hundred and one things they needed for their use: red handkerchiefs, in the middle of which were imprinted designs of famous ships, *Bretagne, Triomphante, Devastation*; ribbons for their bonnets with handsome inscriptions in gold; cords of complicated workmanship destined to close securely those canvas sacks which they have on board for storing their kit; elegant attachments in plaited thread for suspending from the neck of the topmen their large knives; silver whistles for the petty-officers, and finally, red belts and little combs and little mirrors.

From time to time came heavy squalls which sent bonnets flying and made the drunken passers-by stagger. And then the rain came down more heavily, more torrentially, and whipped like hail..

The crowd of sailors steadily increased. They could be seen coming on in groups at the end of the Rue de Siam; they ascended from the port and from the lower town by the great granite stairways, and spread singing into the streets.

Those who came from the roadstead were wetter than the others, dripping with sea-water as well as with rain. The sailing cutters, bending to the cold squalls, leaping amid waves deep-edged with spray, had brought them quickly into port. And joyously they climbed the steps which led to the town, shaking themselves as cats do which have been sprinkled with water.

The wind rushed through the long drab streets, and the night promised to be a wild one.

In the roadstead—on board a ship which had arrived that very morning from South America—on

the stroke of four o'clock, a petty officer had given
a prolonged whistle, followed by cleverly executed
trills, which signified in the language of the sea:
"Man the launch!"   Then a murmur of joy was
heard in the ship, where the sailors were penned, on
account of the rain, in the gloom of the spar-deck.
For there had been a fear for a time that the sea
might be too rough for communication with Brest,
and the men had been waiting anxiously for this
whistle which set their doubts at rest. For the first
time, after three years of voyage, they were about
to set foot on the land of France, and impatience
was great.

When the men appointed, clothed in little
costumes of yellow oilskin, were all embarked in
the launch and had taken their places in correct and
symmetrical order, the same petty officer whistled
again and said: "Liberty-men, fall in!"

The wind and the sea made a great noise; the
distances of the roadstead were drowned in a whitish
fog made of spray and rain.

The sailors who had received permission to go
ashore ascended quickly, issued from the hatches
and took their places in line, as their numbers and
names were called, with faces beaming with the joy
of seeing Brest again.   They had put on their
Sunday clothes; they completed, under the torren-
tial downpour, the last details of their toilet, setting
one another right with airs of coquetry.

When "218: Kermadec!" was called, Yves
appeared, a strapping youngster of twenty-four,
grave in mien, looking very well in his ribbed
woollen jersey and his large blue collar.

Tall, lean with the leanness of the ancients, with

the muscular arms and the neck and shoulders of an athlete, his whole appearance gave an impression of tranquil and slightly disdainful strength. His face, beneath its uniform coat of bronze, was colourless; in some subtle way impossible to define, a Breton face, with the complexion of an Arab. Curt in speech, with the accent of Finistère; a low voice curiously vibrant, recalling those instruments of very powerful sound, which one touches only very lightly for fear of making too much noise.

Hazel eyes, rather close together and very deep-set beneath the frontal bone, with the impassive expression of a regard turned inwards; the nose small and regular in shape; the lower lip protruding slightly as if in scorn.

The face immobile, marmorean, save in those rare moments when he smiles. Then the whole face is transformed, and one sees that Yves is very young. The smile itself is the smile of those who have suffered: it has a childlike gentleness and lights up the hardened features a little as the rays of the sun, falling by chance, light up the cliffs of Brittany.

When Yves appeared the other sailors who were there regarded him with good-humoured smiles and an unusual air of respect.

This was because he wore for the first time on his sleeve the two red stripes of a petty officer, which had just been awarded him. And on board ship a petty officer is a person of consequence. These poor woollen stripes, which, in the army, are given so quickly to the first comer, represent in the navy years of hardship; they represent the strength and the life of young men, expended at every hour of the day and night, high up in the crow's nest, that

B

domain of the topmen which is shaken by all the winds of heaven.

The boatswain, coming up, held out his hand to Yves. Formerly he also had been a topmen inured to hardness, and he was a shrewd judge of strong and courageous men.

"Well, Kermadec," he said. "You are going to water those stripes of yours, I suppose?"

"Yes, bo'sun," replied Yves in a low voice, but preserving a grave and abstracted air.

It was not the rain from heaven that the old boatswain had in mind; for, as far as that went, the watering was assured. No, in the navy, to water your stripes means to get drunk in order to do them honour on the first day they are worn.

Yves remained thoughtful in the face of the necessity of this ceremony, because he had just sworn to me very solemnly that he would be sober, and he wanted to keep his promise.

And then he had had enough, at last, of these tavern scenes which had been repeated so many times in all the countries of the world. To spend one's nights in low pot-houses, at the head of the wildest and most drunken of the crew, and to be picked up in the gutter in the morning—one tires of these pleasures after a time, however good a sailor one may be. Besides the mornings following are painful and are always the same; and Yves knew that and wanted no more of them.

It was very gloomy, this December weather, for a day of return. Of no avail was it to be carefree and young, the weather cast over the joy of homecoming a kind of sinister night. Yves experienced this impression, which caused him, in spite of himself, a mournful surprise; for all this, in sum, was his own Brittany; he felt it in the air and recognised it despite this darkness of dreamland.

The launch moved off, carrying them all towards the shore. It travelled aslant under the west wind; it bounded over the waves with the hollow sound of a drum, and, at each leap that it made, a mass of water broke over them, as if it had been hurled by furious hands.

They made their way very rapidly in a kind of cloud of water, the large salt drops of which lashed their faces. They bowed their heads before this deluge, huddled close one against the other, like sheep in a storm.

They did not speak, all concentrated as they were on the prospect of the pleasure that awaited them. There were among them young men, who, for a year past, had not set foot on land; the pockets of all of them were well-lined with money, and fierce desires bubbled in their blood.

Yves himself thought a little of the women who were waiting for them in Brest, and from among whom presently they would be able to choose. But, nevertheless, he was gloomy, he alone of all the band. Never had so many thoughts at one time troubled the head of this poor simpleton.

It is true that he had had melancholy moods of this kind sometimes, during the silence of the nights at sea; but then the return had appeared to him from the distance in colours of rose and gold. And here, to-day, was the return and, on the contrary, his heart was sadder now than it had ever been before. And this he did not understand, for he had the habit, as the simple and as children have, of suffering his impressions without attempting to interpret them.

With head turned towards the wind, heedless of the water which streamed down his blue collar, he had remained standing, supported by the group of sailors who pressed close against him.

All this coast-line of Brest, which could be distinguished in vague contours through the veil of the rain, awoke in him memories of his years as ship-boy, passed here on this great misty roadstead, pining for his mother. . . . This past had been rough, and, for the first time in his life, his thoughts turned to what the future might be.

His mother! . . . It was true indeed that for nearly two years he had not written to her.   But that is the way with sailors; and, in spite of all, these mothers of theirs are very dear to them. What usually happens is this: they disappear for a few years, and then, one happy day, they return, without warning, to the village, with stripes on their sleeve and pockets full of hard-earned money, and bring back happiness and comfort to the old forsaken home.

They sped on through the freezing rain, leaping over the grey waves, pursued by the whistling of the wind and the roar of the water.

Yves was thinking of many things, and his fixed eyes now saw nothing.   The image of his mother had all at once taken on an infinite tenderness; he felt that she was now quite near to him, in a little Breton village, under this same winter twilight which enveloped him; in two or three days from now, he would go, with an overmastering joy, to surprise her and take her in his arms.

The tossing of the sea, the wind and speed, rendered his changing thoughts incoherent. At one moment he was disconcerted to find his country under a sky so gloomy. During his voyage he had become used to the heat and blue clearness of the tropics, and, here, it seemed that there was a shroud casting a sinister night over the world.

And a little later he was telling himself that he did not want to drink any more, not that there was any harm in it after all, and, in any case, it was the custom among Breton sailors; but, first of all, he had given me his word, and secondly, at twenty-four, one is a grown man and has had a full draught of pleasure, and it seems that one feels the need of becoming a little more steady.

Then he thought of the astonished looks of the others on board, especially of Barrada, his great friend, when they saw him return to-morrow morning, upright and walking straight. At this comical idea, a childlike smile passed suddenly over his grave and manly face.

They had now arrived almost under the Castle of Brest and, in the shelter of the enormous masses of granite, there was suddenly calm. The cutter no longer rocked; it proceeded tranquilly through the rain; its sails were hauled down, and the men in yellow oilskins took over its management with rhythmic strokes of their long oars.

Before them opened that deep and dismal bay which is the naval port; on the quays were alignments of cannon and of formidable-looking maritime things. All around nothing but high and interminable constructions of granite, all alike, overhanging the dark water and staged one above the other with rows of little doors and little windows.   Above these again, the first houses of Brest and Recouvrance showed their wet roofs, from which issued little trails of white smoke.   They proclaimed their damp and cold misery, and the wind rushed all about with a great dismal moaning.

It was now quite dark and the little gas flames began to pink with bright yellow dots these accumulations of dark things.   The sailors could already hear the rumbling of the traffic and the noise of the town which came to them from above the deserted dockyard, mingled with the songs of drunken men.

Yves, out of prudence, had entrusted to his friend Barrada on board all his money, which he was saving for his mother, keeping in his pocket only fifty francs for his night ashore.

CHAPTER IV

" AND my husband also, Madame Quéméneur, when he is drunk, sleeps all day long."

" So you have come out too, Madame Kervella? "

" Yes, I also am waiting for my husband, who arrived to-day on the *Catinat*."

" And my man, Madame Kerdoncuff, the day he returned from China, slept for two whole days; and I, you know, got drunk too, Madame Kerdoncuff.

Oh! and how ashamed of myself I was! And my daughter, also, she fell down the stairs!"

And these things, spoken in the singing and musical accent of Brest, are exchanged under old umbrellas straining in the wind, between women in waterproofs and pointed muslin head-dresses, who are waiting above, at the top of the wide granite steps.

Their husbands have come on that same boat which has brought Yves, and their wives are waiting for them; fortified already by a little brandy, they are on the watch, their eyes half merry and half tender.

These old sailors whom they await were once perhaps gallant topmen inured to hardship; but demoralized by their sojourns in Brest and by drunkenness, they have married these creatures and sunk into the sordid slums of the town.

Behind these women there are other groups again on which the eye rests with pleasure; young women of quiet mien, real sailors' wives these, wrapt in the joy of seeing once more a sweetheart or a husband, and gazing with anxiety into the great yawning cavern of the port, out of which their beloved ones will come to them. And there are mothers, come from the villages, wearing their pretty Breton festival dresses, the wide coif and the gown of black silk embroidered cloth; the rain will spoil them to be sure, these fine trappings, which are renewed perhaps not more than twice in a lifetime; but it is necessary to do honour to this son whom presently they will embrace before the others.

"See there! The men from the *Magicien* are now entering the harbour, Madame Kerdoncuff!"

" And those from the *Catinat* also, do you
see! They are following one another, Madame
Quéméneur!"

Below, deep down, the launches come alongside
the black quay, and those who are awaited are
among the first to ascend.

First the husbands of these good ladies. Way
for the seniors, let them pass out first! Tar, and
wind and sun and brandy have given them the
wrinkled physiognomies of monkeys. . . . And they
go their way, arm in arm, in the direction of
Recouvrance, to some gloomy old street of tall
granite houses; presently they will climb to a damp
room which smells of gutters and the mustiness of
poverty, where on the furniture are shell ornaments
covered with dust and bottles pell-mell with strange
knick-knacks. And thanks to the alcohol bought at
the tavern below, they will find oblivion of this cruel
separation in a renewal of their youth.

Then come the others, the young men for whom
sweethearts are waiting, and wives and old mothers,
and, at last, four by four, climbing the granite steps,
the whole band of wild lads, whom Yves is taking to
celebrate his stripes.

And those who are waiting for them, for this little
band of hot-blooded youth, are in the Rue de Sept
Saints, already at their door and on the watch:
women whose hair is worn with a fringe combed
down to the eyebrows—with tipsy voices and
horrible gestures.

Before the night is out, these women will have
their strength, their restrained passions—and their
money. For your sailormen pay well on the day
of their return, and over and above what they give,

there is what one may take afterwards, when by good luck they are quite drunk.

They look about them undecided, almost bewildered, drunk already merely from finding themselves on shore.

Where should they go? How should they begin their pleasures? This wind, this cold rain of winter and this sinister fall of the night—for those who have a home, a fireside, all that adds to the joy of the return. To these poor fellows it brought the need for a shelter, for somewhere where they could warm themselves; but they were without a home, these returning exiles.

At first they wandered at hazard, linked arm in arm, laughing at nothing, at everything, walking obliquely from right and left—with the movements of captive beasts which have just been set free.

Then they entered *A la Descente des Navires*, presided over by Madame Creachcadec.

A la Descente des Navires was a low tavern in the Rue de Siam.

The warm atmosphere savoured of alcohol. There was a coal fire in a brazier, and Yves sat down in front of it. This was the first time, for two or three years past, that he had sat in a chair. And a real fire! How he revelled in the quite unusual luxury of drying himself before glowing coals. On board ship, there was never a chance of it; not even in the great cold of Cape Horn or of Iceland; not even in the persistent, penetrating rains of the high latitudes were they ever able to dry themselves. For days and nights on end, they remained wet through; doing their best to keep on the move, until the sun should shine.

She was a real mother to the sailors, was this Madame Creachcadec; all who knew her could vouch for it. And she was very exact, too, in the prices she charged for their dinners and their feastings.

Besides, she knew them.   Her large red face flushed already with alcohol, she tried to repeat their names, which she heard them saying among themselves; she remembered quite well having seen them when they were boatmen on board the *Bretagne*; she even thought she could recall their boyhood, when they were ship-boys on the *Inflexible*.   But what tall, fine fellows they had grown since those days!   Truly it was only an eye like hers that could recognize them, altered as they were. . . .

And, at the back of the tavern, the dinner was cooking, on stoves which already sent out an appetising odour of soup.

From the street came sounds of a great uproar. A band of sailors was approaching, singing, scanning at the top of their voices, to a frivolous air, these words of the Church: *Kyrie Christe, Dominum nostrum; Kyrie eleison.* . . .

They entered, upsetting the chairs, and at the same time a gust of wind laid low the flame of the lamps.

Kyrie Christe, Dominum nostrum. . . . The Bretons did not like this kind of song, brought no doubt from the back streets of some great city.   But the discordance between the words and the music was so droll, it made them laugh.

The newcomers, however, were from the *Gauloise*, and recognized, and were recognized by, the others; they had all been ship-boys together.

One of them hastened to embrace Yves: it was Kerboul who had slept in the next hammock to him on board the *Inflexible*. He, too, had become tall and strong; he was on the flagship, and, as he was a steady sort of fellow, he had for a long time worn red stripes on his sleeve.

The air in the tavern was oppressive and there was a great deal of noise. Madame Creachcadec brought hot wine all steaming, the preliminary to the dinner that had been ordered, and heads began to swim.

There was commotion this night in Brest: the patrols were kept busy.

In the Rue de Sept Saints and in the Rue de Saint Yves, singing and shouting went on until the morning; it was as if barbarians had been loosed there, bands escaped from ancient Gaul; there were scenes of rejoicing that recalled the boisterousness of primitive times.

The sailors sang. And the women, their fingers itching for the pieces of gold—agitated, dishevelled in this great excitation of the sailors' homecoming—mingled their shrill voices with the deep voices of the men.

The latest arrivals from the sea might be recognized by their deeper tint of bronze, by their freer carriage; and then they carried with them objects of foreign origin; some of them passed with bedraggled parakeets in cages; others with monkeys.

They sang, these sailors, at the top of their voices, with a kind of naïve expression, things that made one shudder, or perhaps little airs of the south, songs of the Basque country, and, above all, they sang mournful Breton melodies which seemed like old bagpipe airs bequeathed from Celtic antiquity.

The simple, the good, sang part songs together; they remained grouped by village, and repeated in their native tongue the long laments of the country, preserving even in their drunkenness their fine resonant young voices. Others stuttered like little children and embraced one another; unconscious of their strength they smashed doors and knocked down passers-by.

The night was advancing; only places of ill-repute remained open; and in the streets the rain continued to fall on the exuberance of these wild rejoicings.

CHAPTER V

Six o'clock on the following morning. A dark mass having the form of a man in the gutter—by the side of a kind of deserted street overhung by ramparts. It is still dark. The rain still falls, fine and cold; and the winter wind continues to roar. It had "watched," as they say in the navy, and passed the night in groaning.

It was in the lower part of the town, a little below the bridge of Brest, at the foot of the great walls, in that locality where sailors commonly find themselves, who are without a home and who have had the vague intention, blind drunk as they were, of returning to their ship and have fallen en route.

There is already a kind of half light in the air; a wan, pallid light, the light of a winter's day rising on granite. Water was streaming over this human form which lay on the ground, and, right at its side, poured in a cascade into the opening of a drain.

It began to get a little brighter; a sort of light made up its mind to descend along the high granite walls. The dark thing in the gutter was now clearly seen to be the body of a tall man, a sailor, lying with arms outstretched in the form of a cross.

A first passer-by made a sound of wooden sabots on the hard pavé, as of someone staggering. Then another, then many. They followed all the same direction in a lower street which led to the gate of the naval dockyard.

Soon this tapping of sabots became a thing extraordinary; a fatiguing, continuous noise, hammering the silence like a nightmare music.

Hundreds and hundreds of sabots, tramping before daylight, coming from everywhere, and passing along the street below; a kind of early morning procession of evil import: it was the workers returning to the dockyard, still staggering from having drank so much the night before, the gait unsteady, the eyes lustreless.

And there were women also, ugly, pale, and wet, who went to right and left as if seeking someone: in the half light they peered into the faces of the men—waiting and watching there, to see if the husband, or the son, had at last come out of the taverns, if he was going to do his day's work.

The man lying in the gutter was also examined

by them; two or three bent over him so that they might better distinguish his face. They saw features youthful but weatherbeaten, and set now in a corpse-like fixity, the lips contracted, the teeth clenched. No, they did not know him. And in any case he was not a workman, this man; he wore the large blue collar of a sailor.

One of them, nevertheless, who had a son a sailor, tried, out of kindness of heart, to drag him from the water. He was too heavy.

"What a big corpse!" she said as she let his arms drop.

This body on which had fallen all the rain of the night was Yves.

A little later, when it was full daylight, his comrades, who were passing, recognized him and carried him away.

They laid him, all soaked with the water of the gutter, at the bottom of the cutter, itself wet from the spray of the sea, and quickly they put off with canvas spread.

The sea was rough; there was a head wind. They beat to windward for a long time, and were hard put to it to reach their ship.

CHAPTER VI

Yves awoke slowly towards evening. He had first of all sensations of suffering, which came one by one, as after a kind of death. He was cold, cold to the marrow of his bones.

Above all he was bruised and battered and benumbed—stretched for some hours now on a hard bed: and he made a first effort, scarcely conscious, to turn over. But his left foot, in which suddenly he felt a sharp pain, was caught in a rigid thing against which he realized at once it was vain to struggle. And he recognized the sensation: he understood now: he was in irons.

He was already familiar with the inevitable morrow of wild nights of pleasure: to be shackled by a ring to an iron bar for days on end! And this place in which he must be, he divined it without taking the trouble to open his eyes, this recess narrow as a cupboard, and dark, and damp, with its fusty smell, and its dim pale light falling from an opening above: the hold of the *Magicien.*

But he confused this to-morrow with others which had been spent elsewhere—far away, at the other side of the earth, in America, or in the ports of China. . . . Was this for thrashing the alguazils of Buenos Ayres? Or was it that sanguinary fight at Rosario which had brought him to this? Or, again, the affair with the Russian sailors at Hong-

Kong? He was not very clear, to a thousand miles or so, having forgotten in what part of the world he was.

All the winds and all the waves of the sea had carried the *Magicien* to all the countries of the world; they had shaken it, rolled it, battered it from without, but without succeeding in disturbing the various things which were within this hold—without displacing the diver's dress which must be there hanging behind him, with its great eyes and morse-like head, and without changing the smell of rats, of damp, and tar.

He still felt very cold, so horribly cold that it was like a pain in his bones. And he realized that his clothes were wet and his body also. The pitiless rain of the preceding night, the wind, the darkling sky, returned vaguely to his memory. . . . He was not after all in the blue countries of the Equator! He remembered now. He was in France, in Brittany. This was the return of which he had so long dreamed.

But what had he done to be in irons already, almost before he had set foot on his native land? He tried to remember but could not. Then suddenly a recollection came to him, as of a dream: when they were hoisting him on board, he pulled himself together a little, and said that he would climb unaided, and then, as ill-luck would have it, he found himself face to face with a certain old warrant officer whom he held in aversion. And straightway he had fallen to abusing him most vilely; then there had been some sort of scuffle and what happened afterwards he did not know, for at that moment he had fallen inert again and lost consciousness.

But then . . . the leave that had been promised him to go to his village of Plouherzel would not now be given him! . . . All the things for which he had hoped, for which he had longed, during three years of misery, were lost! He thought of his mother and his heart smote him sorely; his eyes opened bewildered, seeing only what was within, dilated in a strange fixity by a tumult of interior things. And, in the hope that it was only an evil dream, he tried to shake his tortured foot in its iron ring.

Then a burst of laughter, deep and resonant, went off like a firework in the dark hold: a man, clothed in a woollen jersey fitting close to his body, was standing beside Yves and looking at him. As he laughed he threw back his handsome head and showed his white teeth with a feline expression.

" Hello! so you are waking up? " asked the man in a sarcastic voice, which vibrated with the accent of Bordeaux.

Yves recognized his friend Jean Barrada, the gunner, and looking up at him he asked *if I knew.*

" Tut! Tut! " said Barrada in his chaffing Gascon way. " Does he know? He has been down three times and even brought the doctor here to have a look at you; you were like a log and we were frightened about you. And I am on duty here to let him know if you move."

" What for? I don't want him or anyone. Don't go, Barrada, do you understand, I forbid you ! "

And so it had happened again. He had come to grief once more, and once more through his old failing. And, on every one of the rare occasions on which he set foot on shore, it fell out thus and it seemed that he could not help it. It must be true, what had been said to him, that this habit was a terrible and a fatal one, and that a man was lost indeed when once it had taken hold of him. In rage against himself he twisted his muscular arms until they cracked; he half raised himself, grinding his teeth; and then he fell back striking his head against the hard planks. Oh! his poor mother, she was now quite near to him and he would not see her, despite his longing of the last three years! . . . And this was his return to France! What anguish and what misery!

"At least you must change your clothes," said Barrada. "To remain wet through as you are won't do you any good. You will be ill."

"So much the better, Barrada! Leave me alone."

He spoke harshly, his eyes dark and menacing; and Barrada, who knew him well, realized that the best thing to do was to leave him.

Yves turned his head and for a time buried his face in his upraised arms. Then, fearful lest Barrada should imagine he was weeping, out of pride he altered his position and gazed straight in front of him. His eyes, in their wearied atony, kept a fierce fixity, and his lower lip, protruded more than usual, expressed the savage defiance which in his heart he was hurling at all the world. He was forming evil projects in his head; ideas which he had already conceived in former days, in hours of rebellion and despair, returned to him.

Yes, he would go away, like his brother Goulven,

like both his brothers.   This time he had made up
his mind, irrevocably.   The life of those sea-rovers
whom he had encountered on the whale-boats of
Oceania, or in places of pleasure in the towns of La
Plata, that life lived in the hazard of the sea without
law and without restraint, had for a long time
attracted him.   It was in his blood for that matter;
it was a thing inherited.

To desert and sail the sea in a trading ship
abroad, or to take part in the ocean fishing, that is
ever the dream which obsesses sailors, and the best
of them especially, in their moments of revolt.

There are good times in America for deserters.
He would not be successful, of that, in his bitterness,
he felt sure; for he was ordained to toil and misfortune; but, if poverty must be his lot, out there at
least he would be free!

His mother!   Yes, in his dash for freedom, he
would steal as far as Plouherzel, in the night, and
embrace her.   In this again like his brother
Goulven, who had done the same thing many years
before.   He remembered having seen him arrive one
night, like a fugitive; he had remained concealed
during the day of farewell which he had spent at his
home.   Their poor mother had wept bitterly, it is
true.   But what was there to do?   It was fate.
And this brother Goulven, how forceful he looked
and how manly!

Except his mother, Yves at this moment held all
the world in hate.   He thought of those years of
his life spent in the service, in the confinement of
ships of war, under the whip of discipline; he
asked himself for whose profit and why.   His heart
overflowed with the bitterness of despair, with desire

for vengeance, with a rage to be free. . . . And, as I was the cause of his re-engaging for five years in the navy, he fumed against me and included me in his resentment against the world in general.

Barrada had left him and the darkness of a December night came on. Through the hatch of the hold the grey light of day was no longer to be seen; only a damp mist now descended, which was icy cold.

A patrol had come and lit a lantern in a wire cage, and the objects in the hold were illumined confusedly. Yves heard above him the evening assembly, the slinging of the hammocks, and then the first cry of the men of the watch marking the half-hours of the night.

Outside the wind was still blowing, and as gradually silence overtook the business of men, the great unconscious voices of things became more perceptible. High up there was a continuous roaring in the rigging; and one heard the sea which lay all about us and which, from time to time, shook everything, as if in impatience. At every shock, it rolled ,Yves' head on the damp wood, and he put his hands underneath so that he might suffer less.

Even the sea, this night, was angry and vicious; it beat against the sides of the ship with a continuous noise.

At this hour no one, surely, would descend again into the hold. Yves was alone, stretched on the floor, fettered, his foot in the iron ring, and his teeth now were chattering.

CHAPTER VII

NEVERTHELESS, an hour afterwards, Jean Barrada reappeared, ostensibly to arrange one of those tackles which are used for the guns.

And this time, Yves called him in a low voice:

"Barrada, you might, like a good fellow, get me a drink of water."

Barrada went quickly to fetch his little mug, which during the day he carried on his belt and which he put away at night in a gun; he poured into it some water which was of the colour of rust, having been brought from La Plata in an iron tank, and a little wine stolen from the steward's room, and a little sugar stolen from the Commander's office.

And then with much kindness and very gently, he raised Yves' head and gave him to drink.

"And now," he said, "won't you change your clothes?"

"Yes," replied Yves, in a meek voice, which had become almost childlike, and sounded odd by contrast with his manner of a short time before.

He helped him to undress, humouring him as one might a child. He dried his chest, his shoulders and his arms, put him on dry clothes, and made him lie down again, first placing a sack under his head so that he might be able to sleep easier.

When Yves murmured his thanks, an amiable smile, the first, passed over his face, changing its

whole expression. It was over now. His heart
was softened and he was himself again. To-day
the change had come more quickly than usual.

He felt an infinite tenderness as he thought of
his mother, and he wanted to cry; something like
a tear even came into his eyes, which were not used
to yield to this weakness. . . . Perhaps after all a
little indulgence would again be shown him, on
account of his good conduct on board, on account
of his endurance in hardship, and of his arduous
work in rough weather. If it were possible—if he
was not given too harsh a punishment, it was certain
he would not repeat his offence and that he would
earn forgiveness.

It was a strong resolution this time. It needed
but a single glass of brandy, after the long abstin-
ences of the sea, to make him lose his head at once;
and then the devil in him drove him to drink
another, and another again. But if he did not
begin, if he never drank again, he would have a
sure means of keeping steady.

His repentance had the sincerity of the repentance
of a child, and he persuaded himself that, if he
escaped this time from the dread court martial which
consigns sailors to prison, this would be his last great
fault.

He hoped also in me and, above all, wanted
earnestly to see me. He begged Barrada to go up
and fetch me.

CHAPTER VIII

Yves had been my friend for seven years when he celebrated in this way his return to his native land.

We had entered the navy by different doors: he two years before I did, although he was some months younger.

The day on which I arrived at Brest, to don there that first naval uniform, which I see still, I met Yves Kermadec by chance at the house of a patron of his, an old Commander who had known his father. Yves was then a boy of sixteen. I was told that he was about to become a probationer after two years as a ship-boy. He had just returned from his home, on the expiration of eight days' leave which had been given him; his heart seemed to be very full of the good-byes he had lately bidden his mother. This and our age, which was almost the same, were two points we had in common.

A little later, having become a midshipman, I came across him again on my first ship. He was then grown into a man and serving as a topman. And I chose him for my hammock man.

For a midshipman, the hammock man is the sailor allotted to hang each evening his little suspended bed and to take it down in the morning.

Before removing the hammock, it is naturally necessary to awaken the sleeper within it and to ask

him to get out.   This is usually done by saying to
him:

" It is réveillé, captain."

This phrase has to be repeated many times before
it produces its effect.   Afterwards, the hammock
man carefully rolls up the little bed and takes it
away.

Yves performed this service very tactfully.   I
used also to meet him daily for the drill, aloft on
the main top.

There was a solidarity at that time between the
midshipmen and the topmen; and, during the long
voyages especially, such as those we were making,
the relations between us became very cordial.   On
shore, in the strange places in which sometimes, at
night, we came across our topmen, we were used
to call them to our aid when there was danger or
an adventure took an ugly look, and then, thus
united, we could lay down the law.

In such cases, Yves was our most valuable ally.

His service records, however, were not excellent.
" Exemplary on board; a most capable and sailor-
like man; but his conduct on shore is impossible."
Or: " Has shown admirable pluck and devotion,"
and then: " Undisciplined, uncontrollable."   Elsewhere: " Zeal, honour, and fidelity," with " Incorrig-
ible " in regard, etc.   His nights in irons, his days
in prison were beyond counting.

Morally as well as physically, large, strong, and
handsome, but with some irregularities in details.

On board he was an indefatigable topman, always
at work, always vigilant, always quick, always clean.

On shore, if there was a sailor out of hand, riotous,
drunk, it was always he; if a sailor was picked up in

the morning in the gutter, half naked, stripped of his clothes as one might strip a corpse, by negroes sometimes, at other times by Indians or Chinese, again it was always he. The sailor absent without leave, who fought with the police, or used his knife against the alguazils, again and always it was he. . . . All kinds of mad escapades were familiar to him.

At first I was amused at the things this Kermadec did. When he went ashore with his friends it would be asked in the midshipmen's quarters: "What fresh tale shall we hear to-morrow morning? In what condition will they return?" And I used to say to myself: "My hammock will not be fixed for me for two days at least."

It did not matter about the hammock. But this fellow Kermadec was so devoted, he seemed so good-hearted, that I began to be genuinely attached to him, rough sea-rover as he seemed to be and tipsy as he so often was. I no longer laughed at his more serious misdeeds, and would gladly have prevented them.

When this first voyage together was ended and we separated, it happened that chance brought us together again on another ship. And then I grew almost to love him.

There were, moreover, two circumstances in this second voyage which helped greatly to unite us.

The first was at Montevideo one morning before daybreak. Yves had been on shore since the previous evening, and I was approaching the quay in a pinnace manned by sixteen men, for the purpose of laying in a supply of fresh water.

I can recall the bleak half light of the dawn, the

sky already luminous but still starry, the deserted quay, alongside which we rowed slowly, looking for the watering place; the large town, which had a false air of Europe, with I know not what of primitive civilization.

As we passed we saw the long straight streets, immensely wide, opening one after the other on the whitening sky.   At this uncertain hour when the night was gradually being dissipated, not a light, not a sound; here and there, some straggler without a home, moving with aimless hesitation; along the sea front, evil-looking taverns, large wooden buildings, smelling of spices and alcohol, but closed and dark as tombs.

We stopped before one called the tavern *de la Independancia.*

A Spanish song coming from within, more or less stifled; a door, half-opened on the street; two men outside fighting with knives; a drunken woman, who could be heard vomiting against the wall. On the quay, heaps of bullock skins freshly flayed, infecting the sweet pure air with an odour of venison. . . .

A singular convoy came out of the tavern: four men carrying another, who seemed to be very drunk, unconscious. They hurried towards the ships, as if they were afraid of us.

We knew this game, which is common enough in the evil places along this coast; to ply sailors with liquor, to make them sign some preposterous engagement, and then to carry them on board by force when they can no longer keep their legs. Then the ship puts to sea as quickly as may be, and when the man comes to his senses he is far from shore; he is fairly caught, under a yoke of iron, and borne away, like a slave, to the whale fisheries, far from any inhabited land. And once there, his escape need no longer be feared, for he is a *deserter* from his country's service, lost. . . .

And so this convoy passing along the quay excited our suspicion. They pressed on like thieves, and I said to the sailors: "Let us follow them!"

Seeing our intention the men dropped their burden, which fell heavily to the ground, and made off as fast as their legs would carry them.

And the burden was Kermadec. While we were occupied in picking him up and establishing his identity, the others had made good their escape and were now locked in the tavern. The sailors wanted to batter in the doors, to take the place by assault, but that would have led to diplomatic complications with Uruguay.

Besides, Yves was saved, and that was the essential thing. I brought him back to the ship, wrapt in a cloak and lying on the goatskins which contained our provision of fresh water.

And to have rendered him this service increased my attachment to him.

The second time was when we were at Pernambuco. I had given a promissory note to some Portuguese in a gambling den. The next day I had to find the money, and as I had none, and as my friends had none either, I was in a difficulty.

Yves took the situation very tragically, and at once offered me the money of his own which he had entrusted to my care, and which I kept in a drawer of my desk.

"It would give me much pleasure, Captain, if you would take it! I have no further need to go

ashore and, as you know well, it would be better
for me if I could not go."

"Yves, my good fellow, I would accept your
money gladly for a few days, since you wish to lend
it me; but, you know, it is short of what I want
by a hundred francs. So you see it's hardly worth
while."

"Another hundred francs? I think I have that
below in my kit-bag."

And he went away, leaving me very much
astonished. That he should have another hundred
francs in his kit-bag seemed very unlikely.

He was a long time in returning. He had not
found them. I had anticipated that.

At length he reappeared.

"Here you are!" he said, handing me his poor
sailor's purse, with a happy smile.

Then a doubt came to me and, to resolve it, I
said to him:

"Yves, lend me your watch, too, like a good
fellow; I left mine in pledge."

He was very confused and said it was broken.
I had guessed right: to get these hundred francs
he had just sold it with the chain, for half its value,
to a petty officer on board.

And so Yves knew that he could call on me in
any circumstances. And when Barrada came for
me on his behalf, I went down to him where he lay,
in irons, in the hold.

But this time, by striking this old warrant officer,
he had got himself in a very serious position; my
intercession for him was in vain, and his punishment
was heavy. Four months afterwards he had to put
to sea again without having seen his mother.

When we were on the point of embarking together
on the *Sibylle* for a voyage round the world in three
hundred days, I took him on a Sunday to Saint Pol-
de-Léon, in order to console him.

It was all I could do for him, for his Plouherzel
was a long way from Brest, in the Côtes-du-Nord,
in the depth of a remote part of the country, and
at that time there was no railway which could take
us there in a single day.

CHAPTER IX

5th May, 1875.

FOR many years Yves had been looking forward to
seeing this Saint Pol-de-Léon, the little town where
he was born.

In the days when we sailed the misty northern
waters together, often as we passed in the offing,
rocked in the grey swell, we had seen the legendary
tower of Creizker upreared in the dark distance,
above the mournful and monotonous stretch of land
which, beyond, represented Brittany, the country of
Léon.

And in the night watch we used to sing together
the Breton song :

> Oh! I was born in Finistère,
> And in Saint Pol first saw the day :|
> My bell tower is beyond compare
> And I love my native land O.
>
> .   .   .   .   .
> Give me back my heather
> And my old bell tower.

But there was as it were a fatality, a throw of the dice against us : we had never succeeded in getting there, to this Saint Pol.   At the last moment when we were on the point of starting out, something interfered to prevent us; our ship received unexpected orders and it was necessary to leave at once.   And at the end we had come to regard with a kind of superstition this tower of Creizker, glimpsed only and always from a distance, in silhouette, on the edge of the mournful horizon.

This time, however, the position seems assured, and we start off in good earnest.

In the coupé of the old country diligence, we take our places next to a Breton Curé.   The horses set off at a good pace towards Saint Pol, and all looks very real.

It is early in the morning, in the first days of May; but it is raining, a fine grey rain like a rain of winter.   Ambling along the winding road, ascending steep hills, descending into damp valleys, we make our way in the midst of woods and rocks. The high ground is covered with dark fir trees. In the valleys are oaks and beeches, the foliage of which, new and wet, is of a tender green.   By the roadside there are carpets of Easter daisies and Breton flowers : the first pink silenes and the first foxgloves.

Turning a rocky corner we find that the rain and the wind have suddenly ceased.   And as if by magic the aspect of things is entirely changed.

We see before us as far as eye commands a great flat country, a barren moor, bare as a desert: the old country of Léon, in the background of

which, far away, stands the granite shaft of the
Creizker.

And yet this mournful country has a charm of
its own, and Yves smiles as he perceives his tower
towards which we are moving.

The gorse is in blossom and the whole plain has
a colour of gold, varied in places by stretches pink
with heather. A veil of pearl-grey mist, of a tint
peculiar to the north, very soft and subtle, entirely
covers the sky; and in the monotony of this pink
and yellow country, on the extreme edge of the far
horizon, nothing but these outstanding points: the
silhouette of Saint Pol and the three dark towers.

Some little Breton girls are driving flocks of
sheep before them through the heather; some young
lads, caracoling on horses which they ride bare-
back, startle them; little traps pass laden with
women in white coifs who are on their way to hear
mass in the town. The bells are ringing, the road
is gaily animated; we arrive.

CHAPTER X

AFTER we had lunched together at the best inn, we
found that the winter's morning had yielded place
to a fine May day. In the empty little streets,
branches of lilac, clusters of wistaria, pink foxgloves
which no one had sown brightened the grey walls;

the sun was really shining and all about was a savour of spring.

And Yves took in everything, marvelling that no recollection of his early childhood came back to him, seeking, seeking in the dim background of his memory, recognizing nothing, and then, little by little, becoming disillusioned.

On the grand'place of Saint Pol the crowd of the Sunday was assembled. It seemed a picture of the Middle Ages. The cathedral of the old bishops of Léon dominated the square, overwhelming it with its dark denticulated mass, throwing over it a great shadow of bygone times. Around were ancient houses with gables and little turrets; all the drinkers of the Sunday, wearing aslant their wide felt hats, were sitting at table before the doors. This crowd in its Breton dress, living and alert here, this, too, might have been a crowd of olden days; in the air, one heard vibrate only the harsh syllables, the northern *ya* of the Celtic tongue.

Yves passed rather distractedly into the church, over the memorial stones and over the old bishops asleep beneath.

But he stopped, suddenly thoughtful, at the door, before the baptismal font.

" Look! " he said. " They held me above this. And we must have lived quite near here; my poor mother has often told me that, on the day of my baptism, on the day, you know, when they so cruelly insulted us by not ringing the bell for me, she had heard, from her bed, the singing of the priests."

Unfortunately Yves had omitted to obtain from his mother, at Plouherzel, the information necessary to identify the house in which they used to live.

He had reckoned on his godmother, Yvonne
Kergaoc by name, who, he understood, lived quite
close to the church. And on our arrival we had
asked for this Yvonne Kergaoc: " Kergaoc." . . .
They remembered her well.

" But from where do you come, my good sirs? . . .
She is dead these twelve years! "

As for the Kermadecs no one had any recollection
of them. And it was scarcely to be wondered at:
it was more than twenty years since they left the
town.

We climbed the tower of Creizker; naturally it
was high, it seemed never to end, this point in the
air. We greatly disturbed the old crows who had
their nests in the granite.

A marvellous lace-work of grey stone, which
mounted, mounted endlessly, and was so slender
it produced sensations of vertigo. We climbed
within it by a narrow and steep spiral staircase,
discovering through all the openings of the " open
tower " infinite vistas.

At the top, isolated, the two of us, in the keen
air and the blue sky, we saw things as a hovering
bird might see them. First, below our feet, were the
crows which whirled in a dark cloud, giving us a
concert of mournful cries; much lower, the old
town of Saint Pol, all flattened out, a Lilliputian
crowd moving about in its little grey streets, like a
swarm of ants; as far as eye could see, to the south,
stretched the Breton country up to the Black
Mountains; and, to the north, was the port of
Roscoff, with thousands of strange little rocks
riddling with their pointed tops the mirror of the sea
—the mirror of the great pale blue sea which

stretched away to mingle in the farthest distance
with the similar blue of the sky.

It pleased us to have succeeded at last in climbing this Creizker, which had so many times watched
us pass in the midst of that infinity of water; it was
so calm, planted there, so permanent, so inaccessible
and unchanging, while we, poor waifs of the sea,
were at the mercy of every angry wind that blew.

This granite lace-work which supported us in the
air had been smoothed and worn by the winds and
rains of four hundred winters. It was of a grey
deepened by warm pinkish tones; and over it, in
patches, was that yellow lichen, that moss peculiar
to granite, which takes centuries to grow and throws
its golden tint over all the old Breton churches.
The ugly-faced gargoyles, the little monsters with
irregular features, who live high up there in the air,
were making faces at our side in the sun, as if they
resented being looked at from so near, as if they
were surprised themselves to be so old, to have
endured through so many tempests and to find themselves once more in the sunlight. It was these
people who had presided from above over the birth
of Yves; it was these people also who from afar
watched us with friendliness as we passed by at sea,
when we, for our part, saw only a vague black shaft.
And now we were making their acquaintance.

Yves was still very disappointed, however, that
he had discovered no trace of his old home nor of his
father; no recollection, either in the memory of
others or his own. And he continued to gaze upon
the grey houses below, especially at those which
were nearest the foot of the tower, awaiting some
intuition of the place where he was born.

We had now only half an hour to spend in Saint Pol before catching the evening diligence. To-morrow morning we should have to be back in Brest, where our ship was waiting to take us once more very far from Brittany.

We sat down to drink some cider in an inn on the *Place de l' Eglise*, and there again we questioned the hostess, who was a very old woman. And she, as chance would have it, started suddenly on hearing Yves' name.

"You are Yves Kermadec's son?" she said. "Oh! Did I know your parents! I should think so, indeed. We were neighbours in those days. Why, when you arrived in the world, they sent to fetch me. But you are like your father, you know! I watched you when you came in. But you are not so handsome as he, bless me, though, to be sure, you are a fine-looking man."

Yves, at this compliment, glanced at me, repressing a strong inclination to smile; and then the old woman, growing very talkative, began to tell him a multitude of things over which more than twenty years had passed, while he listened attentive and greatly moved.

Then she called some other old women, who also had been neighbours, and they all began to talk.

"Bless my soul!" they said. "How is it that no one was able to answer you sooner? Everybody remembers them, remembers your parents. But people are stupid in these parts; and then, when strangers come in this way, it isn't surprising that people should hesitate to talk."

Yves' father had left in the country round a

reputation a little legendary of a kind of giant of rare beauty, who was never able to conform to the ways of others.

"What a pity, sir, that such a man should so often go astray! It was the tavern that ruined him, your poor father; for all that, he was very fond of his wife and children, he was very gentle with them, and in the country round everybody loved him except M. le Curé."

"Except M. le Curé!" Yves repeated to me in a low voice, becoming serious. "You see it is what I told you, on the subject of my baptism."

"One day, there was a battle, here on the square, in 1848, for the revolution; your father withstood single-handed the market people and saved the life of the Mayor."

"He had a big horse," said the hostess, "which was so wild that no one dared to approach it. And people kept out of the way, I assure you, when he passed mounted on the beast."

"Ah!" said Yves, struck suddenly with a recollection which seemed to have come to him from a great distance. "I remember that horse, and I recall that my father used to lift me up and sit me on it when it was tied in the stable. It is the first recollection I have of my father and I can just picture a little his face. The horse was black, was it not, with white hoofs?"

"That's it! That's it," said the old woman. "Black with white hoofs. It was a wild beast, and, bless my soul! what an idea for a sailor to have a horse!"

The inn is full of men drinking cider. They make a cheerful noise of glasses and Breton conversations. And gradually they gather round and make a sort of circle about us.

The hostess has four granddaughters, all alike, and all ravishingly pretty in their white coifs. They do not look like daughters of an inn. They are the perfect type of the handsome Breton race of the north, and they have the calm, thoughtful expression of those women of olden times which the old portraits have preserved for us. They, too, gathered round us, looking and listening.

We are questioned in our turn. Yves replies: " My mother is still living at Plouherzel with my two sisters. My two brothers, Gildas and Goulven, are at sea, on American whalers. I myself have been for the last ten years in the Navy."

There is not much time to lose if we want to see before we go the old home of the Kermadecs. It is quite near, by the very side of the church. They show it to us from the door, and advise us to ask to be allowed to see the room on the left, on the first floor; that is the room in which Yves was born.

At the side of the house is the large abandoned park of the bishopric of Léon, where, it seems, Yves, when he was quite a little child, used to play every day in the grass with Goulven. It is very thick to-day, this grass of May, and full of Easter daisies and silenes. In the park roses and lilac are growing wild now, as in a wood.

We knock at the door of the house which the good women have pointed out to us, and those who live there are a little surprised at the request we make. But we do not inspire distrust, and they ask us only not to make a noise when we enter the first floor room, on account of the old grandmother who

is sleeping there and is on the point of death.   And
then, considerately, they leave us alone.

We enter on tiptoe.   It is a large room, poor and
almost empty.   The things in it seem to have a
presentiment of the grim visitor who is expected;
one is tempted almost to ask whether he has not
already arrived, and our eyes glance uneasily at a
bed, the curtains of which are drawn.   Yves looks
all round, trying to stretch his intelligence into the
past, to force himself as it were to remember.   But
it is no use.   It is finished; and even here he can
find nothing.

We were descending preparatory to leaving, when
suddenly something came back to him like a light
in the distance.

"Ah!" he said, "I think now that I recognize
this staircase.   Wait!   Below there should be a
door on that side leading into a yard, and a well
on the left with a large tree, and, at the back, the
stable where we used to keep the horse with the
white hoofs."

It was as if there had suddenly come a break in
the clouds.   Yves stood still on the stairs, gazing
through this gap which had just been opened on the
past; he was thrilled to feel himself at grips with
that mysterious thing which men call memory.

Below, in the yard, we found everything as he
had described it, the well on the left, the tree, the
stable.   And Yves said to me with an emotion of
awe, removing his hat as if he were by a grave:

"Now I can see quite clearly my father's face."

It was high time to depart, and the diligence was
waiting for us.

Throughout our journey over this golden-coloured

moor, during the long May twilight, our eyes were fixed on the Creizker tower which was disappearing in the distance, and was lost at last in the depths of the limpid darkness. We were bidding it adieu, for we were going to leave to-morrow for very distant seas, where it would no longer be able to see us pass.

" To-morrow morning," said Yves, " you must let me come into your room on board very early, so that I may write at your desk. I want to tell all that we have found out to my mother before leaving France. And, you know, I am sure that tears will come into her eyes when my letter is read to her."

CHAPTER XI

June, 1875.

IT was now the twentieth parallel of latitude, in the region of the trade winds. The hour was about six in the morning. On the deck of a ship which rode solitary in the midst of the immense blue, was a group of young men, stripped to the waist, in the warmth of the rising sun.

It was Yves' band, the topmen of the foremast and those of the bowsprit.

They had thrown over their shoulders, all of them, the handkerchiefs which they had just washed, and they stood there gravely with back to the sun to dry them. Their bronzed faces, their laughter, had still a youthful, almost childlike, grace, and in their movements, in the supple, flexible way in which they placed their bare feet there was something catlike.

And every morning, at this same hour, in this same sunshine, in this same costume, this group foregathered on these same boards which carried them along, all heedless, in the midst of the infinity of the sea.

This particular morning they were talking about the moon, about its human face, which had remained with them since the night as a pale, persistent image graven in their memory. Throughout their watch they had seen it on high, solitary and round, in the midst of the immense bluish void; they had even been obliged to cover their faces (as they slept on their backs in the open) on account of the maladies and evil spells it casts on the eyes of sailors, when they sleep under its gaze.

There were some amongst them who preserved still, and in spite of all, a great air of nobility, a something indescribably superb in their expression and general appearance; and the contrast between their aspect and the simple things they said was singular.

There was Jean Barrada, the sceptic of the company, who broke into the discussion from time to time with a sarcastic burst of laughter, showing his white teeth always and throwing back his handsome head. There was Clet Kerzulec, a Breton from the island of Ushant, who was preoccupied especially with the human features stamped on the pale disc. And then big Barazère, who posed as a thinker and scholar, assuring them that it was a world much larger than ours and inhabited by strange peoples.

They shook their heads, incredulous, at this, and Yves, very thoughtful, said:

"You know, Barazère, there are things . . . there are things about which I don't believe you know very much."

And then he added, with an air which cut short the discussion, that in any case, he was going to find me and get me to explain to him what the moon really was.

There was no doubt in their minds that I should be well-informed about the moon as about everything else. For they had often seen me occupied in watching its progress through a copper instrument in company with a signalman who counted for me out loud, with the monotonous voice of a clock, the tranquil minutes and seconds of the night.

Meanwhile, the little handkerchiefs were drying on the bare backs of the men, and the sun was mounting in the wide blue sky.

Some of these little handkerchiefs were all uniformly white; others had pictures on them in many colours; and some even had great ships printed in the middle in a red frame.

I, whose watch it was, gave the order: " 'Way aloft! Loose the topsail reef!" And the boatswain appeared among the talkers blowing his silver whistle. Then suddenly, in the twinkling of an eye, like a band of cats on whom a dog has been loosed, they all scattered, running, into the masting.

Yves lived aloft in his top. Looking up, one

was sure to see his tall, slim silhouette against the
sky. But one rarely met him below.

It was I who used to climb from time to time to
visit him, although my duty no longer required me
to do so, since I had been promoted from the rank of
midshipman; but I was rather fond of this domain
of Yves where one was fanned by a still purer
air.

In this top, he had his little belongings; a pack
of playing cards in a box, needles and thread for
sewing, stolen bananas, greenstuffs taken during
the night from the Commander's store, anything he
was able to find in his nocturnal marauding that was
fresh and green (sailors are partial to these rare
things which soothe gums parched by salt). And
then he had his " parrot " attached by a claw, its eyes
blinking in the sun.

The " parrot " was a large-headed owl of the
pampas which had fallen on board one day after a
high wind.

There are some strange destinies on the earth,
but few stranger than that of this owl making the
tour of the world at the top of a mast. How unexpected a fate!

He knew his master and welcomed him with little
joyous flappings of his wings. Yves fed him
regularly with his own ration of meat, although he
used to let him loose.

It amused him greatly to peer into its eyes from
quite near, and to see how it shrank away, and
arched its back with an air of offended dignity,
nodding its head after the manner of a bear. Then
he would burst out laughing, and say to it in his
Breton accent:

"Oh! but you are a stupid little fool, my old parrot!"

From aloft one dominated as from a great height the deck of the *Sibylle*, a *Sibylle* flattened out and tapering, very strange to see from this domain of Yves, having the appearance of a long wooden fish, whose colour of new spruce contrasted with the deep and infinite blues of the sea.

And, through all these transparent blues, behind, in our wake, a little grey thing having the same shape as the ship which it followed unceasingly under water: the shark. It is always one shark which follows, rarely two; but if the one is caught, another comes. For days and nights it follows, follows without ever getting tired, waiting for what may fall from the ship: debris of any kind, living men or dead men.

And now and then a number of quite small swallows came also to bear us company, amusing themselves, for a while, in picking up the crumbs of biscuits which we scattered behind us in this watery desert, and then disappeared in the distance describing joyous curves. Little beasts of a rare kind, reddish in colour with a white tail, which live one knows not how, lost amid the great waters, always in the open sea.

Yves, who wanted one, set traps for them, but they were too shrewd to be caught.

We were approaching the Equator, and the regular breath of the trade wind began to die away. There were now erratic breezes which shifted suddenly, followed by times of calm in which everything became immobilized in a kind of immense blue splendour; and then the yards, the tops, and the great white sails were reflected in the water in the form of inverted pictures undulating and incomplete.

The *Sibylle* scarcely moved, she was slow and lazy, she had the movements of one half asleep. In the great moist heat, which even the nights did not diminish, things, as well as men, seemed to be taken with drowsiness. Gradually in the air a strange calm began to reign. And presently clouds, heavy and obscure, gathered over the warm sea like large dark curtains. The Equator was now quite near.

Sometimes flights of swallows, large ones these and strange in movement, rose suddenly from the sea, taking flight in startled fashion with long pointed wings of a glistening blue, and then settled again, and one saw them no more. These were shoals of flying-fish which had lain in our course and which we had disturbed.

The sails, the cordage hung limp, like dead things; we drifted lifeless like a wreck.

Aloft, in Yves' domain, might still be felt some slow movements which were no longer perceptible below. In this motionless air saturated with rays, the crow's nest continued to rock with a tranquil regularity which conduced to slumber. There were long slow oscillations accompanied always by the same flappings of drooping sails, the same creakings of dry wood.

It was intensely hot, and the light had a surprising splendour, and the mournful sea was of a milky blue, of the colour of melted turquoise.

But when the strange dense clouds, which travelled low so as almost to touch the water, passed over us, they brought us night and drenched us with a deluge of rain.

We were now directly under the Equator; and it seemed that there was no breath of air there to carry us forward.

They lasted for hours, sometimes for a whole day, this darkness and these tropical storms. Then Yves and his friends assumed a uniform which they called the "uniform of savages," and sat them down, all heedless, under the warm downpour and let it rain as it would.

And then suddenly the weather changed. The black curtain of clouds drew slowly away, continuing its sluggish progress, over the turquoise coloured sea; and the splendid light reappeared more astonishing than ever after the darkness; and the powerful equatorial sun proceeded to drink up very quickly all this water that had been poured upon us; the sails, the woodwork of the ship, the awnings recovered their whiteness in the sunshine; the *Sibylle* in its entirety took on once more its normal clear colour in the midst of the vast blue monotony which stretched everywhere around.

Looking down from the top in which Yves lived, one saw that this blue world was without limit, that its clear depths were without end. One felt that the horizon, the last line of the waters, was a great distance away, although it did not differ at all from the immediate surroundings, having always the same clearness, always the same colour, always the same mirror-like polish. And one realized then the *roundness* of the earth, which alone set a limit to the vision.

At the hour of sunset there were in the air kinds of vaults formed of successions of tiny golden clouds; they were repeated, in diminishing perspec-

tive, until they almost disappeared in the empty
distance; one followed them to the point of vertigo;
they were like the naves of Apocalyptic temples
having no end.   And the air was so clear that it
needed the horizon of the sea to shut out the vista of
these depths of the sky; the last little golden clouds
formed as it were a tangent to the line of the waters,
and seemed, in their remoteness, as delicate as the
finest of hatching.

At other times there were simply long bands which
traversed the sky, gold on gold: the clouds of a
bright and as if incandescent gold, on a Byzantine
background of dull and tarnished gold.   The sea
below took on a certain shade of peacock blue with
reflections of molten metal.   Afterwards all this
faded very quickly into deep transparencies, into
shadowy colours to which it was not possible to give
a name.

And the nights which followed, even they were
luminous; when everything slept in heavy immo-
bility, in a silence of death, the stars appeared
above more brilliant than in any other region of the
world.

And the sea also was illumined in its depths.
There was a kind of immense diffused light in the
waters.   The slightest movements—of the ship in
its slow progress, of the shark as it turned about in
our wake—disclosed in the warm eddies lights like
that of the glow-worm.   And, besides, on the great
phosphorescent mirror of the sea, there were
thousands of fleeting flames; it was as if there were
myriads of little lamps which lit themselves everywhere, burnt for a few seconds and then went out.
These nights were aswoon with heat, full of phos-

phorus, and all this dimmed immensity was pregnant with light, and all these waters were replete with latent life in its rudimentary state as formerly the mournful waters of the primitive world.

CHAPTER XII

IT was some days now since we had left behind us the tranquillities of the Equator, and we were proceeding slowly towards the south, driven by the south trade wind. One morning Yves entered my room full of business, in order to prepare his lines for catching birds: "We have seen," he said, "the first 'draught-boards' behind us."

These "draught-boards' are birds of the open sea, near relatives of the sea-gull, and the most beautiful of all the tribe: snowy white, the plumage soft and silky, with a black draught-board finely designed on the wings.

The first "draught-boards!" Their appearance reminds us of the distance we have travelled; it is a sign that we have left well behind us our northern hemisphere, and that we are approaching the cold regions which lie on the other side of the earth, in the far south.

They were before their due time nevertheless, these "draught-boards"; for we were still in the blue zone of the trade winds. And all day long, and every day, and every night, was the same breeze, regular, warm, and exquisite to respire; and the same transparent sea, and the same little white fleecy clouds passing peacefully across the lofty heaven; and the same bands of flying fish rising up in foolish alarm with their long wet wings, and shining in the sun like birds of bluish steel.

There were quantities of these flying-fish; and when it happened that one of them was foolish enough to alight on board, the topmen quickly cut off its wings and ate it.

The time when Yves used to like to descend from his crow's nest and come to visit me in my room was in the evening, especially after the assembly at evening quarters. He would come very quietly, without making in his bare feet any more noise than a cat. He would drink some fresh water straight out of a water-cooler which hung at my port-hole, and then set to work putting in order divers things which belonged to me; or, maybe, he would read some novel. There was one especially of George Sand's which enthralled him, " Le Marquis de Villemer." At the first reading I had surprised him on the point of tears, towards the end.

Yves could sew very skilfully, as all good sailors can, and it was quaint to see him engaged in this work, given his size and aspect. During his evening visits he used to overhaul my uniform and do any repairs which he judged were beyond the skill of my servant to attend to properly.

CHAPTER XIII

WE sailed steadily, fully rigged, towards the south.
Now there were clouds of " draught-boards " and
other sea-birds in attendance upon us. They
followed us, wondering and confident, from morning until night, crying, throwing themselves about,
flying in erratic curves—as if in welcome to us,
another great bird with canvas wings, which was
entering their distant and infinite domain, the
Southern Pacific Ocean.

And their numbers increased daily in measure as
we progressed. With the " draught-boards " there
were pearl-grey petrels, the beak and claws lightly
tinted with blue and pink; and black molly-mawks;
and great, heavy albatrosses, dirty in colour, with
their stupid sheepish air, with their immense rigid
wings, cleaving the air, whining after us. There
was one among them which the sailors pointed out
to one another; an Admiral, a bird of a rare and
enormous kind, with *three stars* marked in black on
its long wings.

The weather had changed and become calm,
misty, mournful. The south trade wind had died
away in its turn, and the clearness of the tropics
was no more. A great damp cold surprised our
senses. We were in August and the winter of the
southern hemisphere was beginning. When we
looked round the empty horizon, it seemed that

E

the north, the side of the sun and of living countries, was still blue and clear; while the south, the side of the Pole and of the watery deserts, was dark and gloomy.

As a favour to me, Yves had obtained for his parrot a reserved compartment in the Commander's hen coop, and he used to go every evening to cover it with a piece of sailcloth in order to protect it from the night air.

Every day the sailors used to "fish" with their lines for "draught-boards" and petrels. There were rows of these birds, skinned like rabbits, hanging all red in the foreshrouds, waiting their turn to be eaten. After two or three days, when they had rendered all the oil in their bodies, they were ready for cooking.

These foreshrouds were the larder of the top-men. By the side of the "draught-boards" and the petrels, even rats might sometimes be seen, stripped also of their skin, and hung by the tail.

One night we heard suddenly the rising of a great fearsome voice, and everybody bestirred himself and took to running.

At the same time the *Sibylle* leaned over, shuddering, as if in the grip of a tenebrous power.

Then even those who were not of the watch, even those who were sleeping on the spar deck, understood: it was the beginning of the great winds and the great swell; we had now entered the stormy latitudes of the south, amid which we should have to fight for our existence and at the same time make headway.

And the farther we advanced into this sullen

ocean, the colder became the wind, and the more mountainous the swell.

The fall of the nights became sinister. We were in the neighbourhood of Cape Horn: desolation on the only land that was anywhere near, desolation on the sea, everywhere a desert. At this hour of the winter twilight, when one felt more particularly the need of a shelter, of getting near a fire, of covering under which to sleep—we had nothing, nothing—we kept vigil, for ever on the alert, lost amid all these moving things which made us dance in the darkness.

We tried hard to create an illusion of home in the little cabins rudely shaken, where swung the suspended lamps. But it was no use; there was no stability anywhere: we were in a little frail thing, lost, far from any land, in the midst of the immense desert of the southern waters. And, outside, we heard continuously the roar of the waves and the mournful moaning of the wind which smote the heart.

And Yves, for his part, had no more than his poor swinging hammock, in which, one night out of two, he was allowed the leisure to sleep a little warmly.

CHAPTER XIV

It was one morning, as we were entering the Celebean Sea, that the owl which was Yves' parrot died, a morning of high wind on which we took in the second reef of the topsail.   It was accidentally crushed between the mast and the yard.

Yves, who heard its hoarse cry, rushed to its assistance, but too late.   He came down from the crow's nest carrying the poor thing in his hand, dead, flattened out, having no longer the shape of a bird, a mash of blood and grey feathers, out of which emerged, moving still, one poor curled-up claw.

I could see that Yves was very much upset.   But he did no more than show it to me without a word, biting his disdainful underlip.   Then he threw it into the sea, and the shark which was following us swallowed it as if it had been an ablet.

CHAPTER XV

In Brittany, during the winter of 1876, the *Sibylle* had been back at Brest for two days—after having completed its voyage round the world—and I was with Yves, one evening in February, in a country diligence which was carrying us towards Plouherzel.

It was an out-of-the-way place, this village where Yves' mother lived.   The diligence in which we sat was due to take us in four hours from Guin-camp to Paimpol, where we counted on spending the night; and from there we should have a long way to go on foot.

On we went, jolted over a rough little road, plunging deeper and deeper into the silence of the mournful countryside. The winter's night descended on us slowly, and a fine rain obscured things in a grey mist. We passed trees and more trees, showing one after another their dead silhouette. At wide intervals we passed villages also—Breton villages, dark thatched cottages and old churches with slender granite steeples—little groups of homesteads, isolated and melancholy, which quickly disappeared behind us in the night.

"Do you know," said Yves, "I came this way, at night, eleven years ago—I was then fourteen—and I wept bitterly. It was the first time I had left home, and I was travelling alone to Brest to join the navy."

I was accompanying Yves on this journey to Plouherzel partly for want of something to do. The leave granted me was short, and I had not time, on this occasion, to visit my home, so I was going to visit his, and to see this village of his which he loved so well.

And, at the moment, I was rather sorry I had come. Yves, absorbed in the happiness of his return, kept up a conversation with me out of deference, but his thoughts were elsewhere. I felt that I was a stranger in this world for which we were bound, and this Brittany, which I had not yet learned to love, oppressed me with its sadness.

Paimpol! We roll over cobbles, between old dark houses, and the diligence stops. People are waiting there with lanterns. Breton words and French words are interchanged.

"Are there any travellers for the Hôtel Pendreff?" pipes a small boy's voice.

The Hôtel Pendreff! Surely the name is

familiar to me. And now I remember that nine years before, during my first year in the navy, I had rested there for an hour, on a day in June, when my ship, by chance, had anchored in a bay near by. I recollect it well; an old manor house, turreted and gabled, presided over by two aged sisters named Le Pendreff, both alike, in large white bonnets, making a picture of bygone days. We will get down at the Hôtel Pendreff.

In the house itself nothing is changed. But one of the Le Pendreff sisters is dead. She who remains was already so old nine years ago that she can scarcely have grown older since. Her type, her bonnet, the placid dignity of her bearing, are of a past generation.

It is good to dine before the great roaring fire, and cheerfulness returns to us.

Afterwards, the good dame Le Pendreff, armed with a copper candlestick, leads the way up a stone staircase and ushers us into a very large room, where there are two beds of an old-fashioned type hung with white curtains.

Yves, however, undresses himself very slowly and without conviction.

"Ah!" he says, suddenly putting on his blue collar again. "I am going to continue the journey! In the first place, you understand, I should not be able to sleep. It's true, I shall get home very late, I shall awaken them after midnight, and that will startle them a little—I did that in the year when I returned from the war. But I am so anxious to see them, I cannot wait here."

And I, too, decided that I would follow his example.

Paimpol is asleep when we leave in the pale moonlight. I am accompanying him for a part of his way, to help to pass the hours of the night. We are now in the fields.

Yves walks very quickly; he is very excited, and goes over in his mind the memories of his earlier returns.

"Yes," he said. "After the war I returned like this, about two o'clock in the morning, and woke them up. I had walked from Saint Brieuc; I was returning, very weary, from the siege of Paris. You will realize I was quite young then. I had just become able seaman.

"And, I remember, I got a great fright that night: by the cross of Kergrist, which we shall see in a minute at the turning of this road, I came upon a little old man, very ugly, who stared at me with outstretched arms, but without moving. And I am sure he was a ghost; for he disappeared almost at once, beckoning with his finger as if he wanted me to follow him."

Presently we reached this cross of Kergrist. We saw it rise up before us as if it were someone approaching in the darkness. But there was no ghost at its foot.

It was there I said good-bye to Yves and retraced my steps, for I, for my part, was not going to Plouherzel. When we no longer heard the sound of each other's footsteps in the silence of the winter's night, the ghost of the little old man came back into our minds, and in spite of ourselves we took to peering into the darkness of the undergrowth.

CHAPTER XVI

On the following morning I opened my eyes in the large room of the good dame Le Pendreff. The Breton sun filtered gently through the windows. The day, apparently, was very fine.

After the first few moments which I always spend in asking myself in what corner of the world I am, I remembered Yves and I heard outside the tramping of a crowd in sabots. There was a great fair that day in Paimpol, and I dressed myself up in ordinary sailor's clothes in order that I might not intimidate the many friends to whom I was going to be presented as a south-country sailor. This had been arranged with Yves, both the dressing up and the story attached to it.

I descended the steps of the hotel. The sun was shining and the square was full of people: sailors, peasants, fishermen. Yves, too, was there; he had returned in the early morning for the fête with all his relations from Plouherzel; and he was waiting outside to conduct me to his mother.

She was a very old woman, this mother of Yves, holding herself very upright and rather proudly in her peasant dress. She resembled him a little about the eyes, but her expression was hard. I was surprised to find her so old. She looked over seventy. It is true, of course, that in the country people age very quickly, especially when grief is added to toil.

She did not understand a word of French and scarcely looked at me.

But there was a great number of cousins and friends who all welcomed me warmly and with an air of good humour. They had come from afar, from their little moss-grown cottages scattered about the wild countryside, to assist at the great fête of the town. And with them I needs must drink: cider, wine; there was no end to it.

The noise steadily increased and some hoarse-voiced pedlars of ballads were singing now in Breton, under red umbrellas, woeful and heartrending things.

Presently a personage arrived of whom Yves had often spoken to me, his childhood's friend, Jean; he lived in a neighbouring cottage, and Yves had come across him again in the service, a sailor like himself. He was of our own age, with an open and intelligent face. He embraced Yves affectionately and then introduced us to Jeannie, who, for the last fortnight, had been his wife.

Yves overwhelmed his mother with attentions and caresses; they had many things to tell one another, and they both spoke at once. He made apologies to us from time to time, but it was good to see them and to hear them. Her eyes lost their hard expression when she looked at him.

The good people of the country have always interminable business to transact with the notary; I left them as they all made their way to the one at Paimpol to wait their turn.

In any case I had decided not to establish myself with them until to-morrow, in order that I might not be in the way during their first day, and I went off alone for a long walk.

CHAPTER XVII

I WALKED for about an hour. By chance I had taken the same road as yesterday with Yves, and I had passed again the cross of Kergrist.

Now Paimpol and the sea, and the islands, and the headlands wooded with dark fir trees, had disappeared behind a fold of the ground; a more mournful country stretched before me.

This February day was calm and very dreary; the air was almost mild, and in places the sky was blue, but mainly it was overclouded, as this Breton sky always is.

I made my way along damp lanes, bordered, according to old usage, by high banks of earth, which shut out the view sadly. The short grass, the damp moss, the bare branches told of winter. At the corners of the road old calvaries stretched out their grey arms; they bore simple carvings, quaintly altered by the centuries: the instruments of the Passion, or perhaps a distorted figure of Christ.

At wide intervals were straw-thatched cottages, green with moss, half buried in the earth and the dead branches. The trees were stunted, stripped by the winter, twisted by the wind from the sea. Not a soul in sight and silence everywhere.

A chapel of grey granite with an enclosure of beeches and tombs. . . . Ah! yes, I recognize it without ever having seen it, the chapel of Plouherzel! Yves had often spoken of it to me on board during the night watch, during the clear nights at the other side of the world, when we used to dream of home. " When you reach the chapel," he used to say, " it is quite near; you have but to turn into the path on the left, and two hundred yards away is our home."

I turned to the left and, by the side of the little road, I saw the cottage.

It was solitary, quite low and overshadowed by old beech trees.

It looked out upon a mournful expanse of country, the distances of which were shaded in dark grey. There were interminable, monotonous plains with phantoms of trees; a salt water lake at the hour of low water, an empty lake hollowed out of the granite strata, a deep meadow of seaweed, with an island in the middle.

A strange island, formed of a single piece of polished granite, like a back, having the shape of a large beast sitting. One looked about for the sea, the real sea which with the returning tide must come to fill these abandoned reservoirs, but there was no sign of it anywhere. A cold dark mist was rising on the horizon, and the winter sunshine was beginning to fade.

Poor Yves! So this is his home; a lonely cottage by the roadside; a poor little Breton cottage, in a turning off a remote lane, low-pitched, under a lowering sky, half buried in the earth, with ancient little granite walls overgrown with parietaries and moss.

All his memories of childhood are centred here; it was his cradle, his nest; a cherished home in which his mother lived, a home to which, in far-off countries, in the great cities of America and Asia, his imagination always brought him back. He thought of it with love, of this little corner of the world, during the fine calm nights at sea and during the riotous nights of brutal pleasure which made up his life of adventure. A poor, lonely cottage, at the turning of a road, and that was all.

In his dreams at sea it was this that he saw: under a threatening sky, amid the mournful country of this land of Goëlo, these old damp little walls overgrown with parietaries; and the neighbouring cottages in which kind old women in white Breton head-dresses used to spoil him when he was a child; and then, at the corner of the roads, the granite calvaries, corroded by the centuries. . . .

Merciful heavens! How dreary this country is! How dreary and how depressing!

I knocked at the door and a young girl who resembled Yves appeared on the threshold.

I asked her if this was indeed the house of the Kermadecs.

"Yes," she said, a little surprised and apprehensive. And then, suddenly:

"Ah! you, sir, are the friend of my brother who arrived with him at Brest yesterday evening?"

But she was rather concerned to see that I came alone.

I entered. I saw the cupboards, the Breton beds, the old plates in rows on the plate stand. Everything looked clean and respectable; but the cottage was very small and humble.

"All our relations are rich," Yves had often told me. "It is only we who are poor."

I was shown one of those beds in the form of a

cupboard, with two places, which had been prepared for Yves and me. I was to occupy the upper shelf, which was decorated with thick hangings of reddish cloth, very clean and very stiff.

"Won't you sit down? They will be back from the town very soon now."

But no. I thanked her and went away.

Half-way to Paimpol, as night was falling, I perceived in the distance a large blue collar, in a little trap which was being driven briskly in the direction of Plouherzel: the little carriage of friend Jean bringing back Yves and his mother. I had just time to hide myself behind a hedge; if they had recognized me, there would have been no escape from them, of that I was certain.

It was quite dark when I reached Paimpol, and the little street lamps were lit. I tried to mingle in the crowd which moved about the square and consisted for the most part of those sailors who are known in these parts as Icelanders, men who exile themselves every summer, for six months, in the dangerous fishing expeditions to the cold northern seas.

None of these men was alone. They perambulated the streets, singing, with young women on their arm, sisters, sweethearts, mistresses. And these pictures of happiness and life made me feel my own utter loneliness. I walked about alone, miserable and unknown to them all, in my borrowed clothes which resembled theirs. People stared at me. "Who is that? A stranger in search of a ship? We have never seen him before."

I felt cold at heart and impulsively I turned away to take once more the road to Plouherzel. After all, perhaps I should not be greatly in the way of my simple friends there, if I went and warmed myself a little among them.

I had forgotten all about dinner and walked rapidly, fearful lest I should arrive too late, fearful lest I should find the cottage shut up for the night and my friends in bed.

CHAPTER XVIII

AT the end of about an hour I was in the midst of fields, absolutely lost. Around me nothing but darkness, and the silence of a winter's night. I wandered along muddy lanes; not a soul of whom I could ask the way, not a hamlet, not a light. But always the dark silhouettes of trees, and, at intervals, calvaries; some of these calvaries were very large, and I had no recollection of having seen them in my walk during the day.

I retraced my steps hurriedly. For a long time I tried different directions, running. An icy rain began to fall, driven by the wind which had risen suddenly. It did not distress me much that I had lost my way, but I felt the need of seeing someone friendly, and I made haste in my efforts to find Yves.

It must have been very late when I recognized ahead of me the chapel of Plouherzel and the sea-water lake, on which the moonlight was now falling, and the dark mass of the granite isle on the pale water, the back of the great couchant beast.

Near the chapel I heard voices. In the darkness two men, one of athletic build, holding each other by the hand and talking to each other very affectionately, in the manner of men in the early stage of intoxication: Yves and Jean; and I hastened to them.

They were greatly surprised and pleased to see me. And Jean, taking each of us by the arm, insisted that we should both accompany him to his home.

Jean's cottage, isolated also, was in the neighbourhood of Yves', but it was much larger and better furnished.

You realized at once that you were in the home of people comfortably off: the presses and the beds had clasps of figured steel which shone like armour. At the farther end was a monumental fireplace, in which blazed a large oak log.

Two women were sitting before this fire, Jeannie, the young wife, and the old grandmother, in tall head-dress, busy at her spinning-wheel.

She would have made a fine study for an artist, this mother of Jean. She had also, in some measure, brought up Yves, whom she called in Breton " her other son," and whom she kissed very affectionately on both cheeks.

The women, for the past hour, had been sitting up anxiously for them. They received them with indulgence, although they were tipsy (it was what commonly happened when old friends met), scolded them just a little, and then set to work to make pancakes and soup for the three of us.

A wild wind, which had begun to blow from the sea, roared outside, in the darkness of the deserted countryside. From time to time, it rushed down the chimney, driving before it the bright flames of the fire; and then little flakes of ash, very light, began to dance a round-dance about the hearth, very low, skimming the floor, like those unhappy souls of dwarfs which circle the whole night long about the Great Rocks.

We were very comfortable before this fire which dried our clothes soaked with rain, and we waited eagerly for the hot soup which was being prepared for us.

CHAPTER XIX

THE pancakes, which were being made for us, resembled the moon, so large were they; they were passed to us in turn, piping hot, at the end of a long oak spoon shaped like the oar of a cutter.

Yves let one fall on a large hen which we had not noticed on the floor. The hen retreated hurriedly to a dark corner, shaking its feathers with a peevish and offended air. I wanted to laugh and so did Jeannie, but we dared not, knowing as we both did that it was a sign of misfortune.

" That old black one again! " said the old grand-mother, letting go her spinning-wheel, and looking at Yves with an air of consternation. " Jeannie, you must remember to send it to market to-morrow morning; it is for ever wandering about when all the others are in bed; it will end by bringing unhappiness upon us."

We cut our pancakes in small pieces and put them in our soup-bowls, and then we eat them, well-soaked, with our wooden spoons. And Jeannie made us drink, all three out of the same large mug, some very good cider.

Afterwards, when we had eaten and drunk our fill, Jean began to sing, in a fine tenor voice, a sea chanty known to all Breton sailors. Yves and I sang bass, and the old grandmother beat time with her head and the pedal of her spinning-wheel. We no longer heard the mournful refrains which the wind sang, all alone, outside.

The ditty ran:

> We were three sailor lads of Groix,
> We were three sailor lads of Groix,
> A sailing on the *Saint François.*
> How the wind blows!
> The wind is the plague o' the sailor.
>
> Heave to! There's a man overboard;
> Heave to! There's a man overboard;
> The others are in sore distress.
> How the wind blows!
> The wind is the plague o' the sailor.
>
> The others are in sore distress,
> The others are in sore distress,
> They hoist the white flag on the mast.
> How the wind blows!
> The wind is the plague o' the sailor.
>
> They hoist the white flag on the mast.
> They hoist the white flag on the mast.
> But all they find is his poor hat.
> How the wind blows!
> The wind is the plague o' the sailor.

F

But all they find is his poor hat,
But all they find is his poor hat,
His 'baccy pipe and his jack-knife.
　　How the wind blows!
The wind is the plague o' the sailor.

The mother dear he left behind,
The mother dear he left behind,
She prays Saint Anne of Auray.
　　How the wind blows!
The wind is the plague o' the sailor.

O! good Saint Anne send back my son,
O! good Saint Anne send back my son,
The good Saint Anne she makes reply .
　　How the wind blows!
The wind is the plague o' the sailor.

The good Saint Anne she makes reply,
The good Saint Anne she makes reply,
" You'll find him again in Paradise! "
　　How the wind blows!
The wind is the plague o' the sailor.

Home she goes to her cottage lone,
Home she goes to her cottage lone,
And dies, poor soul, on the morrow.
　　How the wind blows!
The wind is the plague o' the sailor.

CHAPTER XX

WHEN it was time to go, I found that Yves was
much more tipsy than I could have believed. Outside he stumbled up to his knees in puddles of water,
and reeled from side to side. To get him home I

put my right arm round his waist and his left arm over my shoulder and almost carried him. We could see nothing but the intense blackness of the night; a strong wind lashed our faces, and, in the dark lanes, Yves no longer knew where he was.

They were uneasy in his cottage and were sitting up for him. His mother scolded him, in her stern way, speaking loud and angrily as one might to a naughty child; and he went very crestfallen and sat down in a corner.

However, we were forced to partake of a second supper; it is the custom and there was no escape. An omelette, more pancakes, and slices of brown bread and butter. Afterwards we proceeded to retire for the night, the men first and then, the light having first been extinguished, the women. Under our mattresses there were thick litters made of a mass of branches of oaks and beeches; these subsided with a crackle of dry leaves when we lay down, and we felt ourselves sink into a little hollow, which kept us warm.

" Hoo! hoo-oo-oo! Hoo! hoo-oo-oo! " sang the wind outside, with a voice like an owl's, as if it were angry, as if it were indignant, then as if it were complaining and dying.

When the candle was put out and the cottage was in darkness, came the sound of a small voice beginning a Breton prayer; it was the voice of a little girl of four who had been adopted by the family; she was in fact the child of Gildas by a girl in Plouherzel, begotten during his last visit to his home.

A very long prayer, broken by solemn responses of the old grandmother; all the Saints of Brittany :

Saints Corentin and Allain, Saints Thénénan and Thégonnec, Saints Tuginal and Tugdual, Saints Clet and Gildas were invoked, and then there was silence.

Quite near me, the scarcely perceptible breathing of Yves, already sunk in deep sleep. At the foot of our bed the hens at roost dreaming on their high perch. A cricket giving out from time to time, in the still warm hearth, a mysterious little crystal note. And outside, around the solitary cottage, the continuous noise of the wind: an immense groaning which swept over all the Breton country: an unceasing pressure which came from the sea with the night and stirred the country to a monotonous dark movement, at the hour when the dead appear and ghosts walk.

CHAPTER XXI

" Good morning, Yves ! "

" Good morning, Pierre ! "

And we throw open to the light of the morning the shutters of our cupboard.

This " Good morning, Pierre ! " preceded by a little smile of intelligence, is said with hesitation, in a shy voice; it is " Good morning, Captain ! " that Yves is accustomed to say, and he is rather disconcerted at finding himself on awakening, so near me and under the necessity of calling me by my name. To impose upon the good people of Plouherzel and preserve the character given me by my borrowed clothes, we had concerted this show of intimacy.

The sunshine of yesterday had departed and the high wind of the night was no more. It was typical Brittany weather and the whole country was enveloped in the same immense grey cloud. The light was the light of twilight, and was so pale and wan that it seemed that it had not strength enough to enter through the little windows of the cottages. Of distant things one could distinguish nothing; a fine drizzle, like a watery dust, filled the air.

We had to make the promised round of visits to uncles, cousins, old friends of boyhood; and these little homesteads were very scattered, for Plouherzel is not a village, but a region around a chapel.

Often we had far to walk, along muddy lanes, between moss-covered banks, under the vault of old dead beech trees and under the veil of the grey sky.

And all these cottages were alike, low, sunk in the earth, gloomy; their thatched roof, their rough granite walls, made green with scurvy grass, with lichen and the fresh moss of winter. Within, dark, primitive, with press-beds protected by pictures of the saints or statues of the Blessed Virgin.

We were received everywhere in most cordial fashion, and everywhere we needs must eat and drink. There were long conversations in Breton, with which, in my honour, was mingled, with indifferent success, a little French. It was of the childhood of Yves that these good people loved most to talk. Dear old men and dear old women recounted with glee the pranks he used to play; and, by all accounts, they were very numerous.

"Oh! he was a terrible fellow, you may take our word for it!"

Yves received these compliments with his big, placid air and drank at every opportunity.

The devil-may-care sea-rover was taking shape already, it seemed, in the heart of the little wild boy; the little Yves, who ran barefoot about these lanes of Plouherzel, was the unconscious germ of the sailor of later days, wild, truant, uncontrollable.

Towards evening, at low tide, we descended, Yves and I, into the bed of the salt-water lake, into the meadow of brown seaweed. We carried, each of us, a slice of black bread well buttered, and a large knife for opening shell-fish. A feast of his boyhood which he wanted to renew with me: shell-fish eaten raw with bread and butter.

The sea had receded for many miles, laying bare the vast fields of seaweed, the deep meadow in which the herbage was brown and briny, with strange living flowers. All around, granite walls enclosed this immense pond, and the isle shaped like a couchant beast, stripped to its feet, disclosed the bottom of its black base. There were many other granite blocks also, which had been hidden under water at high tide and now were visible, rising up, with their long trimmings of seaweed hanging like wet bedraggled hair. On the mournful plain many of them might be seen scattered all about, in strange attitudes of awakening.

The cold air was impregnated with the acrid odour of sea-wrack. Night came on slowly, with

silent stealth, and all these large backs of stone
began to take on the appearance of herds of
monsters. We took the shell-fish on the end of
our knives and ate them as they were, all living, with
our slices of bread, being both hungry and in haste
to be done before the light should fail.

"It's not so good as it used to be," said Yves
when he had finished eating. "And somehow it
seems to me melancholy here. . . . When I was
little, I remember, there were times when I had the
same feeling, but not so strongly as to-night. Let
us go, shall we?"

Rather surprised by what he said, I replied to
him :

"My poor Yves, I think you are becoming like
me!"

"Like you, do you say?"

And he looked at me with a long melancholy
smile, which revealed to me new things in him, new
and indefinable things. And I realized that evening that he had in fact, much more than I should
have thought, ways of thinking, ideas, sensations,
similar to mine.

"And do you know," he continued, as if following still the same train of thought, "do you know
there is one thing which troubles me often when we
are far away, at sea or in countries overseas? I
scarcely dare to tell you. . . . It is the idea that
I might die perhaps and not be buried in our
cemetery here."

And he pointed to the steeple of Plouherzel
Church, which could be seen above the granite cliffs
in the far distance, like a grey arrow.

"It is not from any religious feeling, as you will

understand; for you know that I have no love for the clergy. No, it is just an idea that comes to me, I cannot tell you why. And when I am unhappy enough to think of this thing, I cease somehow to be brave."

CHAPTER XXII

IT was in the evening, after supper, that Yves' mother solemnly recommended her son to my care. It was a trust that has endured until now.

She had understood, with her mother's instinct, that I was not what I appeared to be, and that I should be able to exercise over the destiny of her last son a very important influence.

"She says," translated her daughter, "that you are deceiving us, sir, and that Yves, too, is deceiving us to please you; that you are not one like ourselves. . . . And she asks, since you voyage together, if you will look after him."

Then the old woman began to tell me the story of Yves' father, a story which I had heard long before from Yves himself. I listened to it willingly, nevertheless, recited by this young girl, before the wide Breton fireplace where the flames danced over a beech log.

"She says that our father was a very handsome sailor, so handsome that no one in the country had ever seen so handsome a man walk the earth. He died, leaving thirteen of us, thirteen children. He

died as many sailors of our country die.   One
Sunday when he had been drinking he put to sea
at night in his boat, in spite of a strong wind that
blew from the north-west, and he never returned.
Like his sons, he was a man without fear; but his
head was not good. . . ."

And the poor mother looked at her son
Yves.

"She says," continued the daughter, "that my
parents lived at Saint Pol-de-Léon, in Finistère,
that Yves was one year old, and that I was not yet
born when our father died, that she then left Saint
Pol and returned to Plouherzel in Goëlo, her native
country.   My father left his affairs in great disorder;
almost all the money that at one time we had had
been spent in the tavern, and my mother had no
longer wherewithal to feed us.   It was then that my
two elder brothers, Gildas and Goulven, left to
become ship-boys on ocean-going ships.

"We have not seen much of them in the country
here since their departure, and yet it cannot be said
that they have ceased to care about us.   They
many times surrendered their sailors' pay in order
to help my mother to bring us up, us younger ones,
Yves, my sister who is here, and me.

"But Goulven deserted, sir, more than fifteen
years ago, in a fit of temper."

"They, too," said the old woman, "are handsome
and brave sailors, their heart is true as gold. . . .
But they have their father's head, and already they
have taken to drinking heavily."

"My brother Gildas," the daughter went on,
"served for seven years on board an American ship
engaged in whale fishing in the great ocean.   That

voyage made him very rich; but it seems that it is
a hard calling, is it not, sir?"

"Yes, a hard calling indeed. . . ." I have seen
them at work in the great ocean, these sailors in
question, half whale fishers and half pirates, who
pass years in the great swell of the southern seas
without ever touching inhabited land.

"He was so rich, my brother Gildas, when he
returned from this fishing, that he had a large sack
filled full with pieces of gold."

"He poured them here on to my knees," said the
old woman, holding out the skirt of her dress as if
to receive them again, "and my apron was filled
with them. Large golden coins of other countries,
marked with all sorts of heads of kings and birds.[1]
There were some of them quite new, with the
portrait of a woman wearing a crown of feathers,[2]
a single one of which was worth more than a
hundred francs. Never had we seen so much gold.
He gave a thousand francs to each of his sisters and
a thousand to me, his mother, and bought me this
little house in which we live. He squandered the
rest in amusing himself at Paimpol and in doing
things which, certainly, were not good. But they
are all like that, sir, you know it better than I. For
two months they spoke of none but him in the town.

"Then he left us again and we have not seen
him since. He is a brave sailor, sir, is my son
Gildas, but he has been ruined as his father was
by his fondness for liquor."

And the old woman bowed her head sadly as

[1] The Chilian *Condors*.
[2] The twenty piastre piece of California (the whalers
usually turn their savings into this money).

she spoke of this incurable plague which destroys the families of Breton sailors.

There was silence for a time, and then she spoke again to her daughter in an earnest voice, looking at me the while.

" She asks, sir, if you will make her this promise . . . about my brother. . . ."

Her anxious, searching gaze, fixed on me, affected me strangely. It is no doubt true that all mothers, however far apart in station they may be, have, in certain hours, the same expression. . . . And now it seemed to me that this mother of Yves had some resemblance to mine.

" Tell her that I swear to look after him *all my life, as if he were my brother*."

And the daughter repeated, translating slowly into Breton:

" He swears that he will look after him all his life as if he were his brother."

The old mother had risen, upright as ever, stern and brusque; she had taken from the wall a picture of Christ and had advanced towards me, addressing me as if she wished to take me at my word, there and then, with naïve, impulsive simplicity:

" It is on this, sir, that she asks you to swear."

" No, mother, no! " said Yves, in confusion, trying to interpose, to stop her.

But I held out my arm towards this picture of Christ, a little surprised, a little moved, perhaps, and I repeated:

" I swear to do what I have said."

But my arm trembled a little because I foresaw that my responsibility would be a heavy one in the future.

And then I took Yves' hand. His head was bowed in thought:

"And you will do what I tell you, you will follow me . . . *brother?*"

And he replied, in a low voice, hesitating, his eyes turned away, but with the smile of a child:

"Why, yes . . . of course I will."

CHAPTER XXIII

WE had not long to sleep that night, *my brother and I*, in our little beds in the cupboard.

As soon as the old cottage cuckoo had announced four o'clock in its cracked voice, quickly, we had to get up. We were due at Paimpol before daybreak, to catch there at six o'clock the diligence for Guincamp.

At half-past four, on this cold winter's morning, the poor little door opened to let us out; it closed on a last kiss for Yves from his weeping mother, on a last handshake for me. We set off in the cold rain and the dark night, and for five years we saw them no more.

That is what happens in the families of sailors.

When we were half-way on our road we heard the Angelus sounding behind us at Plouherzel. We thought we were late and began to run. Our faces were bathed in perspiration when we reached Paimpol.

But we had been mistaken; the hour of the Angelus had been put forward.

We found a refuge in a tavern already open, where we had breakfast with some Icelanders and other seafaring folk.

And on the night of the same day, at eleven o'clock, we arrived back in Brest to put to sea once more.

CHAPTER XXIV

I was aware that I had accepted a heavy responsibility in adopting this refractory brother, the more so because I took my oath very seriously.

But fate separated us on the second day following, and soon we were half the world apart.

Yves set sail for the Atlantic, and I left for the Levant, for Stamboul.

It was not until fifteen months later, in May, 1877, that we met again on board the *Médée*, which was cruising between India and China.

CHAPTER XXV

On board the *Médée*, *May*, 1877.

"This suits me as gaiters suit a rabbit," said Yves, with a boyish air, as he contemplated his pagoda sleeves and his blue robe of Burmese silk.

It was at Yé, a Siamese town, on the Bay of Bengal. He was sitting in the background of a sailors' tavern on a stool of Chinese design.

He was very drunk, and after he had smiled thus to see himself clothed in the fashion of a Chinese mandarin, his eyes became dull and lustreless, his lip curled and disdainful. At such moments there was nothing he might not do, as in his bad days of old.

By his side was big Kerboul, also a foresail topman, who had just had brought to him fifteen glasses of a very expensive Singapore liquor, and had drained them one after the other, breaking them afterwards with blows of his fist, in the deadly serious way characteristic of the drunken Breton. And the debris of these fifteen glasses covered the table on which now he had put his feet.

And Barrada, the gunner, was there too, handsome and calm as usual, smiling his feline smile. The topman had invited him, exceptionally, to their feast. And Le Hello also, and Barazère, and half a dozen others of the mainsail and four of the bowsprit—all attitudinizing, with superb airs, in their Eastern robes.

And even Le Hir was there, a half-witted fellow from the island of Sein, whom they had brought as a laughing-stock, and who was drinking refuse mixed with his bowl of rum. And, to complete the tale, two sea-rovers, two blacklisters, deserters from every flag, old acquaintances of Yves', who had found them, that evening, on the beach and, out of kindness, brought them along.

It was to celebrate the feast of Saint Epissoire, the patron saint of the topmen, that they had foregathered here, and custom required that I should put in an appearance among them, as navigating officer.

For a year past they had not put foot on land. And the Commander, who was well satisfied with his crew, had permitted them, as being the most meritorious, to celebrate as in France the anniversary of their patron saint. He had selected this town of Yé, because it seemed to him the least dangerous for us, the people there being more inoffensive than elsewhere and more easily appeased.

In this room, which was large and low-pitched, with paper walls, there was, at the same time as us, a band of sailors from an American merchantship, who were drinking with sandy-haired, long-toothed women escaped from the brothels of British India.

And these intruders annoyed the topmen who wanted to be alone and let them see it.

Eleven o'clock. The candles had just been renewed in the coloured lanterns, and outside the Siamese town was asleep in the warm night. Inside one felt that trouble was brewing, that arms and fists were itching for a fight.

"Who are these fellows?" said one of the Americans, who spoke with a Marseilles accent. "Who are these Frenchies who come here to lay down the law? And that one who is with them "— this was meant for me—" the youngest of them all, who gives himself airs and seems to be in command?"

" That one," said Yves, with the air of one who did not deign to turn his head, " that one—any one who touches him will need to be a man!"

" That one!" said Barrada. " Do you want to

know who he is? Wait a moment and we will tell
you, without troubling him to speak for himself; and
you will see, my boys, *if that will enlighten you!* "

Yves had already hurled at them his Chinese
stool, which had burst the wall just above their
heads, and Barrada, with a first blow, had knocked
over two of them. The others overthrown in turn
on top of the first two, all struggling on the ground.
Kerboul began to belabour the mass unmercifully
with his table, scattering over his enemies the debris
of his fifteen glasses.

Then we heard outside the sounding of gongs
and the ringing of bells, rustlings of silk and shrill
little laughs of women.

And the dancing-girls entered. (The topmen had
asked for dancing-girls.)

The fighting stopped when they appeared, for
they were strange to see. Painted like Chinese
idols, covered with gold and glistening stones, the
eyes half-closed, looking like little white slits, they
advanced into our midst with the smiles of dead
women, holding their arms in the air and spreading
out their slender fingers, the long nails of which
were enclosed in golden sheaths.

At the same time came perfumes of balm and
incense; little sticks had been set alight in a
warming-dish, and an odorous, languorous smoke
spread in a blue cloud.

The gongs sounded louder now and the phantoms
began to dance, keeping their feet motionless,
executing a kind of rhythmic movement of the
stomach with twistings of the wrists. Always the
same set smile, the same white mask of death. It
seemed that the only life there was in them was

concentrated in their rounded hips and arched stomachs which moved with lascivious wrigglings; and in the rigid arms, the disturbing outspread hands which writhed unceasingly.

Le Hello who, for some time past, had been asleep on the floor, hearing the loud sounding of the gongs, woke up, startled.

" Why, you fool, it's the dancing-girls! " explained Barrada, jeering, laughing at him.

" Oh! yes! the dancing-girls! "

He got up and with his large paw, which groped in the air, uncertain, he tried to beat down these upraised arms and these gilded claws, stuttering, thick-voiced.

" It's not good, you white faced guy, it's not good to move your hands like that, it's vulgar. . . . I think it's . . . I think it's . . . damnation! " And he sank to the floor again and went to sleep.

Barrada, who also this evening had drunk more than was usual with him, reproached them for their yellow skin and told them about his, which was white. " White! White! White! " He insisted over and over again on this whiteness, which as a matter of fact he much exaggerated, and proceeded presently to show it to them. First his arm, then his chest. " Look! " he said. " Is it not true? "

The little yellow dolls of Asia continued their slow, lugubrious, beast-like wrigglings, preserving always the mystery of their rictus and of their white elongated eyes. And now Barrada, completely nude, was dancing before them, looking like a Greek marble which had suddenly taken life for some ancient bacchanal.

But the Burmese ladies, wound up like automata,

G

danced on and on for long after he was tired.   And presently, when all was over and the gongs were silent, the sailors were seized with fear at the idea that these women, paid for their pleasure, were waiting for them.   One after another they slunk away in the direction of the shore, not daring to approach them.

CHAPTER XXVI

THIS Barrada, who had " wangled " things so that he sailed for a third time on the same ship with us, was the great friend of Yves.

An illegitimate child, born and reared in the open on the quays of Bordeaux.   Very vicious, but with a good heart; full of contrasts, certain elementary notions of human dignity were entirely wanting in him; it was his pride to be better-looking than the others, more agile, stronger, and a more artful " wangler."   (" Wangler " and " wangling " are two words which resume in themselves almost the whole life of the navy; they have no academic equivalent.)

In return for payment, Barrada taught on board every kind of exercise in vogue among sailors: boxing, single-stick, fencing, with gymnastics into the bargain, and singing and dancing.   Supple as a clown; the friend of all the travelling strongmen who posed in the studios of sculptors; fighting for money in mountebank shows.

An outstanding personality at the sailors' feastings, but always as a guest, drinking freely, but never paying; drinking freely, but never beyond his capacity, and passing through all sorts of revelry, without losing his upright carriage, his smile, or his freshness.

He was always ready with a mocking repartee which would never have occurred to anyone else; his Gascon accent rendered his sallies more comical; and then he used to punctuate his phrases with a kind of noise that was peculiarly his own; a half laugh which sounded in his deep chest like the hoarse yawning of a lion.

Withal, honest, grateful, obliging to everyone, and faithful to his friends; unequivocal in speech and answering always with the disconcerting frankness of a child.

And yet making money by any and every means, even by his beauty when the occasion offered. And that, naïvely, with his unspoilt good nature, in such a way that the others, who knew it, pardoned him as they would one more like a child than themselves. Yves contented himself with saying:

"That's not good, Barrada, I assure you . . ." and loved him none the less.

And all this was amassed, was condensed as it were in the form of large pieces of gold sewn about his waist in a leathern belt. And its object was to enable him, after his five years' re-engagement, to marry a little Spanish dressmaker at Bordeaux, who worked in a large shop in the Passage Sainte Catherine; a refined little workwoman whose photograph he always carried with him, a photograph showing her in profile with a fringe and an elegant fur toque trimmed with a bird's wing.

"What can one do! She was my little sweetheart when I was a boy," he used to say, as if it was necessary to make an excuse.

And, while he was waiting for this little sweetheart, he abandoned himself to many others, deliberately often, but sometimes in sheer goodness of heart in the manner of Yves, because he shrank from giving pain.

CHAPTER XXVII

AT SEA, *May,* 1877.

FOR two days now, the great sinister voice had been groaning round us. The sky was very dark. It was like the sky in that picture in which Poussin has tried to paint the deluge; only all the clouds were moving, tormented by a wind that awakened fear.

And this great voice continued to swell, growing deeper, incessant; it was like a fury which was becoming exasperated. In our progress we ran into enormous masses of water which came on in white-crested volutes and passed as if in pursuit one of another; they rushed upon us with their full force; and then there were mighty shocks and great dull sounds.

Sometimes the *Médée* reared, mounted over

them, as if she, too, in turn, was seized with fury against them. And then she descended again, head first, into the treacherous hollows which lurked behind; she touched the bottom of these kinds of valleys which opened rapidly between high walls of water; and then made haste to climb once more, to escape from between these curved, glistening, greenish walls, which threatened to overwhelm her.

An icy rain streaked the air with long white arrows, whipping, stinging, like the blows of a lash. We had drawn nearer the north, in advancing along the Chinese coast, and the unexpected cold bit into us.

Aloft, in the rigging, they were trying to take in the topsails already close hauled; the stormsail was already hard to carry and now, it was necessary, at any cost, to make head against the wind, on account of the doubtful countries which lay behind us.

For two long hours the topmen were at work, blinded, lashed, stung by all that fell over them, sheets of spray from the sea, sheets of rain and hail from the sky; trying, with hands cramped with cold and bleeding, to take in the stiff wet canvas which bellied in the furious wind.

But one saw nothing, heard nothing.

It was difficult enough merely to prevent oneself from being swept away, merely to hold fast to all these moving, wet and slippery things—but they had besides to work high up in the air on their yards which, swaying, had sudden, irregular movements, like the last beating of wings of a great wounded bird in its death-throes.

Cries of pain came from aloft, from this kind of hanging bunch of human grapes. Cries of men, hoarse cries, more ominous than those of women, because one is less accustomed to hear them; cries of horrible suffering: a hand caught somewhere, fingers jammed, from which the flesh was torn as they were drawn away—or maybe, some unfortunate fellow, less strong than the others, numbed with cold, who felt that he could hold out no longer, that his head was beginning to swim, that he was about to let go and fall. And the others, out of pity, bound him and tried to lower him to the deck.

For two hours this lasted; they were exhausted, beat; flesh and blood could do no more.

Then they were ordered down, and in their place were sent up the men of the larboard watch, who had been resting and were not so cold.

They came down, pale, wet, with icy water streaming down their chest and down their back, hands bleeding, nails torn, teeth chattering. For two days they had lived in water, had scarcely eaten, had scarcely slept, and their vitality was at an ebb.

It is this long watching, this long labour in the damp cold, which are the true horrors of the sea. Often poor fellows die, who, before they utter their last cry, their last sob of agony, have remained for days and nights wet through, dirty, covered with a muddy coating of cold sweat and salt, with a kind of veneer of death.

And still the wind increased. There were times when it whistled, shrill and strident, as in a paroxysm of evil exasperation; and others again, when its voice became deep, cavernous, powerful as the immense sounds of cataclysm. And we continued to leap from wave to wave, and, save for the sea which preserved still its unholy whiteness of foam and froth, everything was becoming darker. A glacial twilight was falling upon us; behind these dark curtains, behind all these masses of water which climbed to the sky, the sun had disappeared at its due hour; it abandoned us, and left us to find our way as best we could in the darkness. . . .

Yves had climbed with the larboard men into the disarray of the rigging, and then I kept my eyes aloft, blinded myself also, and only seeing momentarily now the human cluster in the air.

And, suddenly, in a lurch more violent than any that had gone before, the silhouette of this group was broken brusquely and changed its form; two bodies broke away from it and fell with outspread arms into the roaring volutes of the sea, while another crashed on the deck, without a cry, falling as a man might who was already dead.

" The foot-rope broken again! " said the officer of the watch, stamping his foot with rage. " Some rotten rope which they gave us in that damned port of Brest! Big Kerboul in the sea. And the other one, who was he? "

Others, clinging to ropes, swung for some moments in the void and then climbed, hand over hand, very rapidly, as monkeys might.

I recognized Yves as one of the climbers, and breathed again.

They threw out life-buoys as a matter of course for those who were in the sea. But what was the use? The hope rather was that we should not see them reappear, for if we did, on account of the danger of getting broadside on to the rollers, we should not have been able to stop to rescue them and should have needed the horrible courage to abandon them. But a roll was called of those who remained in order to find out the name of the second who had been lost: he was a very steady little apprentice, whom his mother, a widow well on in years, had commended to the care of the boatswain before the departure from France.

The other, the one who had crashed on the deck, they carried below as best they could, with great difficulty, letting him fall again on the way; and lay him in the infirmary which had become a foul sink in which swirled two feet of filthy, dark water, with broken bottles and odours of all sorts of spilt remedies. Not even a place where he might die in peace, for the sea had no pity on the sufferer; it continued to make him dance, to toss him more than ever. A kind of sound came now from his throat, a rattling which persisted for some little time, lost in the great uproar of things. One might have been able to succour him perhaps, to prolong his agony, with a little calm. But he died there quickly enough, in the hands of the sick-berth attendants who had become stupid with fear, and tried to make him eat.

Eight o'clock at night. At this time the responsibility of the watch was heavy and it was my turn to take it.

We carried on as best we might. We could see nothing now. We were in the midst of so much noise that the voices of the men seemed no longer to have any sound; the blasts of the whistles, blown with full might, came faintly, like the flute-like pipings of very small birds.

We heard terrible blows struck against the sides of the ship, as by some enormous battering-ram.

And everywhere and always great hollows opened, gaping wide; we felt ourselves being hurled into them, head lowered, in the pitch darkness. And then a force struck us with a brutal strength, carrying us high into the air, and the *Médée* vibrated in its whole being, as it were, like a monstrous drum. In vain then we tried to hold fast; we were forced to let go and quickly cling more strongly to something else, shutting our mouths and eyes as we did so, because we knew by instinct, without seeing, that it was the moment when a great mass of water would sweep through the air and maybe sweep us away with it.

And this went on continuously, these headlong plunges, followed by these leaps with their accompanying terrifying drum-like sounds.

And, after each of these shocks came again the streaming of water pouring in from all sides; the sound of a thousand things breaking, a thousand fragments rolling in the darkness. And all this prolonged in a sinister trail the horror of the first concussion.

And the topmen and my poor Yves, what were they doing aloft? We could see the masts, the yards, now and then in the darkness, in silhouette, when the smarting pain caused by the hail allowed us to open our eyes and look; we could see the shapes of the great crosses, with double arms, after the fashion of Russian crosses, rocking in the darkness with movements of distress, with crazy gestures.

"Bring them down," said the Commander, who preferred the danger of the unfurled sail to the fear of losing more of his men.

I gave the order quickly, with a feeling of relief.

But Yves, from aloft, replied to me with the help of his whistle, that they had almost finished; that they had only to replace one gasket which was broken, by a makeshift knot, and then they would all come down, having taken in their sail and completed their work.

Afterwards when they were all down I breathed more freely. No one now aloft, nothing more to be done up there, nothing to be done now but to watch and wait. Then it seemed to me that the weather was almost fair, that it was almost comfortable on this bridge, now that I was relieved of the heavy weight of my anxiety.

CHAPTER XXVIII

Midnight. The end of the watch; the hour when we could go and seek shelter.

Below, in the padded gun-room, one saw another aspect of the tempest, the grim reality of the misery it caused in the entrails of the ship.

Seen from end to end it was a kind of long dark hall dimly lighted by flickering lanterns. The big guns, supported on their mountings, remained more or less in position by virtue of their lashings of iron cables. And this whole place was in motion; it had the movements of a thing which is shaken in a sieve, shaken without respite, without mercy, perpetually, with a blind rage; it creaked everywhere, it trembled like an animate thing in pain, racked, exhausted, as if it were about to burst and die.

And the great waters outside, for ever seeking to enter, penetrated here and there in little streams, in sinister spoutings.

You were lifted up so quickly that your knees gave way—and then suddenly things slipped from under you, sank beneath your feet—and you descended with them, stiffening in spite of yourself, as for a kind of resistance.

There were shrill, discordant, alarming noises which came from all round; all this framework in the form of a fish which was the *Médée* was loosening little by little, and groaning under the terrible strain. And outside, on the other side of the wooden wall, always the same immense deep sound, the same deep voice of horror.

But all held fast nevertheless. The long gun-room remained intact, one saw it still from end to end, sometimes tilted, half-overturned, sometimes rising almost upright in a concussion, looking longer still in this darkness in which the lanterns were lost, seeming to change its shape and grow larger, in all this noise, as if it were some vague place of dreamland.

On the low ceiling were hung interminable rows of canvas pockets, swollen all of them by their heavy contents, looking like the little pockets which spiders hang to walls—grey pockets enclosing each a human being, the sailors' hammocks.

Here and there one saw an arm hanging out, or a bare leg. Some slept peacefully, exhausted by their labours; others moved restlessly and talked aloud in bad dreams. And all their hammocks swung and jostled one another in a perpetual movement, and sometimes came in violent collision and heads suffered.

On the floor, beneath the hapless sleepers, was a lake of dark water which swirled this way and that, carrying with it soiled articles of clothing, pieces of bread and biscuit, spilt porridge, every sort of debris and unclean refuse. And from time to time came men, pale, exhausted, half-naked, shivering in their wet shirts, who wandered beneath these rows of grey hammocks, seeking theirs, seeking their poor little suspended bed, the only place where they might find a little warmth, a little dryness, and what would have to serve for rest. They stumbled as they passed, holding on to anything that offered to prevent themselves from falling, and bumping their heads against those who slept. Every man for himself in times such as this; none cared what happened to another. Their feet slipped in the pools of water and filth; they gave no more thought to their dirtiness than animals in distress.

A suffocating reek filled the gun-room; all this filth which slid about the floor gave the impression of a lair of sick beasts, and one smelt the acrid stench which is peculiar to the hold of a ship in times of bad weather.

At midnight, Yves, in turn, descended into the gun-room with the other men of the larboard watch; their spell of duty had been extended for an hour on account of the necessity for securing the boats. They slid down through the half-opened hatchway which closed upon them, and mingled with this floating misery below.

They had spent five hours at their rough work, rocked in the void, lashed by the furious winds above, and soaked to the skin by the stinging rain which seared their faces. They made a grimace of disgust as they entered this closed place where the atmosphere savoured of death.

And Yves said, in his big disdainful way:

"It's those Parisians[1] again, I'll bet, who have made this place stink."

They were not ill, these fellows who were real sailors: their lungs were still filled with the wind of the masthead, and the healthy fatigue which they had just endured assured them now of a wholesome sleep.

They stepped on the rings, on the angle-blocks, on the ends of the gun-carriages, with precaution, in order to avoid the dirty water and the filth—placing their bare feet on any projection that offered, using the precarious footholds of cats. Near their hammocks they undressed, hung up their caps, hung up their large leather-chained knives, their soaked clothing, hung up everything and hung up themselves; and when they were stripped they brushed off with their hands the water which trickled still down their muscular chests.

After that, they raised themselves to the ceiling with the lightness of acrobats, and stretched themselves, against the white beams, in their narrow little canvas beds. Overhead, above them, after each shock, one heard what seemed the passage of a cataract: the waves, the great masses of water which

---

[1] "Parisian" is a term of insult as used by sailors; it means: no sailor, a weakling, a sick man.

swept the bridge.   But the row of their hammocks assumed nevertheless the slow swinging motion of the neighbouring rows, grinding on the iron hooks, and they slept soundly in the midst of the mighty uproar.

Soon, around Yves' hammock, the Burmese women came and danced.   In the midst of a cloud of incense, rendered more murky by his dream, they came one after another with their dead smile, in strange silken costumes, covered with glistening stones.

They swayed their haunches slowly, to the sound of the gong, their hands upraised in the air, their fingers outspread, like so many phantoms.   They twisted their wrists in epileptic movements, and their long nails enclosed in the golden sheaves became entangled.

The gong—it was the tempest which sounded it, outside, against the sides. . . .

CHAPTER XXIX

I, too, at midnight, when my watch was over and I had seen Yves descend, returned to my room to try to sleep. After all, the fate of the ship concerned us now no longer, me no more than them. We had done our spell of watching and of work. We might sleep now with that absolute freedom from care which one has at sea when the hours of duty are finished.

In my own room, which was on the bridge, there was no lack of air—on the contrary. Through the broken panes the wind and the furious rain entered freely: the curtains twisted themselves into spirals and mounted to the ceiling with the sound of wings.

Like Yves, I hung up my wet clothes. The water streamed down my chest.

Although my little bed could scarcely be said to be comfortable I fell quickly asleep nevertheless, worn out by fatigue. Rolled, shaken, half thrown out of bed, I felt myself swung from right and from left, and my head bumped against the wood, painfully. I was conscious of all this in my sleep, but I slept on. I slept on and dreamt of Yves. Seeing him fall during the day had left me with a kind of uneasiness, as if some sinister thing had brushed against me in passing.

I dreamt I was lying in a hammock, as formerly

during my first years at sea. Yves' hammock was near mine. We were swinging violently and his became unhooked. Beneath us there was a confused movement of something dark which it seemed to me was deep water, and he, Yves, was about to fall into it. I stretched out my hands to save him, but they seemed to have no strength, they were nerveless as in dreams. I tried then to seize him round the body, to knot my hands about his chest, remembering that his mother had entrusted him to me; and I realized with anguish that I could not do it, that I was no longer capable of it; he was going to slip from me and to disappear in all this moving blackness which roared beneath us. . . . And then, what struck me with a horror of fear, was that he did not waken and he was icy cold, with a cold which penetrated me also, to the marrow of my bones; and the canvas of his hammock had become rigid like the sheath of a mummy. . . .

And I felt in my head the real concussions, the real pain of all these shocks, I mixed the real with the imaginary of my dream, as happens in conditions of extreme fatigue, and on this account the sinister vision assumed all the more intensity and life.

Afterwards, I lost consciousness of everything, even of the movement and noise, and then only did my rest begin.

When I awoke it was morning. The first light was of that yellow colour which is peculiar to the sunrise on days of tempest; and the roaring of the wind persisted still.

Yves came and opened my door a little and looked in. He propped himself in the doorway, holding on by one hand, bending his body now this way and now that, according to the needs of the moment, in order to preserve his equilibrium. He had put on again his damp clothes, and was covered with sea salt which was deposited in his hair, in his beard, in the form of a white powder.

He smiled, looking very calm and good-humoured.

"I wanted to see you," he said, "for I dreamt about you a lot in the night. All night long I saw those good Burmese ladies with their long golden nails, you know. They surrounded you with their evil monkeyings, and I could not drive them away. At last they wanted to eat you. Fortunately the réveillé sounded then; I was in a cold sweat when I awoke."

"And I, too, am very glad to see you, my dear Yves, for I have dreamt a lot about you also. Is it as rough as yesterday?"

"Perhaps a little more manageable. And, anyhow, it's day. As long as it's light, you know, it's always easier to work at the masthead. But when it's as black as the devil's pit, as last night, I don't like it at all."

Yves glanced with satisfaction all round my room, arranged by him in anticipation of bad weather. Nothing had budged, thanks to his contrivance. On the floor there was indeed a pool of salt water in which divers things floated; but the objects to which I attached more or less value had remained suspended or fixed, like furniture, to the panels of the walls by bolts or angle-irons. Everything had been corded, tied, secured with an extreme care by means of tarred rope of various thicknesses. Arms and bronzes had been wrapped in articles of clothing in a strange higgledly-piggledly. Japanese masks with

H

long human hair gazed at us through a network of
tarred thread; they had the same remote smile, the
same tilting of the eyes as the golden-nailed Burmese
women who, in Yves' dream, had wanted to
eat me. . . .

A bugle-call suddenly, brisk and joyful: the
summons to "wash deck!"

The bugle sounded a little thin, a little silvery,
in the formidable bellowing of the wind.

To wash the deck when the seas were breaking
over it might seem a somewhat senseless operation
to people who live on land.   But we found nothing
very extraordinary in it; it was done every morning,
without fail and in all circumstances; it is one of the
primordial rules of life at sea.   And Yves left me
saying, as if it was the most natural thing in the
world:

" I must be off to my washing station."

Nevertheless the bugle had sinned by excess of
zeal, and sounded without order, at its usual hour;
for this morning the deck was not to be washed.

One felt that things were more manageable, as
Yves had said; the movements were longer, more
regular, more like the rollings of the swell.   The
sea was less angry, and the deep, heavy-sounding
concussions were less frequent.

And then it was day—a vile day, it is true, with a
strange livid yellowness, but day nevertheless, less
sinister than the night.

Our hour, it seemed, had not yet come, for on the
second day following we ran into calm water, in a
port in China, at Hong Kong.

CHAPTER XXX

September, 1877.

THE *Médée* had been homeward bound for many a day.

Wind and current had favoured her. She sailed rapidly, so rapidly, for days and nights on end, that one lost the notion of places and distances. Vaguely we had seen pass the Straits of Malacca, taken in our course; the Red Sea, ascended under steam in a blaze of sunlight; then the point of Sicily, and at last the great couchant lion of Gibraltar. Now we are watching the horizon and the first land, which may appear at any moment, will be the land of Brittany.

I had joined the *Médée* only during the latter part of the voyage and, this time, my tour with Yves will have lasted less than five months.

Amid the grey expanse little white lines now appear; then a tower with dark little islets scattered about: all this still very distant and scarcely visible in the dull wan daylight which envelopes us.

We might imagine without any trouble that we were still at the other side of the world, in that extreme Asia which we have lately left; for things on board have not changed, nor faces either. We are still encumbered with Chinese knick-knacks; we continue to eat fruits gathered on the other side and still green; we carry with us odours, savours of China.

But no; our house has been translated very quickly; this tower and these islets are the Pierres-Noires; Brest is there, quite near us, and before night we shall have anchored there.

Always an emotion of remembrance, when this great roadstead of Brest appears, imposing and solemn, and these great sailing ships which one rarely sees elsewhere. All my first impressions of the navy, all my first impressions of Brittany—and then, too, it is France.

There is the *Borda* beyond; as I look at it, I can see again in my mind's eye the desk over which I have pored in long hours of study; and the blackboard on which I wrote feverishly, before the examination, the complicated formulæ of mechanics and astronomy.

Yves at that time was a small boy with a very serious and thoughtful air, a little round-faced Breton apprentice, who dwelt in the near-lying ship, the *Bretagne*, the neighbour and companion of the *Borda*. We were children then—to-day we are grown men—to-morrow . . . old age—the day after, death.

CHAPTER XXXI

SUNDAY, a day of great " boozing " in Brest.

Ten o'clock. A calm night, with a moonlit, tranquil sea; on board the *Médée* the sailors have finished singing their endless songs and silence has supervened.

Since the fall of darkness my eyes have been turned in the direction of the lights of the town. I am awaiting with uneasiness the return of the cutter of which Yves is in charge: it went ashore and has not returned.

At last I see its red light approaching, two hours late!

The sea is sonorous at night; in the distance I can hear cries mingling with the sound of the oars; strange things seem to be happening in the cutter.

She has scarcely come alongside when three drunken petty officers, in a state of fury, hasten on board and demand of me the head of Yves:

" He must be put in irons straightway; he must be tried and shot afterwards, for he has struck his superior officers."

Yves was standing there, trembling from the conflict in which just now he was engaged. These three petty officers have fought with him, or at any rate have tried to make him fight.

" They wanted to put me in the wrong! " he said disdainfully; and he swore that he had not returned the blows of the three men; for that matter he could have knocked all three of them over with his open hand. No; he let them lay hold of him and pull him about; they scratched his face and tore his clothes into ribbons, because he refused to allow them to take charge of the cutter, drunk as they were.

All the crew of the cutter were drunk also, by the fault of Yves, who had allowed them to drink.

And the three petty officers remained standing there, quite near him, continuing to shout, to revile, to threaten, three old drunkards, grotesque in their stuttering fury, very ridiculous if discipline, that implacable thing, had not been on their side to make the scene terribly grave.

Yves, upright, his fists clenched, his hair over his forehead, his shirt torn, his chest all bare, tried almost beyond endurance by these insults, itching to strike, appealed to me with his eyes, in his distress.

Oh! discipline, discipline! There are times when it is harsh indeed. I am the officer of the watch and it is contrary to all rules that I should interfere except to speak non-committal words, and to hand them all over to the justice of the ship's police.

Contrary to all rules, however, I leap down from the bridge and throw myself on Yves—it was none too soon!—I pass my arms round his arms, and thus restrain him at the very moment when he is about to strike.

And I fix my eyes on the others, who then, in the presence of this turn in the situation, beat a retreat in the manner of dogs before their master.

Happily it is dark—and there are no witnesses. Only the cutter's crew and they are drunk—and, moreover, I am sure of them: they are good fellows all and if it is necessary to go before a courtmartial, they will not bear witness against us.

Then I take Yves by the shoulders and passing in front of his three enemies, who fall back to let us pass, I lead him to my room and lock him in. There for the moment he is safe.

I am summoned before the Commander who has been awakened by the noise. Unfortunately I have to explain the matter to him.

And I explain, extenuating as much as possible the fault of my poor Yves. I explain; and then, for some mortal minutes, I beg; I believe that never in my life had I begged before, it seems to me that it is no longer I who am speaking. And all I can say and all I can do breaks down against the cold logic of this man who holds in his hands the very existence of Yves, which has been entrusted to me.

I have, however, succeeded in removing the gravest of the matters, the question of striking a superior officer; but the insults remain and the refusal to obey. Yves has done these things: in substance, the charges are unfair and revolting; in the letter, they are true.

He is ordered to be put in irons at once, to begin with, and to be sent below under guard, on account of the disturbance and scandal.

Poor Yves! An unrelenting fatality has pursued him, for, this time, he was not really culpable. And this misfortune came upon him at the very time when he was becoming steadier, when he was making great efforts to give up drinking and behave himself.

CHAPTER XXXII

WHEN I returned to my room to tell him that he was to be put in irons, I found him sitting on my bed, his fists and teeth clenched with rage. His passionate Breton temper had got possession of him.

Stamping his foot, he declared that he would not go—it was too unjust!—unless they carried him by force, and that he would kill the first man that came to take him.

Then I saw that he was lost indeed, and my heart ached for him. What could be done? The guard was there, outside my door, waiting to lead him away and I dared not open; seconds and minutes passed and I could find no pretext for further delay.

An idea came to me, suddenly: I entreated him very gently, in the name of his mother, reminding him of my oath and, for the second time in my life, calling him brother.

Yves wept. It was over; he was vanquished and docile.

I threw some water over his forehead, adjusted his shirt a little and opened my door. All this had not lasted three minutes.

The guard appeared. He rose and followed, meek as a child. He looked back and smiled at me, went and replied with calmness to the interrogatory of the Commander, and proceeded peacefully to the hold to be put in irons.

About midnight, when this arduous watch was over, I went to bed, sending to Yves a blanket and a cloak. (For the nights already were cold.) And this in my helplessness was all that I could now do for him.

CHAPTER XXXIII

THE next day, a Monday, the Commander sent for me early, and I entered his room with a feeling of resentment in my heart, with bitter words ready on my lips, which I would have uttered at the outset in revenge for my supplications of yesterday, if I had not feared to aggravate Yves' lot.

I was mistaken, however: he had been touched the previous night and had understood me.

" You may go to your friend. Give him a good talking to, but say that I pardon him. The affair will go no farther and will be put right by a simple disciplinary punishment. He will remain eight days in irons, and that will be all. I inflict on the three petty officers, at your instance, the equivalent punishment of eight days' close arrest. I do this for you, who look upon him as a brother, and for his sake also, for, after all, he is the best man we have on board."

And I went away with feelings very different from those with which I had come, regarding him indeed with gratitude and affection.

CHAPTER XXXIV

A CORNER of the hold of the *Médée*, in all the disarray of laying up. A lantern illumines a vast medley of heterogeneous objects more or less nibbled by rats.

A dozen or so sailors—Barrada, Guiaberry, Barazère, Le Hello, all the little band of friends—are grouped about a man lying on the floor. It is Yves in irons, stretched on the damp boards, his head supported on his elbow, his foot in the padlocked ring of the " bar of justice."

The most implacable of his three enemies, Petty Officer Lagatut, stands before him, threatening him in his old drunken voice. He threatens him with revenge for that affair of the cutter, in which, to his mind, I had taken too large a part.

He has quitted his close arrest to come and abuse him—and I, whose watch it is and who am making a round, enter from behind and find him there—the old rogue is very neatly caught! The sailors who saw me enter, chuckle quietly in their sleeves, in anticipation of what is about to happen. Yves makes no reply, contenting himself with turning over and presenting his back to his tormentor with supreme insolence. For he, too, had seen me enter.

" We have begun a game of écarté together," said Petty Officer Lagatut; " you, Kermadec, boatswain; I, Lagatut, chief gunner, decorated with the Legion of Honour. Thanks to certain officers who protect you, you have taken the first two tricks: it remains to see who is going to take the three others."

" Petty Officer Lagatut," said I from behind, "we will play a three-handed game, if you are agreeable: a game of *rams*, that will be more amusing. And you, my good Yves, take another trick."

A chicken finding a knife, a thief who stumbles against a policeman, a mouse, which, by inadvertence, puts its paw on a cat, have not a longer face than Petty Officer Lagatut at that moment.

This little pleasantry of mine was not perhaps in the best of form. But the gallery, which was very friendly to us, greatly enjoyed this triumph of Yves.

CHAPTER XXXV

EIGHT days afterwards our frigate was completely disarmed and laid up in a remote part of the dockyard, the crew was paid off and the *Médée* might be described as a dead ship.

I was going away, and Yves accompanied me to the railway. The station was crowded with sailors; all those of the *Médée* who also were leaving; and others again who, taking French leave, had come to see them off.

Amongst them were many old acquaintances of ours, protégés and friends of Yves. And all these good fellows, rather tight, doffed their caps and bade us good-bye with effusion. It was a scene such as is usual when a ship is paid off; for a ship which finishes in this way is something apart; it marks the end of so many acquaintances, so many rancours, so many hates, so many sympathies.

At the entrance to the waiting-room, as I gripped Yves' hand, I said to him:

"You will write to me at any rate?"

And he replied:

"I was going to explain to you," and he hesitated still, with an amiable, shamefaced smile. "Well, here goes! I was going to explain to you that I do not know what to put at the beginning."

And it was true that the appellations "Captain," "Dear Captain," and others of the same kind, would scarcely any longer do. What should it be, then? I replied:

"Why, but that's very simple," and I cast about for a long time for this simple thing and could not find it. "That's very simple. Put . . . put: 'My dear brother'; that will be true in the first place, and, for the purpose of a letter, very suitable."

CHAPTER XXXVI

I<small>T</small> was about six weeks after the *Médée* had been laid up at Brest and I had separated from Yves, when one day, at Athens, I think, I received this surprising letter:

"B<small>REST</small>, 15*th September*, 1877.

"M<small>Y</small> D<small>EAR</small> B<small>ROTHER</small>,—I write you these few words, in haste to let you know that I got married yesterday. And, you may be sure, I would have asked your advice in advance, but, you must understand, I had no time to lose having been named to join the *Cornélie*, and having only eight days before me to spend with my wife.

"I think that you will find, you also, my dear brother, that this is better than being always moving about, as you know, from one ship to another. My wife's name is Marie Keremenen; I may tell you I am very proud of her and think we shall get on very well together if only I can settle down.

"I will write you a longer letter before I leave, my dear brother, and I can assure you I am very sad at the idea of embarking without you.

"I end by embracing you with all my heart.
"Your loving brother,
"Y<small>VES</small> K<small>ERMADEC</small>.

"P.S.—I have just learnt that my destination is

altered; I am embarking on the *Ariane* which does
not leave until the middle of November.   That
gives me nearly two months to spend with my wife.
We shall have good time in which to get to know
one another, and you may be sure I am very
pleased."

On their return from their voyages, sailors are
wont to do all sorts of stupid things with their
money; it is a thing excused by tradition.   And
seaport towns have reason to know their rather wild
eccentricities.

Sometimes, even, they marry, by way of pastime,
the first woman that offers in order to have an occasion for donning a black coat.

And Yves, who had already in times past
exhausted all kinds of foolishness, he, too, for a
change, had finished by marrying.

Yves married!   And to whom in heaven's name?
Perhaps some shameless hussy of the town, picked
up by chance in an hour when he was tipsy!

I had good reason to be uneasy, remembering a
certain creature in a feathered hat whom he had been
on the point of marrying for a lark—when he was
twenty—in this same town of Brest.

CHAPTER XXXVII

Two months later, when the *Ariane* was about to depart, fate decreed that I, too, should be appointed, at the last moment, to join its staff.

CHAPTER XXXVIII

AT the moment of leaving I saw this Marie Keremenen, whom I had half dreaded to meet. She was a young woman of about twenty years of age, dressed in the costume of the village of Toulven, in lower Brittany.

Her fine dark eyes were clear and frank. Without being absolutely pretty, she had a certain charm in her embroidered bodice, her white wide-winged head-dress, and her large collarette recalling a Medici ruff.

There was about her something candid, something wholesome which it did you good to see. It seemed to me that she was exactly what I should have looked for if it had fallen to me to choose for my brother Yves.

CHAPTER XXXIX

CHANCE had brought the two together, one day when she was on a visit to her godmother in Brest.

The lover lost no time, and she, won over by Yves' manly air, by his honest, winning smile, had been induced to consent—not without a certain uneasiness, nevertheless—to this precipitate marriage, which was going, for a start, to make her a widow for some seven or eight months.

She had a little fortune as they say in the country, and was going to return, as soon as we had left, to her parents' home in her village of Toulven.

Yves confided to me that they were expecting the arrival of a child.

"You will see," he said. "I bet that he will arrive just in time for our return."

And he embraced his wife, who was weeping. We departed. Once more we were going to cruise in the blue domain of the flying fish and dorados.

CHAPTER XL

15th November, 1877.

ON the day before we sailed, Yves had obtained a special permission to go ashore during the day in order that he might see, in the naval hospital, his eldest brother, Gildas, the fisher of whales, who had just arrived in a half dead condition, and whom he had not seen for ten years.

Gildas Kermadec was a man of about forty, tall, with features more regular than Yves'. In his eyes there was still a kind of dead fire. He must at one time have been exceedingly handsome.

He was paralysed and dying, destroyed by alcohol and excess of all kinds; he had lived a life of pleasure, sown his wild oats, and spent his strength on all the world's highways.

He came forward slowly, leaning on a stick, upright and well-set still, but dragging a leg, and with haggard eyes.

"Oh, Yves!" he said, and he repeated it three times: "Oh, Yves! Oh, Yves!"

It was scarcely articulate; for he was paralysed in speech also. He opened his arms to embrace Yves and tears ran down his bronzed cheeks.

There were tears in Yves' eyes also. . . . And then, quick, it was time to go. The leave that had been given him was only for an hour.

For that matter, Gildas found nothing more to say. He had made Yves sit down beside him on a hospital bench, and, holding his hand, looked at him with bewildered eyes that were near to dying. At first indeed he did try to say many things which seemed to press in his head; but there issued from his lips only inarticulate sounds, hoarse, deep, painful to hear. No, he could speak no more; and he contented himself with holding Yves' hand and gazing at him with an infinite sadness.

   .   .   .   .

Yves carried away a profound impression of this

last interview with his brother Gildas. They had only seen each other twice since Gildas had gone to sea. But they were brothers, brothers of the same cottage and of the same blood, and in that there is something mysterious, a bond which nothing can break.

A month later, at our first place of call, we learnt that Gildas was dead. And Yves put a band of mourning on his woollen sleeve.

CHAPTER XLI

ON BOARD THE *Ariane, May*, 1878.

THE island of Teneriffe appears before us like a kind of large pyramidal edifice, placed on an immense reflecting mirror which is the sea. The rugged sides, the gigantic ridges of the mountains are brought near, in little, by the extreme, unbelievable clearness of the air. One can distinguish everything: the sharp angles touched with rose, the hollows touched with blue. And the whole rests on the sea like a picture in a child's scrap-book, infinitely light, weightless. A sharp line of clouds pearly-grey in colour cuts Teneriffe horizontally in two, and, above, the peak rears its great cone bathed in sunlight.

The gulls are making an extraordinary racket around us; they cry and beat the air with their white wings in one of those accessions of frenzy, which seize them sometimes for what reason it is impossible to say.

Midday. The crew had just finished dinner. The whistle had sounded: " The port watch will clear away! " And Yves, who was on the port watch on board the *Ariane,* came up on deck and approached me, blowing his whistle softly to assure himself that it was still in good order.

" What is the matter with the gulls to-day? They were puling all the time during dinner, did you hear them? "

To be sure I did not know what was the matter with the gulls. But, since it was necessary, out of politeness, to make some sort of reply to Yves, I answered him in this wise:

That the gulls had asked to speak to the officer of the watch, who to be precise was myself. They wanted news of their little cousin Pierre Kermadec; and I had replied to them: " My good sirs, little Pierre Kermadec, my godson, is not yet born; you are too soon, come back in a few days' time, when we are at Brest." On that, as you see, they have departed. Look over there how they have all made off.

" You have given me a very pretty answer," said Yves, who did not often smile. " But I tell you, I dreamt much about this again last night and, do you know, a fear has come to me. It is that it may be a little girl."

It would indeed be a sad disappointment if the expected godson should turn out to be a little girl! It would not then be possible to call the newcomer Pierre.

This kinship of Yves' little child with the gulls was not of my invention: " gull " was the name given to the topmen on board the *Ariane,* and the name they gave to one another amongst themselves. It was not surprising, therefore, that my little godson should be deemed a blood relation of this bird of the sea.

And so, when we talked of him in our conversations at night, we used always to say:

" When will the ' little seagull ' arrive? "

And we never referred to him in any other way.

CHAPTER XLII

BREST, 13*th June*, 1878.

WE are staying for to-day at a casual lodging in the Rue de Siam at Brest, where the *Ariane* anchored this morning.

In reply to the advice of his arrival, Yves received from Toulven, from his wife's father, the following telegram:

" Little son born last night. Is going on very well. Marie also.

" CORENTIN KEREMENEN."

When night came and we were in bed it was impossible to sleep. I heard Yves turning in his bed, " going about " as he said in his Breton accent. At the thought that on the morrow he would be on the road to Toulven to see his little firstborn, his honest manly heart overflowed with all kinds of sentiments which were quite new to him.

Two days after him, I, too, would be due at
Toulven for the baptism.

And he made a thousand and one projects for
this ceremony:

" I hardly dare to say it, but, if you would like,
at Toulven, to stay with us. . . . At my father-in-
law's place, you know. . . . To be sure it is not like
the town, as I need not tell you. . . ."

CHAPTER XLIII

BREST, 15*th June*, 1878.

IN the early morning I set out for Toulven where
Yves has been awaiting me since yesterday.

The weather is magnificent.   Old Brittany is
green and decked with flowers.   Along the road are
large woods and rocks.

Yves is waiting for me on the arrival of the diligence which I caught at Bannalec.   Beside him is
a girl of eighteen or nineteen, who blushes, looking
very pretty in her large coif.

" This is Anne," says Yves to me, " my sister-in-
law, the godmother."

There is still some distance between the little
town and the cottage in which they live at Trémeulé
in Toulven.

Some village lads lift my luggage on their
shoulders, and I set out to make my visit to the
sea-gull which has just been born; to make the
acquaintance also of this Breton family, into which

Yves has entered in his headlong way without very clearly knowing why.

What will they be like, these new relations of my brother Yves—and this new country which is to become his?

CHAPTER XLIV

WE make our way all three along sunken lanes, which vanish in front of us under the shade of beech trees and are overgrown with ferns.

It is evening; the sky is overcast, and in these lanes there is a kind of night which is perfumed with honeysuckle.

Here and there, on the roadside, are grey cottages, very old and covered with moss.

From one of them comes a lullaby, sung in slow cadence by a voice which also is very old:

> "Boudoul, boudoul, galaïchen!¹
> Boudoul, boudoul, galaïch du!"¹

"It is *he* they are rocking," said Yves, smiling. "Come in!"

This cottage of the old Keremenen people is half-buried and overgrown with moss. Above it the oaks and beeches spread their green vault; it seems as old as the earth of the lanes.

¹ These words have no meaning in Breton, any more than "mironton, mirontaine" in the old French lullaby. They were probably invented by the old woman who sang them.

Inside the light is dim; one sees the press-beds in line with cupboards along the rough granite of the walls.

A grandmother in a large white collarette is within, singing beside the new-born son, singing an air of the time of her own childhood.

In an old-fashioned Breton cradle, which, before him, had rocked his forbears, lies the little sea-gull: a fat baby three days old, very round, very dark, already tanned like a mariner, and sleeping now with his closed fists under his chin. He has a growth of short hair, which appears below his bonnet on his forehead, like the coat of a mouse. I kiss him affectionately, for he is Yves' baby.

"Poor little sea-gull!" I say as I touch as gently as possible the little mouse's coat, "he has not so far got many feathers."

"That's true!" says Yves, smiling. "And look," he added, opening with infinite precaution the little closed fist and spreading it on his rough hand. "I have not been very successful: he is not web-footed."

We are told that Marie Keremenen is lying in one of the beds, the little perforated wooden door of which has been closed on her, because she has just fallen asleep; we lower our voices for fear of awakening her, and Yves and I go out, for we have many things to see to in the village in view of to-morrow's ceremony.

CHAPTER XLV

IT seems odd to us to find ourselves performing the formal duties of citizens in the way of the world in general. At the Mairie, and at the parish priest's house, we feel very awkward and at moments are hard put to it not to laugh.

The little sea-gull is definitely registered in the records of Toulven under the Christian names of Yves-Pierre—his father's name and mine, in accordance with the custom of the country. And it is arranged with the priest that he will await us at nine o'clock to-morrow morning, at the church, and that there shall be a *Te Deum*.

" And now let us go straight home," says Yves. " The old man is probably in already and they will be waiting supper for us."

CHAPTER XLVI

THE June night was falling slowly, bringing peace and silence over the Breton countryside. In the sunken lanes it was becoming difficult to see.

Old Corentin Keremenen had in fact returned from his work in the fields and was waiting for us at his door. He had had time even to change his clothes: he was wearing now his large silver-buckled hat and his feast-day jacket of blue cloth ornamented with metal spangles and, on the back, with an embroidery representing the Blessed Sacrament.

There is an air of joyous movement in the cottage, an air of celebration. The copper candlesticks are on the table which has been covered with a handsome cloth. The presses, the stools, the old oak woodwork shine like mirrors. One guesses that Yves has been busy.

The candles illumine only the centre of the room, leaving the rest in gloom. There are movements of large white things which are the wide-winged coifs and pleated collarettes of the women; but otherwise the backgrounds are dark; the light dies as it flickers on the granite of the walls, on the irregular and time-blackened beams which support the thatch of the roof. This thatch and this rough granite still preserve in the Breton villages a note of the primitive epoch.

Supper is served and we take our places, Yves on my left, Anne on my right.

It is a plenteous repast: chickens served with different sauces, wheaten cakes, savoury and sweet omelettes; and wine and golden cider which foams in our glasses.

Yves says to me aside in a low voice:

" He is a very good man, my father-in-law; and my mother-in-law Marianne, you cannot imagine what a good woman she is! I am very fond of them both."

During the evening a girl brings from the village clean starched things of voluminous dimensions. Anne hastens to conceal them in a press, while Yves, with a glance of intelligence, says:

" You see what preparations are being made in your honour! "

I had guessed what they were: the ceremonial head-dress and the immense, embroidered, thousand-pleated collarette, with which she was going to adorn herself for to-morrow's festival.

And I, on my side, have a number of little packets which I want to bring out, unperceived, with Yves' help from my trunk: sweets, sugar-plums, a gold cross for the godmother. But Anne has seen it all from the corner of her eye and starts to laugh. So much the worse! After all it is difficult to succeed in making mystery in a dwelling which has only one door and only one room for everybody.

Little Pierre, round as ever, a little bronze baby, continues to sleep in the same position, his closed fists under his chin. Never was a new-born baby so beautiful and so good.

When I take my leave of them, Yves gets up also in order to accompany me as far as the village, where I am going to sleep at the inn.

Outside, in the sunken lane, under the branches, it is now pitch dark; we are enveloped by a double obscurity, that of the trees and that of the night.

It is a kind of peace to which we are not accustomed, the peace of the woods. And there is no sea; the country of Toulven is far away from it. We listen; it seems to us still that we ought to hear in the distance its familiar sound. But no; all about is silence. Nothing but scarcely perceptible rustlings in the thick greenery, soft sounds of wings opening, slight quiverings of birds dreaming in their sleep.

There is still the perfume of honeysuckle; but,

with the night, have come a penetrating freshness and odours of moss, of earth, of the dampness of Brittany.

All this sleeping countryside, all these wooded hills which surround us, all these slumbering trees, all these tranquillities oppress us. We feel rather like strangers in the midst of it all, and we miss the sea, the sea which, after all, is the great open space, the great unconfined field over which we are accustomed to run.

Yves suffers these impressions and tells me of them in a naïve way, a way peculiarly his own, which would scarcely be intelligible to anyone but me. In the midst of his happiness, an uneasiness troubles him this evening, almost a regret that he should unthinkingly have fixed his destiny in this remote little cottage.

And presently we come upon a calvary, stretching out in the darkness its two grey arms, and we think of all these old granite chapels which lie here and there around us, isolated in the beech woods . . . in which the souls of the dead keep vigil.

CHAPTER XLVII

On the following day, Thursday, the 16th of June, 1878, in radiant weather, the baptismal party gets ready in the cottage of the Keremenens.

Anne, her back turned towards me in a corner, adjusts her coif before a mirror, a little embarrassed to be obliged to do so in my presence; but the cottages of Brittany are not large, and they have no other separations within than the little cupboards in which one sleeps.

Anne is dressed in a costume of black cloth, the open corsage of which is embroidered with different coloured silks and silver spangles; she wears an apron of blue moire, and, overflowing her shoulders, a white thousand-pleated collarette which remains rigid like a ruff of the sixteenth century. For my part, I have put on a uniform with bright gold facings and, certainly, we shall make a pretty picture presently, arm in arm, in the green lane.

In attendance on the baby this morning is a new personage, a very ugly and very extraordinary old woman, who assumes an air of much importance and receives general obedience: she is the nurse, it appears.

" She looks rather like a witch," says Anne, who guesses my thought. " But she is really a very good woman."

" Oh! yes, a very good woman indeed," confirms old Corentin. " Her appearance is not attractive, it is true, but she is attentive to her religion and in fact, last year, obtained great blessings in the pilgrimage of Saint Anne."

Bent double like Hecate, with a nose hooked like the beak of an owl and little grey eyes rimmed with red, which blink very rapidly in the manner of those of fowls, she goes this way and that, very busily, in her large stiff ceremonial collarette; when she speaks, her voice startles like a sound of the night; you might imagine you heard the brown owl of the tombs.

Yves and I at first did not like this old woman's attentions to the newcomer; but we found consolation in the thought that, for fifty years, she had been presiding at the birth of children in this region of Toulven, without having brought harm to any one of them. Quite the contrary in fact. Besides, she observes conscientiously all the ancient rites, such as making the little one drink before the baptism a certain wine in which its mother's wedding ring has been dipped, and many others which must on no account be neglected.

In this little cottage, deep-sunken in the ground and very much in shadow, one sees just as much as is necessary and no more. A little daylight enters by the door; at the back there is also a dormer window sparingly contrived in the thickness of the granite, but the ferns have invaded it. They are seen, in transparency, like the intricate figurings of a green curtain.

At last little Pierre's toilet is finished and without so much as a cry. I should have liked him better dressed as a little Breton; but no, this son of Yves is all in white, with a long embroidered robe and bows of ribbon, like a little gentleman of the town. He looks more vigorous and browner than ever in this doll's dress; the poor little town babies, who go to their baptism in similar attire, are not, as a rule, so strong and lusty.

Nevertheless, I am constrained to recognize that at present he is not a beauty; probably he will improve as time goes on; but at the moment he has the bloated look of a new-born kitten.

Outside, in the fern-clad lane, under the green vault, are moving already several large white coifs and embroidered cloth bodices similar to those of Anne. They belong to young women who have come out of neighbouring cottages and are waiting to watch us pass.

Anne and I set out, arm in arm. Little Pierre leads the way, in the arms of the old woman, with the birdlike beak, who hurries on with short quick steps, waddling strangely like some old hag. And big Yves brings up the rear, in his wedding clothes, very serious, a little surprised to find himself at such a ceremony, a little shy, too, at having to walk alone as custom, however, prescribes that he must.

In the fine June morning we make our way gaily down the Breton lane; above our heads the covering of the oaks and beeches sifts little rounds of light which fall in thousands, like a white rain, through the verdure. The hanging clematis is intertwined with honeysuckle, and the birds are singing a welcome to this little sea-gull who is making his first appearance in the sun.

We are now in Toulven which is almost a little town. The good people are at their doors and we pass slowly along the main street on our way to the church.

It is very old, is Toulven church. It stands up all grey in the blue sky, with its tall perforated granite steeple, which in places is yellowed by lichen. It overlooks a large pond, motionless and water-lilied, and a series of uniformly wooded hills which form, in the background, an immemorial horizon.

All around, an ancient enclosure: the cemetery. Crosses border the sacred pathway; they emerge from a carpet of flowers, carnations and white Easter daisies. And in the more neglected parts where time has levelled the little mounds of turf, there are still flowers for the dead: silenes, and the foxgloves of the fields of Brittany; the ground is pink with them.   The tombs are thick near the door of the age-old church, as on the mysterious threshold of eternity; this tall grey thing rising up here, this steeple uplifted in eager aspiration, it seems as if it does in fact protest a little against annihilation; in raising itself into the sky, it appeals, it supplicates; it is like an eternal prayer immobilized in granite. And the poor tombs buried in the grass await there, with greater confidence, at this threshold of the church, the sound of the last trump and the voice of the Apocalypse.

There, also, no doubt, when I am dead or broken by old age, there also will they lay my brother Yves; he will give back to the Breton earth his unbelieving head and the body which he had taken from it. Later again little Pierre will find there his last resting-place—if the great sea shall not have kept him from us—and, on their tombs the pink flowers of the fields of Brittany, the wild foxgloves, the luxuriant grasses of June, will flourish as they do to-day, in the warm summer sunshine.

In the porch of the church were all the children of the village looking very solemn.   And the parish priest was there too, awaiting us in his ceremonial vestments.

The architecture of the porch was very primitive, and the stones had been worn by many Breton generations; there were shapeless saints, carved in the granite, who were aligned like so many gnomes.

There was a protracted ceremony at the door.

The owl-faced old woman had placed little Pierre in our hands and we held him between us, the godmother, according to prescribed usage, holding the feet and I the head. Yves, leaning against a granite pillar, watched us with an air of reverie, and indeed Anne looked very pretty, in this grey porch, with her handsome dress and her large ruff, caught in the full light of a ray of the sun.

Little Pierre made a slight grimace and passed the end of his tiny tongue over his lip with an air of distaste, when the salt, the emblem of the sorrows of life, was put in his mouth.

The priest recited long *oremuses* in Latin, after which he said in the same language to the little sea-gull: *Ingredere, Petre, in domum Domini.* And then we entered the church.

The saints there, in niches, dressed in the costume of the sixteenth century, watched little Pierre make his entry, with the same placid and mystic air with which they have seen born and die ten generations of men.

At the baptismal font there was again a very long ceremony and then Anne and I had to take our places before the screen of the choir, kneeling like a newly-wedded pair.

Finally it fell to me to take unaided this son of Yves, whom I was fearful of breaking in my unaccustomed hands, and, climbing the steps of the altar with this precious little burden, to make him kiss the white cloth on which the Blessed Sacrament rests. I felt very awkward in uniform; it seemed as if I were carrying a weight of great heaviness. I had not imagined that it would be so difficult to hold a new-born babe; and yet he was asleep: if he had been moving I should never have been able to manage it.

All the children of the village were waiting for us as we came out, little Bretons with shy looks, round cheeks and long hair.

The bells sounded joyously from the top of the old grey steeple and the *Te Deum* burst out behind us, sung lustily by little choir boys in red cassocks and white surplices.

We were allowed to pass, still tranquil and devout, along the flowered alley bordered by the tombs—but, afterwards, when we were outside!

Little Pierre, the cause of all this commotion, had gone on ahead, carried away more and more quickly by the hook-nosed beldam and sleeping still his innocent sleep. And the assault fell upon Anne and me: little boys and little girls surrounded us, shouting and jumping; there were some of these little girls who could be no more than five years old, and who yet wore already large collars and large head-dresses similar to those of their mothers; and they skipped around us like very comical little dolls.

It was a strange thing, the joy of these little Breton people, pink-cheeked with long curls of yellow silk; mere buds of life, and dressed already in the costume and fashion of olden times— bubbling over with a heedless joy—as once upon a time their forbears, and they are dead! Joy of a new overflowing life, joy such as kittens have, and kids, and, after ten years, they die; puppies and lambkins know this self-same joy and gambol as these children here—and time passes and they are killed!

We scattered among them handfuls of sugar-

K

plums, and our whole route was sown with sweets.
The baptism of the little sea-gull will be remembered
in Toulven for many a long year.

Afterwards, we found once more the quiet of the
Breton lane, the long green alley, and, at the end
of it, the primitive hamlet.

It was now near noon; butterflies and flies made
merry in the air all along our road.   The day was
very warm for Brittany.

In broad daylight the roof of the cottage of the
old Keremenens was a veritable garden: a quantity
of little flowers, white, yellow and red, were
installed there with a great variety of ferns, and the
whole was sprinkled with sunlight, which filtered
through the overhanging oaks.

Inside it was still cool, in the slightly green half-
light, under the low black roof of the old beams.

Dinner was on the table, and Yves' wife, who
had got up for the first time, was awaiting us, seated
in her place, in her brave holiday dress.   In the
course of the last few days, her beauty had deserted
her, and she was pale and thin.   Yves looked at
her with an air of disillusionment which did not
escape her; and, realizing that this was not as it
should be, he went over to her and kissed her
affectionately with rather a lordly air.   And I
augured sad things from this glimpse of disen-
chantment.

Nevertheless this baptismal dinner was a gay
affair.   It consisted of a great number of Breton
dishes and lasted a very long time.

During the dessert, we heard outside two voices
murmuring a kind of litany very rapidly, in the
language of lower Brittany.   It was two old women,

two old beggar-women, linked arm in arm and leaning on sticks, in the manner of the fairies when they take decrepit shape for the purpose of disguise.

They asked to be allowed to enter, having come to wish good luck to little Pierre. At the oaken cradle in which he was being gently rocked they predicted very fortunate things, and then withdrew with a blessing for everyone.

Generous alms were given them, and Anne cut them slices of bread and butter.

CHAPTER XLVIII

In the afternoon there was a scene: my poor brother Yves was tipsy and wanted to go to Bannalec and take train to rejoin his ship.

We had wandered some considerable distance and were in a wood, Anne, Yves, and I, when suddenly, without apparent cause, the idea seized him. He had turned back and left us, saying that he was going away for good; and we had followed him in some anxiety fearful of what he might do.

When, a few minutes after him, we reached the cottage of the old Keremenens, we found that he had thrown off his fine white shirt and his wedding clothes, and, stripped to the waist, in the usual style of sailors on board ship during the morning, he was looking everywhere for his jersey which had been hidden from him.

"Good Lord Jesus, have pity on us," Marie, his wife, was saying, joining her poor white invalid's hands.   "How has this happened, Lord?   For really he has drunk but little!   Oh, sir, prevent him," she begged, turning to me.   "What will people say in Toulven when he passes, when they see that my husband will not stay with me!"

It was a fact that Yves had drunk very little; happiness, no doubt, had turned his head at dinner, and, what made the matter worse, we had taken him for a walk in the heat of the sun: it was not altogether his fault.

Sometimes, though rarely, it was possible to arrest these moods of his by dint of kindness.   I knew that, but I did not feel able to-day to use this means.   For really, it was too bad of him!   Even here, in this place of peace and on this happy day of festival, to introduce a scene of this kind!

I said simply:

"Yves shall not leave!"

And to bar his way, I stood before the door, buttressing myself against the old oak mullions which were massive and solid.

He did not dare to answer me.   He moved this way and that, continuing to look for his sailor's clothes, turning about like a wild beast which is held captive.   He muttered under his breath that nothing would prevent him from going, as soon as he should have found his sailor's bonnet.   But all the same the idea that he would have to touch me before he could get out served also to restrain him.

I, too, was in no very amiable mood, and I felt nothing now of the affection which had lasted so many years and forgiven so many things.   I saw before me the drunken sea-rover, ungrateful and in revolt, and that was all.

Deep down in every man there is always a hidden savage who keeps vigil—especially perhaps amongst us who have lived on the sea. And it was the savage in each of us who now confronted one another, who had just come into collision one with the other, as in our worst days in the past.

Outside, all round us, was still the peace of the countryside, the shade of the oaks, the tranquil *green night.*

Poor old Keremenen was quite helpless, and the affair came very near to being utterly odious and pitiful, when we heard Marie weeping; they were the first tears of her wifehood, urgent, bitter tears, the forerunners, no doubt, of many others; and sobs which were distressing to hear amid the silence which we all preserved.

And presently Yves was vanquished and drew near slowly to embrace her:

" Come, come! I am wrong," he said, "and I ask you to forgive me."

And then he came to me and used a name which he had sometimes written, but which until then he had never pronounced:

" You must forgive me again, *brother!* "

And he embraced me also.

Afterwards he begged forgiveness of the old Keremenens, who kissed him in a fatherly and motherly way; and forgiveness also of his son, the little sea-gull, as he pressed his lips against the little closed fists which peeped out of the cradle.

He was quite sobered and the evil hour had passed; the real Yves, my brother, had returned; there was as always in his repentance something simple and childlike which won forgiveness **without** reserve, so that all was forgotten.

He proceeded now to pick his clothes up from the floor, to brush them, and to dress himself again, without saying a word, miserable, exhausted, wiping his forehead which was beaded with a cold perspiration.

An hour later I watched Yves as he stooped, the very figure of an athlete, over the cradle of his son; he had been rocking him and had just succeeded in putting him to sleep; and now, little by little, progressively, with many precautions, he was stopping the movement of the little oak basket, to leave it at last motionless, seeing that sleep had indeed come. Then he stooped lower still and gazed intently at his son, examining him with much curiosity, as if he had never seen him before, touching his little closed fists, his growth of little mouse's hair which peeped still from beneath the little white bonnet.

And as he gazed his face assumed an expression of infinite tenderness; and the hope came to me that this little child might one day be his safeguard and salvation.

CHAPTER XLIX

In the evening after supper, we went for a walk, Anne, Yves and I, a walk much more peaceful than that of the day.

And, at nine o'clock, we sat down by the side of a wide road which traversed the woods.

It was not yet dark, so prolonged in Brittany are the evenings in the beautiful month of June; but we began, nevertheless, to talk of phantoms and the dead.

Anne said:

" In winter when the wolves come we can hear them from our home; but sometimes ghosts, too, utter cries like theirs."

On this particular evening, however, we only heard the passing of cockchafers and stagbeetles which flew through the warm air in eccentric curves, and the small buzzings of summer.   And, also, from a distant part of the wood: " Hoot! . . . Hoot . . ." a mournful call, given out very softly in the voice of an owl.

And Yves said:

" Do you hear, brother?   The parakeets of France are singing." (This was an allusion to the *parakeet* he had on the *Sibylle*.)

The slender grasses, with their flowers of grey dust, spread over the ground a deep, scarcely palpable covering into which the feet sank, and the last moths, at the end of their evening's exercise, plunged one after another into the thickness of this herbage, to take their sleeping posts on the slender stems.

And darkness came, slow and tranquil, with an air of mystery.

Passed a young Breton lad who carried a knapsack on his shoulder. He was returning rather tipsy from Lannildu, a peacock's feather in his hat. (I do not know what this has to do with the story of Yves: I relate at hazard things which have remained in my memory.) He stopped and began to address us. Finally, by way of peroration, he showed us his knapsack, saying:

" Look here! I have two cats in this." (This had no sort of relation to what he had been saying to us before.)

He placed his burden on the ground and threw his hat upon it. Thereupon the knapsack began to *swear*, with the strong voices of angry tom-cats, and to move in somersaults along the road.

When he had convinced us in this way that they were indeed cats, he put the whole on his shoulder again, saluted, and went his way.

CHAPTER L

17th June, 1878.

WE rose early to go into the woods and gather
" luzes " (little blue-black fruits which are found in
the deepest of the thickets, on plants which resemble
the mistletoe).

Anne no longer wore her gay festival attire : she
had put on a large smooth collarette and a simpler
head-dress. Her Breton dress of blue cloth was
ornamented with yellow embroidery : on each side
of her bodice were designs imitating rows of eyes
such as butterflies have on their wings.

Along the sunken lanes, in the green night, we
met women who were going into Toulven to hear
the early morning mass. From the end of these
long corridors of verdure, we saw them coming with
their collarettes, their tall white head-dresses, the
sides of which fell symmetrically over their ears, like
the bonnets of the Egyptians. Their waists were
tightly compressed in bodices of blue cloth which
resembled the corselets of insects and on which were
embroidered always the same designs, the same rows
of butterfly eyes. As they passed they gave us
good-day in Breton and their tranquil faces wore an
expression of primitive times.

And at the doors of old grey granite cottages
which were almost hidden in the trees, we found old

women sitting and minding little children; old women with long unkempt white hair, in tattered blue cloth cut in the fashion of long ago, with the remains of Breton embroideries and rows of eyes: the poverty and primitiveness of olden times.

Ferns, ferns, all along these lanes—ferns of the most elaborate kind, the finest, the rarest, which have flourished there in the damp shade, forming sheaves and carpets—and pink foxgloves, too, shooting up like pink rockets, and, pinker even than the foxgloves, the silenes of Brittany, scattering over all this fresh verdure their little carmine-coloured stars.

To us, maybe, the verdure seems greener, the woods more silent, the perfumes more penetrating, to us who live in wooden houses in the midst of the sound of the sea.

" It seems to me very pleasant here," said Yves. " A little later on when little Pierre is big enough for me to lead him by the hand, we will go together to pick all kinds of things in the woods—and, later again, we can shoot. To be sure! I will buy a gun, as soon as I have saved a little money, to kill the wolves. I don't think I shall ever be bored in this country here."

I knew well, alas! that sooner or later he would weary of it; but it served no purpose to tell him so and it was better to let him, as one lets children, cherish his illusion.

Besides, he also was about to depart; two days after me, he was due at Brest, to embark once more. This was only a very brief rest in our life, this sojourn at Toulven, only a little interlude of

Brittany, after which we must resume once more our business of the sea.

We were in the heart of the woods. No pathways now, no cottages. Nothing but a succession of hills following one another into the distance, covered with beeches, with brushwood, with oaks and heather. And flowers, a profusion of flowers; the whole countryside was flowered like an Eden: honeysuckle, tall asphodels with white distaffs and foxgloves with pink distaffs.

In the distance, the song of cuckoos in the trees, and, around us, the humming of bees.

The berries grew thick here and there, on the stony soil, mingled with flowering heather. Anne always found the best and gave them to me in handfuls. And big Yves watched us with a grave smile, conscious that he was playing, for the first time, a kind of rôle of mentor, and finding it very surprising.

The place had a wild air. These wooded hills, these carpets of lichen, resembled a landscape of olden times, though bearing the mark of no precise epoch. But Anne's costume was clearly of the Middle Ages and the impression that one had was of that period.

Not the gloomy and twilight Middle Ages as understood by Gustave Doré, but the Middle Ages sunlit and full of flowers, of these same eternal flowers of the fields of Gaul, which bloomed as now for our ancestors.

It was eleven o'clock when we returned to the cottage of the old Keremenens for dinner. It was very warm that summer in Brittany; the ferns and the little red flowers of the roadside bowed down under the unaccustomed sun, which exhausted them, tempered though it was by the green branches.

One o'clock. For me, the hour of departure. I went first of all to kiss little Pierre, asleep still in his old oaken cradle, as if these four days had not sufficed him for recovering from the fatigue he had suffered in coming into the world.

I bade good-bye to all. Yves, thoughtful, leaning against the door, was waiting to accompany me as far as Toulven, whence the diligence would take me to the station at Bannalec. Anne and old Corentin also insisted on escorting me.

And, when I saw Toulven disappearing in the distance, its grey steeple and its mournful pond, my heart contracted. How many years would it be before I should return to Brittany? Once more we were separating, my *brother* and I, and both of us were going away into the unknown. I was uneasy about his future, over which I saw dark clouds gathering. . . . And I thought also of these Keremenens whose welcome had touched me. I asked myself whether my poor Yves, with his terrible failings and his uncontrollable character, was not going to bring unhappiness upon them, under their roof of thatch covered with little red flowers.

CHAPTER LI

November, 1880.

A LITTLE more than two years later.

Little Pierre was cold. He cried as he clasped his two little hands, which he tried to hide under his pinafore. He was in a street in Brest, before daybreak, on a November morning. A fine rain was falling. He pressed close to his mother who, also, was weeping.

There, at a street corner, Marie Kermadec was waiting, loitering in the darkness like some unfortunate. Would Yves come home? . . . Where was he? . . . Where had he spent the night? In what low tavern? Would he return to his ship at any rate, when the gun sounded, in time for the roll-call.

And other women were waiting also.

One passed with her husband, a petty officer like Yves; he came out of a tavern which had just been opened. He was drunk. He tried to walk, staggered a few steps and then fell heavily to the ground. His head made a sickening sound as it struck the hard granite.

"Oh! my God!" wailed his wife. "Jesus, Holy Virgin Mary, have pity on us! Never have I seen him like this before! . . ."

Marie Kermadec helped her to get him on his feet again. He was a good looking man, kindly and serious.

" Thank you, madam! "

And his wife contrived to make him walk, supporting him with all her strength.

Little Pierre was crying quietly, as if he understood already that something shameful overshadowed them and that it behoved him not to make a noise. He bowed his little head and continued to hide under his pinafore his little hands which were so cold. He was well enough wrapped up, but he had been standing for a long time, without moving, at this damp street corner. The gas lamps had just been extinguished and it was very dark. Poor little plant, healthy and fresh, born in the woods of Toulven, how came it, to be stranded in the misery of this town? For his part he saw no sense in the change; he could not understand why his mother had wanted to follow her husband to this Brest, and to live in a cold and dismal lodging, at the end of a court, in one of the low-lying streets abutting on the harbour.

Another passed; he was struggling with his wife, this one, he was not going to be taken home. It was a horrible sight. Marie uttered a cry as she heard the dull sound of a blow struck by a fist; and covered her face, unable to bear more. Yves at any rate had never done that! But would it come to that in time? Would it come to pass, one of these days, that they would sink to this last misery?

CHAPTER LII

YVES appeared at last, walking straight, carrying himself well, his head high, but his eye lustreless, bewildered. He saw his wife, but pretended that he did not, throwing on her as he passed an angry, troubled glance.

It was not he—as he used to say himself afterwards, in the good moments of repentance which still came to him.

In fact, it was not he: it was the savage beast within him which drunkenness awakened, when his real self was obscured and submerged.

Marie refrained from saying a word, not only from uttering a reproach, but even from an entreaty. It was better not to speak to Yves in these moments when his head was gone: he would go away again. She knew that; she was forced into this silence.

She followed, with downbent head, in the rain, dragging by the hand her little Pierre who was trying to cry even more quietly now since he had seen his father, and whose poor little feet were getting wet in the mud of the gutter.

How could she let him walk thus? How could she even have brought him out like this, before daybreak? What was she thinking of? Had she gone mad? . . . And she picked him up and hugged him to her breast, warming him against her body, kissing him in passionate affection.

Yves pretended to pass his door, by way of aggravation—a piteous piece of brutish foolery—and then looked back at his wife with a stupid smile which was not good to see, as one who should say: "That was a little joke of mine, but you see I am going in."

She followed at a distance, hugging the wall of the dark staircase so as not to be seen, making herself small, lowly. Happily it was not yet daylight, and the neighbours no doubt would still be abed, and so would not be witnesses of this disgrace.

She followed him into their room and shut the door.

There was no fire and the room had an air of poverty which smote the heart.

When the candle was lit, Marie saw that Yves had again torn his new clothes, which once already she had mended with so much care; and his big blue collar was crumpled and stained and his jersey unravelled, the broken stitches gaping on his chest.

He walked up and down, turning about like a caged beast, making confusion, upsetting brusquely things which she had arranged, pieces of bread which she had saved up.

And she, having put their child in his cradle and covered him up, pretended to occupy herself with domestic duties. At times such as these it was necessary to appear as if nothing had happened; otherwise, if one seemed to be taking too much thought of him, he would become suddenly exasperated, like a wild beast which has scented blood; and he would want to go out again. And when once he had said: "I am going out! I am going out to join my friends!" out he would go with the obstinacy of a brute; not force, nor prayers, nor tears were able to restrain him.

CHAPTER LIII

SOMETIMES Yves would fall suddenly like a log and sleep for several hours; and then it would be over. This depended on the particular kind of liquor he had taken.

At other times he held out, somehow or other, and returned to his ship in the harbour.

On this particular morning, at seven o'clock, Yves, a little sobered, had the idea unprompted of bathing his head in cold water. Then he went out and took the road to the dockyard.

CHAPTER LIV

THEN Marie sat down, broken, utterly powerless, beside the cradle in which their little son was sleeping.

Through the curtainless windows a whitish light began to enter, a pale, pale light which made one feel cold.

Another day! In the street below could be heard the characteristic sound of the lower quarters of Brest at the hour of the return to work: thousands of wooden sabots hammering on the hard granite pavé. The workers were returning to the dockyard, stopping on their way for one last drink, in the taverns but just now opened which mingled with the growing daylight the yellow light of their little lamps.

Marie remained there, motionless, perceiving with a painful acuteness all these already familiar sounds of the winter mornings which ascended from the street, voices husky with alcohol and the rumblings of sabots. It was in one of those old many-storeyed houses, tall, immense, with dark yards, rough granite walls as thick as ramparts, sheltering all sorts of people, workmen, pensioners, sailors; at least thirty families of drunkards. It was now four months since—on Yves' return from the Antilles— she had left Toulven to come and live there.

A growing light entered through the windows, fell on the dirty, dilapidated walls, penetrated little by little the whole of the large room in which their modest little household furniture, now in disorder, seemed lost. Clearly the day had come; and, out of thriftiness, she went and blew out the candle, and then returned to sit by the window.

What was she going to do with this new day; should she work? No, she had not the heart, and, then, what was the use?

Another day to be passed without a fire, with a heart that was dead, watching the rain falling, watching and waiting! Waiting, waiting in an anxiety that grew from hour to hour, waiting for the coming of the darkness, for the moment when the hammering of the sabots would begin once more in the grey street below, when the workers' day was done. For Yves and the other sailors whose ships were in the

port were released at the same time as the workers
in the dockyard; and then, every evening, leaning
out of her window, she would watch the flood of
humanity pass, searching, with anxious eyes, among
all these groups, looking for him who had taken from
her her life.

She could recognize him from afar, by his tall
figure and his bearing; his blue collar towered over
the others.   When she had discovered him, walking
quickly, hastening towards their lodging, it seemed
to her that her poor heart overflowed, that she
breathed better; and when she saw him at last
beneath her, entering the old low doorway, she was
almost happy.   He had come—and when he was
there and had embraced them both, her and little
Pierre, the danger was past, he would not go out
again.

But if he was late, gradually she felt herself wrung
with anguish. . . . And when the hour was passed,
and night came and the crowd had dispersed and
he had not returned, oh! then began those sinister
evenings she knew so well, those mortal evenings
of waiting which she spent, the door open, seated in
a chair, her hands joined, saying her prayers, her
ear straining at all the sailors' songs which came
from outside, trembling at every sound of footsteps
which she heard on the dark staircase.

And then, very late, when others, her neighbours,
were in bed and could no longer see her, she
descended; in the cold, in the rain, she went out
like one possessed to wait at street corners, listen
at the doors of pot-houses where men were drinking
still, press her pallid cheek against the window-
panes of taverns.

CHAPTER LV

LITTLE Pierre was still asleep in his cradle, making up for the sleep he had lost in the early morning. And this morning his mother also dozed near him in her chair, exhausted as she was by fatigue and watching.

It was broad daylight when she awoke, her limbs numb with cold. And with returning consciousness came once more the weight of her anxiety.

Why had she left Toulven? Why did she marry? Daughter of the country as she was what was she doing in this Brest where people stared at her peasant's dress? Why had she come to wear in the streets of the town her large white collarette, often soaked with rain, which in despair, in utter weariness, she allowed now to hang crumpled and limp on her shoulders.

She had done everything she could to reform Yves. He was still so kind, so good, he was so fond of his little Pierre in his sober hours, that often she was encouraged still to hope! He had moods of repentance that were quite sincere and lasted for several days; and those days were days of happiness.

" You must forgive me," he used to say, " for you can see that I was not myself! "

And she forgave him. Then he would stay at home, and when by chance the weather was reasonably fine, they dressed little Pierre in his new clothes, and went for a walk, the three of them, in Brest.

And then, one fine evening Yves would not return, and all was to be begun again, and she fell back into despair.

Things went from bad to worse; the stay at Brest exerted over him the same influence as it usually does over all sailors. Every week now almost, the dread thing happened; it was becoming a habit. What room was there for hope?

There was no money left in their drawer. What was to be done? Borrow from these women, her neighbours, who from time to time used to drink also, and whom she disdained to know! Of that she was ashamed! Nevertheless she was at her wits' end to know how to hide her distress from her parents, who knew nothing, and had taken Yves to their heart as if he had been their own son.

Very well then, she would tell them, tell them he was unworthy of them. She was in revolt at last. She would leave him; he had gone too far, and he had no heart.

CHAPTER LVI

AND yet, yes!—something told her that he had a heart, but that he was just a big boy whom the life of the sea had spoilt. And with a great tenderness she recalled his handsome, gentle face, his voice, his smile in those hours when he was sober. . . .

Abandon him? . . . At the idea that he should go his ways alone, utterly lost then, and throwing care to the devil, delivered up to his vices and to the vices of others, to begin again his life of deba chery with other women, to sail distant seas, and en to grow old alone, forsaken, exhausted by a'co 'l! . . . Oh! at this idea of leaving him, she was seized with an anguish more terrible than all: she felt that she was bound to him now by a bond stronger than any reason, than any human will. She loved him passionately, without realizing the strength of her love. . . . No, rather than that, if she was not able to draw him back, she would let herself sink with him to the last degradation in order that she might still hold him in her arms until the hour of death.

CHAPTER LVII

LITTLE Pierre, for his part, did not like Brest at all. He found it a most uncomfortable place, ugly and dark.

He had lived there only for four months, and already his round cheeks had paled a little under their bronze.   Before, they were like those ripe nectarines of the south country which are of a warm golden colour, a red stained with sun.

His eyes were black and shone with the sparkle of jet, like those of his mother, from between beautiful long eyelashes.   In his little eyebrows there was already a suggestion of seriousness, which came from Yves.

He would have made a pretty picture, with his thoughtful expression and the manly and forceful little air which he had already like a grown lad.

Now and then he had still his moments of noisy gaiety; he jumped and skipped about the gloomy room, making a great commotion.

But this did not happen so often as at Toulven. He missed, in his already vague baby memory, he missed the little playmates of the beech-bordered lane, and the petting of his grandparents, and the songs of his old great-grandmother. There, everybody took notice of him, while here he was nearly always alone.

No, he did not like the town. And then he was always cold, in this bare room and on these old stone staircases.

CHAPTER LVIII

" You must forgive me; you can see that I am not myself."

When once Yves had said that, the storm was finally over; but it was often a long time before he said it. When the fit of drunkenness had passed, for two or three days, he would remain gloomy, depressed, without speaking; until suddenly, at some quite negligible thing, his smile would appear once more with an expression of childlike embarrassment.

Then the clouds would break for poor Marie and she would smile too, a smile of her own, without ever uttering a word of reproach; and that was the end of the ordeal.

Once she dared very softly to ask him :

" But what is the need for sulking for three days, when it is over."

And he, more softly still, with a naïve half-smile, looking at her sideways, in obvious embarrassment :

" What is the need for sulking for three days, do you say?   Why, Marie, do you think I am pleased with myself when I have these bouts. . . . Oh! but it's not against you, my poor Marie, I assure you."

Then she came very close to him and leaned against his shoulder, and he, answering her silent appeal, kissed her.

" Oh! drink! drink! " he said slowly, averting his half-closed eyes with a savage expression. " My father! my brothers!   Now it's my turn! "

He had never said anything like this before. He had never alluded to the terrible vice which possessed him, nor given any sign that he realized its consequences.

How was it possible not to have still brief moments of hope seeing him afterwards so sensible, so dutiful, playing at the fireside with his son; dropping then all his domineering ways, alert with a thousand kindly thoughts for his wife, in his effort to make her forget her suffering?

And how believe that this same Yves would presently and fatally become once more that *other*, the Yves of the bad days, the Yves of the vacant gaze, the Yves depressed and brutal, the beast bewildered by alcohol, whom nothing could move?

Then Marie surrounded him with tenderness, concentrated on him all the force of her will, watched over him as over a child, trembling as she followed him with her eyes whenever he so much as descended into the street where his blue-collared comrades passed and where the taverns opened their doors.

On shore Yves was lost; he knew it well himself, and used to say sadly that he would have to try to get to sea again.

He had grown up on the sea, at random, as wild plants grow. It had been nobody's business to give him notions of duty or conduct, nor of anything in the world. I alone perhaps, whom fate and his mother's prayer had put in his way, had been able to speak to him of these new things, but too late no doubt, and too vaguely. The discipline of the ship, that was the great and only curb which had directed his material life, maintaining it in that rude and healthy austerity which makes sailors strong.

The *shore* had for long been for him but a place of passage, where for a time he was free from restraint and where there were women; he descended on it as on a conquered country, between long voyages; and he came well supplied with money and found, in the quarters of pleasure, everything compliant to his whim and will.

But to live a regular life in a little household, to reckon up each day's expenses, to behave himself and have thought for the morrow, his sailor's ways could no longer adapt themselves to these unexpected obligations. Besides, around him, in this corrupt, degenerate Brest, alcohol seemed to ooze from the walls with the unwholesome damp. And he sank to the depths like so many others, who also once had been good and brave; he became debased, slipping down little by little to the level of this population of drunkards; and his excesses became repulsive and vulgar like those of a workman.

CHAPTER LIX

ONE day, I received a letter which called me to his assistance.

It was very simple, very much like a letter from a child :

" MY DEAR BROTHER,—I do not know how to tell you, but it is true, I have taken to drink again.   Also I do not want to remain in Brest, as you will understand, for I am afraid of this thing.

" I have already been punished three times with irons in the Reserve, and now I do not know how to get away from the ship, for I realize that if I remain on board some misfortune will happen to me.

" But it seems to me that if I could embark once more with you, that would be exactly what I need. My dear brother, since you will soon be going away again, if you would come to Brest and take me with you, it would be much better for me than here, and I feel sure that that would save me.

" You have done me a great wrong in saying in your letter that I did not love my wife or my son;

because for her and little Pierre there is nothing I would not do.

"Yes, my dear brother, I have wept and I am weeping now as I write, and I cannot see for the tears that are in my eyes.

"I only hope that you will be able to come. I embrace you with all my heart, and beg you not to forget your brother, in spite of all the disappointments he has caused you.

"Ever yours,
"YVES KERMADEC."

CHAPTER LX

ONE Sunday in December I returned to Brest unannounced and made my way into the low-lying quarters of the Grand 'Rue, looking for Yves' house. Reading the numbers on the doors, I passed all those high granite buildings which once were houses of the rich and now are fallen into the hands of the people; below, everywhere open taverns; above, the curtained windows of poverty, with last sickly flowers on the sills; dead chrysanthemums in pots.

It was morning. Bands of sailors were about already, looking very smart in their clean clothes, singing, beginning already the Sunday holiday.

One breathed a white mist, a damp coldness—a first sensation of winter. Newly-arrived as I was from the Adriatic, where the sun was still shining, the colours of Brest seemed to me greyer than ever.

At number 154—above the sign : *A la pensée du beau canonnier*—I climbed three flights of stairs in an old wide staircase, and came upon the room of the Kermadecs.

I could hear through the door the regular sound of a cradle. Little Pierre, very spoilt in spite of all, had retained this habit of being rocked to sleep, and Yves, alone with his son, was sitting near him, rocking the cradle with one hand, very slowly.

He raised pathetic eyes, moved at seeing me, but hesitating to come to me, his expression saying:

" Ah, yes, brother, I know. You have come to take me away; it is true that this is what I asked of you; but . . . but I did not expect you perhaps so soon; and to go away . . . that will be very hard to bear. . . ."

Physically, Yves had greatly changed. He had become paler, sheltered as he had been from the tanning of the sea; his expression was different, less assured, almost mournful. It was plain that he had suffered; but on his face, marmorean still and colourless, vice had not succeeded yet in imprinting any trace.

I looked around with an impression of surprise, and a contraction of the heart. I had not, in fact, foreseen what the dwelling of my brother Yves, on shore and in a town, would be like. It was very different from that sea dwelling in which I had so long known him: the masthead, full of wind and sun. Here, now, amid this reality of poverty I felt as he no doubt felt himself, out of place and ill at ease.

Marie was outside, at the pump, and little Pierre was sound asleep, his long baby's eyelashes resting on his cheeks. We were alone together and as he was uncomfortable in my presence, he began hurriedly to talk of embarking, of departure.

A change in the list had called me to Brest prepared for immediate departure: two or three ships were about to be put into commission—for the China station, for the Southern Seas, for the Levant—and it was necessary to hold myself in readiness, from hour to hour, for one of these destinations.

The week which followed was one of those agitated periods which are common enough in a sailor's life: living at the hotel as in a flying camp, amid the disorder of half-unpacked trunks, not knowing to-morrow's destination; busy with a number of things, official business at the port and preparations for the voyage;—and then these comings and goings, applications on Yves' behalf, in order to secure his withdrawal from the Reserve, and to keep him near me, ready to depart with me.

The December days, very short, very gloomy, sped quickly. I climbed often, three steps at a time, the sordid old staircase of the Kermadecs; and Marie, anxious always about the first words I might say, smiled at me sadly, with a respectful and resigned confidence, awaiting the decision I should bring.

CHAPTER LXI

IN THE ROADSTEAD OF BREST,
23rd December, 1880.

A NIGHT in December, clear and cold; a great calm over the sea, a great silence on board.

In a little ship's cabin, which is painted white and has iron walls, Yves is sitting near me amid open trunks and cases. We are still in the disarray of arrival; we have yet to instal ourselves, to make a little home, in this iron box which presently is going to carry us through the waves and storms of winter.

All the embarcations we had foreseen, all the long voyages we had projected, had come to nothing. And I find myself simply on board this *Sèvre* which is not going to leave the Brittany coast. Yves is among the crew and we shall be together again, in all human probability, for a year. Given our calling it is a stroke of good luck; it might have happened to us at any moment to be separated for ever. And Yves has very gladly given a hundred francs out of his purse to the sailor who consented to give up his place to him.

Let us make the best of this *Sèvre*, since fate will have it so. It will remind us at any rate of the times already distant when we sailed together over the misty northern sea under the protecting eye of the Creizker tower.

But I should have liked it better if we had been

sent elsewhere, to somewhere in the sun; for Yves'
sake especially, I should have preferred to be going
farther from Brest, farther from his evil companions
and the taverns of the coast.

CHAPTER LXII

AT SEA *25th December, Christmas Day.*
IT was the second day following, very early, at
daybreak.   I came up on deck, having scarcely
slept a moment, after a very trying watch from midnight to four o'clock: we had been buffeted throughout the night by a gale of wind and a heavy sea.

Yves was there, wet through, but in his element
and very much at ease; and, as soon as he saw me
appear, he pointed out to me, smiling, a singular
country which we were approaching.

Grey cliffs walled the distant horizon like a long
rampart.   A kind of calm fell upon the waters,
although the wind continued to buffet us furiously.
In the sky, dark heavy clouds slid one over the
other, very rapidly: a leaden vault in movement;
immense, dark things, which changed shape, which
seemed in haste to pass, to reach a goal elsewhere,
as if seized with the vertigo of some impending and
formidable convulsion.   Around us, thousands of
reefs, dark heads which rose up everywhere amid
this other silvered commotion made by the waves;
they seemed like immense herds of sea monsters.
They stretched as far as eye could see, these

dangerous dark heads, the sea was covered with them. And then, beyond, on the distant cliff, the silhouettes of three very old towers, looking as if they had been planted alone there in the midst of a desert of granite, one of them greatly overtopping the two others, and rearing its tall figure like a giant who watches and presides. . . .

Yes! I recognize it well, and, like Yves, salute it with a smile; somewhat puzzled, nevertheless, to see it reappear so close to us, and in the midst of this festival of shadows, on a morning when I was not expecting it. . . . What were we going to do there, in its neighbourhood? This was no part of our original plan and I could not understand it.

It was a sudden decision of the captain, taken during my hour of sleep : to make for the entrance to the roadstead of Taureau, hard by Saint Pol, and seek a shelter there from the south wind, the open sea being now too rough for us.

And that was how it came about that, on his return to the northern waters, Yves' first visit was to the Creizker tower.

CHAPTER LXIII

CHERBOURG, *27th December*, 1880.
AT seven o'clock in the morning word is brought to me that Yves, dead-drunk, is in a boat alongside. Some old friends of his, topmen on the *Vénus*, have kept him drinking through the night in

low taverns—to celebrate their return from the Antilles.

I am of the watch. There is no one yet on deck, save some sailors busy with their furbishing—but devoted fellows these, known for many a day and to be counted on. Four men get him aboard, and furtively carry him down a hatch and hide him in my room.

A bad beginning, truly, on board this *Sèvre*, where I had taken him under my charge as on a kind of probation, and where he had promised to be exemplary. And the black thought came to me for the first time that he was lost, beyond redemption, no matter what I might do to save him from himself. And also this other thought, more desolating still, that perhaps he was deficient in certain qualities of heart.

Throughout the day Yves was like a dead man.

He had lost his bonnet, his purse, his silver whistle, and there was a dent in his head.

It was not until about six o'clock in the evening that he showed sign of life. Then, like a child awakening, he smiled—a sign this that he was still drunk, for otherwise he would not smile—and asked for food.

Then I said to Jean-Marie, my faithful servant, a fisherman from Audierne:

" Go to the ward-room kitchen and see if you can get him some soup."

Jean-Marie brought the soup, and Yves began to turn his spoon this way and that, as if he did not remember which way to hold it:

" Come on, Jean-Marie, make him eat it! "

" It is too salty! " said Yves suddenly, lying back,

M

making a wry face, his accent very Breton, his eyes again half-closed.

" Too salty! Too salty! " . . .

Then he fell asleep again, and Jean-Marie and I burst out laughing.

I was in no frame of mind for laughter, but this notion and this spoilt child's air were too comical. . . .

Later, at ten o'clock, Yves came round, got up furtively, and disappeared.

For two days he remained hidden in the crews' quarters in the bow of the ship, only showing himself for his watch and for drill, hanging his head, not daring to look at me.

Oh! these resolutions taken twenty times and as many times broken. . . . We dare not take them again or at any rate dare not say that we have taken them. The will flags, and the days slip by while we wait inert for the return of courage and self-respect.

Slowly, however, we came back to our normal manner of existence. I used to call him in the evenings and we would walk up and down the deck together for hours on end, talking almost in the old way, in the mournful wind and the fine rain. He had still the same fashion of thinking and speaking as before, very naïve and at the same time very profound; it was the same, but with just the least suggestion of constraint; there was something frigid between us which would not thaw. I waited for a word of repentance which did not come.

Winter was advancing, the winter of the Channel, which envelopes everything—thoughts, and men, and things—in the same grey twilight.

The cold dark days had come, and our evening walk was taken at a quicker pace in the damp wind of the sea.

There were times when I wanted to grip his hand and say to him: "Come, brother, I have forgiven you; let us forget all about it." But I checked the words on my lips; after all it was for him to ask forgiveness; and there remained a kind of haughty coldness in my manner which kept him at a distance from me.

This *Sèvre* was not a success for us at all, that was clear.

CHAPTER LXIV

LITTLE Pierre is at Plouherzel, trying to play in front of his grandmother's door—quite lost as he looks at the motionless sheet of water before him, with the large beastlike shape which seems to be asleep in the centre, behind a veil of mist. There is free air and open sky here, to be sure, but the wind is keener than at Toulven, and the country more desolate; and children feel these things by instinct; in the presence of things forlorn, they have involuntary melancholies and silences—as birds have.

Here now are two little comrades who have come from a neighbouring cottage to take stock of him, the little new-comer. But they are not those of Toulven; they do not know the same games; the few little words which they are able to speak are not of the same Breton. And, therefore, not venturing much on one side or the other, they remain all three at gaze, with shy smiles and comical little airs.

It was yesterday that little Pierre arrived at Plouherzel with Marie Kermadec. Yves had written to his wife bidding her make this journey as soon as she could; the thought had come to him suddenly, the hope indeed, that this might reconcile them with his mother. For the old woman, always hard and headstrong, after having in the first instance flatly refused her consent to their marriage, had accepted it subsequently with bad grace, and, since, had not even troubled to answer their letters.

Poor forsaken old woman! Of thirteen children whom God had given her, three had died in infancy. Of the eight sons who had reached manhood, all of them sailors, the sea had taken seven—seven who had been lost in shipwreck, or else had disappeared abroad, like Gildas and Goulven.

Her daughters, too, had left her. One of them had married an Icelander, who had taken her away to Tréquier; the other, her head turned by religion, had entered the convent of the Sisters of Saint Gildas du Secours.

There remained only the little grandchild, the forsaken little daughter of Goulven. And all the old woman's love was centred in her—an illegitimate child, it is true, but the last survivor of that long shipwreck which had bereft her, one after another, of the others. This little child loved to watch the incoming tide from the shore of the sea water lake.

She had been forbidden to do it, but one day she went thither alone and did not return. The next tide brought in a stiff little corpse, a little body of white wax, which was laid to rest near the chapel, under a wooden cross and a mound of green turf.

She still cherished a hope in her son Yves, the last, the best beloved, because he had remained the longest at home. . . . Perhaps he, at least, would return one day to live near her!

But it was not to be. This Marie Keremenen had stolen him from her; and, at the same time— a thing which counted in her rancour—she had taken from her also the money which this son had previously sent to help her to live.

And for two years now, she had been alone, quite alone, and would be alone to her last day.

In obedience to Yves, Marie had come yesterday, after two days' journeying, and knocked at this door with her child. An old, hard-featured woman, whom she recognized at once without ever having seen her, had opened to her.

" I am Marie, Yves' wife. . . . How do you do, mother? "

" Yves' wife! Yves' wife! So this then is little Pierre? This is my little grandson? "

Her eye had softened as she looked at the little grandson. She had made them enter, given them to eat, seen that they were warm and comfortable, and prepared for them her best bed. But for all that there was a coldness, an ice which nothing could thaw.

In the corner, surreptitiously, the grandmother embraced her grandchild with affection. But before

Marie she gave no sign and remained always stiff and hard.

Now and then they spoke of Yves, and Marie said timidly that, since their marriage, he had reformed greatly.

"Tra la la! . . . Reformed!" repeated the old woman, assuming her ill-tempered air. "Tra la la! my child! . . . Reformed! . . . He has his father's head, they are all the same, they are all alike, and you have not seen the last of it in him; mark my words!"

Then poor Marie, her heart heavy, not knowing what to reply, nor what else to say during the long day, nor what to do with herself, waited impatiently for the time fixed by Yves for their departure. Very surely she would not return.

CHAPTER LXV

At Paimpol Marie, with her son, has climbed into the diligence which moves off and is bearing them away. Through the door she watches her mother-in-law who has had the grace to accompany them from Plouherzel to see them off, but who has said good-bye briefly and coldly, a good-bye to chill the heart.

She watches her and is puzzled; for the old woman is running now, running after the diligence—and her face, too, is working; she seems to be making some kind of grimace. What can she want of them? And as she watches Marie becomes almost afraid. For she is grimacing still. And see! now

she is crying! Her poor features are quite con-
torted, and her tears fall fast. . . . And now she
understands!

"For the love of heaven! stop the diligence, sir,
if you please," says Marie to an Icelander, who is
sitting near her and who, too, has understood; for
he passes his arm through the little window in front
and pulls the conductor by the sleeve.

The diligence stops. The grandmother, who has
continued to run, is at the back, almost on the step;
she stretches out her hands to them, and her face is
bathed in tears.

Marie gets down and the old woman throws her
arms round her, embraces her, embraces little
Pierre.

"My dear child! may God in His goodness be
with you."

And she weeps and sobs.

"My child, with Yves, you know, you must be
very gentle, you must take him by the heart; you
will see that you can be happy with him. Perhaps
I was too hard with his poor father. God bless
you, my dear daughter!"

And there they stand, united in the same love for
Yves, and weeping together.

"Now then, my good women!" cries the conductor, "when will you have finished rubbing
noses?"

They had to drag them apart. And Marie,
seated once more in her corner, watches as she draws
away, with eyes filled with tears, the old woman,
who has sunk down, sobbing, on a milestone, while
little Pierre waves good-bye with his plump little
hand from the window.

CHAPTER LXVI

1st January, 1881.

In the heart of the docks at Brest, a little before dawn, on the first morning of the year 1881. A mournful place, these docks; the *Sèvre* has been moored there now for a week.

Above, the sky has begun to brighten between the high granite walls which enclose us. The lamps, few and far between, shed in the mist their last meagre yellow light. And already one may discern the silhouettes of formidable things which are taking shape, awakening ideas of a grim and cruel rigidity; machines high perched, enormous anchors upturning their black arms; all sorts of vague and ugly shapes; and, in addition, laid-up ships, with their outline of gigantic fishes, motionless on their chains, like large dead monsters.

A great silence prevails and a deadly cold. There is no solitude comparable with that of a naval dockyard at night, especially on a night of holiday. As the time approaches for the gun to sound the signal to cease work, everybody flees as from a place of pestilence; thousands of men issue from every point, swarming like ants, hastening towards the gates. The last of them run, actuated by a fear lest they should arrive too late and find the iron gates closed. Then calm descends. Then night. And there is no longer a soul, no longer a sound.

From time to time a patrol passes on his round,

challenged by the sentries, giving in a low voice the password. And then the silent population of rats debouches from all the holes, takes possession of the deserted ships, the empty yards.

On duty on board since the previous day I had got to sleep very late, in my icy, iron-walled room. I was worried about Yves, and the songs, the shoutings of sailors which came to me in the night from the distance, from the low quarters of the town, filled me with foreboding.

Marie and little Pierre were to make their journey to Plouherzel in Goello, and Yves had wanted, nevertheless, to spend the night on shore in Brest, to celebrate the New Year with some old friends. I could have stopped him by asking him to stay and keep me company; but the coldness between us persisted; and I had let him go. And this night of the 31st December is of all nights perhaps the most dangerous, a night when Brest gives itself up wholly to a riot of alcohol.

As I climbed on deck, I saluted rather sadly this first morning of the New Year, and I began the mechanical promenade, the hundred paces of the watch, thinking of many past things.

And especially I thought of Yves, who was my present preoccupation. During the last fortnight, on this *Sèvre*, it seemed to me that the affection of this simple brother who had long been the only real friend I had in the world, was slowly, hour by hour, drifting from me. And then, also, I was angry with him for not behaving himself better, and it seemed to me, that, for my part, too, I loved him less. . . .

A black bird passed above my head, uttering a mournful croaking.

" Good luck to you! " said a sailor who was making his morning ablution in cold water. " Here's some one come to wish us a happy New Year! . . . You ugly croaker! Anyhow, you are a sign that better things are to follow."

Yves returned at seven o'clock, walking very straight, and answered the roll-call. Afterwards he came to me, as usual, to wish me good morning.

I quickly saw, from his eyes slightly dulled and his voice slightly altered, that he had not been as abstemious as he should. And I said to him in the tone of a curt order:

" Yves, you will not return to shore to-day."

And then I affected to speak to others, conscious that I had been unduly severe and none too pleased with myself.

Midday. The dockyard, the ships are emptying, becoming deserted as on days of holiday. Everywhere the sailors may be seen on their way out for the day, all very smart in their clean Sunday clothes, brushing off with eager hand the least trace of dust, adjusting for one another their large blue collars. Walking briskly they soon reach the gates and press forward into Brest.

When it comes to the turn of those on the *Sèvre* Yves appears with the others, well brushed, well washed, and very bare about the neck, in his best clothes.

" Yves, where are you going? "

He gave me an angry glance such as I had not had from him before. It seemed to defy me and I read in it still the fever and bewilderment of alcohol.

" I am going to join my friends," he said.

"Sailors from my country, whom I have arranged to meet, and who are expecting me."

Then I attempted to reason with him, taking him aside, obliged to say what I had to say very quickly, for time pressed, obliged to speak low and to maintain an appearance of complete calm, for it was necessary that the others who were standing quite near us should not know what was passing. And I began to feel that I had taken a wrong road, that I was no longer myself, that my patience was exhausted. I spoke in the tone which irritates and does not persuade.

"I am going, I am going, I tell you," he said at the end, trembling, his teeth clenched. "Unless you put me in irons to-day, you will not stop me."

He turned away, defying me to my face for the first time in his life, and moved to rejoin the others.

"In irons? Very well then, Yves; in irons you shall be."

And I called a sergeant-at-arms, and gave him out loud the order to lead him away.

Oh! the glance he gave me as he turned away, obliged to follow the sergeant-at-arms who prepared to take him below, before all his fellows, to descend into the hold in his brave Sunday clothes! He was sobered, assuredly; for his gaze was penetrating and his eyes were clear. It was I who hung my head under this expression of reproach, of sorrowful and supreme amazement, of sudden disillusion and disdain.

And then I went back to my room.

Was it all over between us? I thought it was. This time I had lost him indeed.

I knew that Yves, with his obstinate Breton

character, would not return; his heart, once closed, would never open again.

I had abused my authority over him, and he was of those, who, before force, rebel and will not yield.

I had begged the officer on duty to let me continue in charge for this day, not having the courage to leave the ship—and I continued my endless walk up and down the deck.

The dockyard was deserted within its high walls. There was no one on deck. The sound of distant singing came from the low-lying streets of Brest. And, from the crew's quarters below, the voices of the sailors of the watch calling at regular intervals the *Loto* numbers with the little jokes usual among sailors, which are very old and always gain a laugh.

" —22, the two quartermasters out for a walk! "

" —33, the legs of the ship's cook! "

And my poor Yves was below them, at the bottom of the hold, in the dark, stretched on the floor in the cold, with his foot in an iron ring.

What should I do? . . . Order him to be set free and sent to me? I foresaw perfectly well how this interview might turn out: He standing before me, impassive, sullen, his bonnet, respectfully doffed, braving me by his silence, his eyes downcast.

And, if he refused to come—and he was quite capable of this in his present mood—what then? . . . How could I save him from the consequences of such a refusal of obedience? How could I then extricate him from the mess I should have made between our own private affairs and the blind rules of discipline?

Now, night was falling and Yves had been nearly

five hours in irons. I thought of little Pierre and of Marie, of the good folk of Toulven, who had put their hope in me, and then of an oath I had sworn to an old mother in Plouherzel.

And above all, I realized that I still loved my poor Yves as a brother. . . . I went back to my room and began hurriedly to write to him; for this must be the only means of communication between us; with our characters, explanations would never be successful. I wrote quickly, in large letters, so that he could still read them: darkness was coming on quickly, and, in the dockyard, a light is a thing forbidden.

Then I said to the sergeant-at-arms:

"Bring Kermadec to speak to *the Officer of the Watch*, here in my room."

I had written:

"DEAR BROTHER,—I forgive you and I ask that you too will forgive me. You know well that we are now brothers, and that, in spite of everything, we must stick together through thick and thin. Are you willing that all that we have done and said on the *Sèvre* should be forgotten, and are you willing to make one more firm resolution to be sober? I ask this of you in the name of your mother. If you will write 'Yes' at the bottom of this paper, all will be over and we will not speak of it again.

"PIERRE."

When Yves came in, without looking at him, and without waiting for a reply, I said to him simply:

"Read this which I have just written for you."
And I went out, leaving him alone.

He came out quickly, as if he had been afraid of my return, and, as soon as I heard that he was some distance away, I re-entered my room to see what he had answered.

At the bottom of my letter—in letters still larger than mine, for it was growing darker—he had written: "Yes, brother," and signed: "YVES."

CHAPTER LXVII

"JEAN-MARIE, go as quickly as you can and tell Yves that I am waiting for him on shore, on the quay."

This was ten minutes later. It was clearly necessary that we should meet—after having written one another thus—in order to make the reconciliation complete.

When Yves arrived, his face had changed and he was smiling as I had not seen him smile for many a long day. I took his hand, his poor topman's hand, in mine; it was necessary to squeeze it very hard to make it feel the pressure, for work had greatly hardened it.

"But why did you do that? It wasn't kind, you know."

And this was all he found to say to me by way of reproach.

The guard at night on the *Sèvre* was not very strict.

"Look here, Yves, we are going to spend this

first night of the New Year on shore, in Brest, and you are going to have dinner with me, as my guest. That is a thing we have never done and it will be fun. Quickly, go and brush your clothes (for he had got very dirty in irons in the hold), and let us go."

"Oh! but we must be quick, though. Let me rather brush myself when we get on shore. The gun will sound directly, and we shall not have time to get out."

We were in a remote part of the docks, very far from the gates, and we started off at once almost running.

But, as luck would have it, when we were but half-way, the gun sounded and we were too late.

There was nothing for it but to return to the *Sèvre*, where it was cold and dark.

In the wardroom there was a pitiful lantern in a wire cage, which had been lit by the fireman patrol, but no fire. And it was there we passed the first night of the new year, dinnerless through our own fault, but content nevertheless that we had found each other again and had made friends.

Nevertheless something still worried Yves.

"I did not think of it before: but perhaps it would have been better if you had left me in irons until the morning, on account of the others, you know, who won't be able to make out what has happened. . . ."

But about his future conduct, he had no misgiving at all; to-night he felt very sure of himself.

"In the first place," he said, "I have found a sure method; I will never go ashore again except with you, and you will take me where you will. In that way, you see. . . ."

CHAPTER LXVIII

Sunday, 31*st March,* 1881.

TOULVEN, in spring; the lanes full of primroses. A first warm breeze stirs the air, a surprise and a delight; it stirs the branches of the oaks and beeches, and the great leafless woods; it brings us, in this grey Brittany, the scent of distant places, memories of sunlit lands. A pale summer is at hand, with long, mild evenings.

We are all outside at the cottage door, the two old Keremenens, Yves, his wife, and Anne, little Corentine, and little Pierre. Religious chants, which we had first heard in the distance, are slowly drawing near. It is the procession coming with rhythmic step, the first procession of spring. It is now in the green lane. It is going to pass in front of us.

" Lift me, godfather, lift me! " says little Pierre, holding out his hands for me to take him in my arms, so that he may see better.

But Yves forestalls me and raising him very high, places him standing on his shoulders; and little Pierre smiles to find himself so tall and thrusts his hands into the mossy branches of the old trees.

The banner of the Virgin passes, borne by two young men, thoughtful and grave of mien. All the men of Trémeulé and of Toulven follow it, bareheaded, young and old, hat in hand, with long hair, brown or whitened by age, which falls on Breton jackets ornamented with old embroideries.

And the women come after: black corselets embroidered with eyes, a little restrained hubbub of voices pronouncing Celtic words, a movement of large white things of muslin on the heads. The old nurse follows last, bent and hobbling, always with her witch-like movements; she gives us a sign of recognition and threatens little Pierre, in fun, with the end of her stick.

It passes on and the noise with it.

Now, from behind and from a distance, we see the long procession as it ascends between the narrow walls of moss, a long lane of white wide-winged head-dresses and white collarettes.

It moves on, in zigzags, ascending always towards Saint Eloi of Toulven. It is a strange sight, this long procession.

"Oh! what a lot of coifs!" says Anne, who is the first to finish her rosary, and who begins to laugh, struck with the effect of all these white heads enlarged by the muslin wings.

And now it has disappeared—lost in the distances of the vault of beech trees—and one sees only the tender green of the lane and the tufts of primroses scattered everywhere: eager growths which have not waited for the sun, and which cluster on the moss in large compact masses, of a pale sulphur yellow, a milky amber colour. The Bretons called them "milk flowers."

I take little Pierre's hand and lead him with me into the woods, in order to leave Yves alone with his relations. They have very serious matters, it seems, to discuss together: those interminable questions of profits and distribution which, in the country, take so large a place in life.

This time it has to do with a dream Yves and his wife have dreamt together: to realize all their possessions and build a little house, covered with slate, in Toulven. I am to have my room there in this little house, and in it are to be put the old-fashioned Breton things I love, and flowers and ferns. They do not want to live any more in the large towns, not in Brest particularly—*it is not good for Yves*.

" It is true," he says, " that I shall not often be at home; but when I am, we shall all be very happy there. And then, you know, later on when I take my pension . . . it is for then really; I shall settle down very nicely in my house and my little garden."

His pension! That is ever the sailor's dream. It begins in early youth, as if the present life were only a time of trial. To take his pension, at about forty; after having traversed the world from pole to pole, to possess a little plot of earth of his own, to live there very soberly and to leave it no more; to become someone of standing in his village, in his parish church—a churchwarden after having been a sea-rover; the devil turned monk and a very peaceful one. . . . How many of them are mown down before they reach it, this more peaceful hour of ripe age? And yet, if you ask them, they are all thinking of it.

This *sure method* which Yves had discovered for keeping sober had succeeded very well; on board he was the exemplary sailor he had always been, and, on shore, we were never apart.

Since that miserable day which began the year 1881, the relations between **us** had completely changed, and I treated him now in every respect as a brother.

On board this *Sèvre*, a very small boat, we officers lived in a very cordial intimacy. Yves was now of our band. At the theatre, in our box; sharing our enterprises which for the most part were insignificant enough. Rather shy at first, refusing, slipping away, he had ended by accepting the position, because he felt that he was loved by us all. And I hoped by this new and perhaps unusual means to attach him to me as much as possible, and to raise him out of his past life and win him from his former friends.

That thing which it is usual to call education, that kind of polish which is applied thickly enough, it is true, on so many others, was entirely wanting in my brother Yves; but he had naturally a kind of tact, a delicacy much rarer, which cannot be assumed. When he was in our company, he kept himself always so well in his place, that in the end he himself began to feel at ease. He spoke very little, and never to say those banal things which everybody says. And when he put off his sailor's clothes and dressed himself in a well-fitting grey suit with grey suède gloves to match, then, though preserving still his careless sea-rover's carriage, his high-held head and his bronzed skin, he had all at once quite a distinguished air.

It used to amuse us to take him with us and present him to smart people upon whom his silence and bearing imposed and who found him rather haughty. And it was comical, next day, to see him once more a sailor, as good a topman as before.

Little Pierre and I, then, were in the woods of

Toulven, looking for flowers during the family council.

We found a great many, pale yellow primroses, violet periwinkles, blue borage, and even red silenes, the first of the spring.

Little Pierre gathered as many as he could, in a state of great excitement, not knowing which way to run, panting hard, as if in the throes of a very important work; he brought them to me very eagerly in little handfuls, very badly picked, half-crushed in his little fingers, and too short in the stalk.

From the height we had reached we could see woods as far as eye could command; the black-thorns were already in flower; all the branches, all the reddish sprigs, full of buds, were waiting for the spring. And, in the distance, in the midst of this country of trees, Toulven church raised its grey spire.

We had been out so long that Corentine had been placed on the look out in the green lane to announce our return. We saw her from a distance, jumping, dancing, playing all sorts of tricks alone, her big head-dress and her collarette fluttering in the wind. And she shouted loud:

"They are coming, big Peter and little Peter, hand in hand."

And she turned it into a rhyme and sang it to a lively Breton air as she danced in time:

> " See here they come together
> And they hold each other's hand,
> Peter big and Peter little
> Are coming hand in hand."

Her big head-dress and her collarette aflutter in the breeze, she danced like some little doll which had become possessed. And night was falling, a night of March, always mournful, under the leafless roof of the old trees. A sudden chill passed like a shudder of death over the woods, after the sunny warmth of the day:

> " And they hold each other's hand,
>   Peter big and Peter little!
>   And little black man Peter! "

" Little black man " was the nickname Yves had borne, and she gave it now to her little cousin Pierre, on account of the bronzed colouring of the Kermadecs. Thereupon I called her " Little Miss Golden Locks," and the name stuck to her; it suited her well, on account of the curls which were for ever escaping from her head-dress, curls like skeins of golden silk.

Everybody in the cottage seemed very pleased, and Yves took me aside and told me that matters had been arranged very satisfactorily. Old Corentin was giving them two thousand francs and an aunt was lending them another thousand. With that they would be able to buy a piece of land for a term of years and begin to build immediately.

We had to leave immediately after dinner in order to catch the diligence at Toulven and the train at Bannalec. For Yves and I were returning to Lorient, where our ship was waiting for us in the harbour.

At about eleven o'clock, when we had got back to the chance lodging we had booked in the town, Yves, before going to bed, began to arrange in vases the flowers we had gathered in the woods of Toulven.

It was the first time in his life that he had ever

done anything of the kind; he was surprised at himself that he should find pleasure in these poor little flowers to which he had never before given a thought.

" Well, well! " he said. " When I have my own little house at Toulven, I shall have flowers in it, for it seems to me that they look very well. But it is you, you know, who have given me the idea of these things. . . ."

CHAPTER LXIX

AT sea, on the following day, the first of April. Bound for Saint Nazaire. A full spread of canvas; a strong breeze from the north-west: the weather bad; the lighthouses no longer visible. We came into dock in the small hours, with a damaged bow and a broken foretopmast.

The 2nd is pay day. Drunken men stumble in the hold in the dark and there are broken heads.

A little liberty of two days, quite unexpected. On the road with Yves for Trémeulé in Toulven. This *Sèvre* is a good boat which never takes us away for long.

At ten o'clock at night, in the moonlight, we knock at the door of the old Keremenens and of Marie, who were not expecting us.

They wake up little Pierre in our honour, and sit him on our knees. Surprised in his first sleep he smiles and says how do you do to us very low.

but afterwards does not make much ado about our visit. His eyes close in spite of himself and he cannot hold up his head. And Yves, disturbed at this, seeing him hanging his head, and looking at us in sidelong fashion, his hair in his eyes:

" You know, it seems to me that he has . . . that he has . . . a sly look."

And he looks at me anxious to know what I think of it, conceiving already a grave misgiving about the future.

Nobody in the world but my dear old Yves would have felt concern on such ludicrous grounds. I shake little Pierre, who thereupon becomes wide awake and bursts out laughing, his fine big eyes well opened between their long lashes. Yves is reassured and finds that in fact he does not look at all sly.

When his mother strips him, he looks like a classic baby, like the Greek statues of Cupid.

CHAPTER LXX

TOULVEN, 30*th April.*

THE cottage of the old Keremenens, as darkness is falling on an evening of April. Our little party has just returned from a walk: Yves, Marie, Anne, little Corentine " golden locks," and " little black man " Pierre.

Four candles are burning in the cottage (*three* would be unlucky).

On an old table of massive oak, polished by the years, there are paper, pens and sand. Benches have been placed round. Very solemn things are about to happen.

We put down our harvest of herbs and flowers, which shed a perfume of April in the old cottage, and take our places.

Presently two dear old women enter with an important air: they say good evening with a curtsey, which makes their large starched collarettes stand upright, and sit down in a corner. Then Pierre Kerbras, who is engaged to Anne. At last everybody is placed and we are all complete.

It is the great evening for the settlement of the family arrangements, when the old Keremenens are going to fulfil the promise they have made to their children. The two of them rise and open an old chest on which the carvings represent Sacred Hearts alternating with cocks; they remove papers, clothing, and from the bottom, take a little sack which seems heavy. Then they go to their bed, lift up the mattress and search beneath: a second sack!

They empty the sacks on the table, in front of their son Yves, and then appear all those shining pieces of gold and silver, stamped with ancient effigies, which, for the last half century, have been amassed one by one and put in hiding. They are counted out in little piles; the two thousand francs promised are there.

Now comes the turn of the old aunt who rises and empties a third little sack; another thousand francs in gold.

The old neighbour comes last; she brings five

hundred in a stocking foot. And all this is lent to Yves, all this is heaped before him. He signs two little receipts on white paper and hands them to the two old lenders who make their curtsey preparatory to leaving, but who are detained, as custom ordains, and made to drink a glass of cider with us.

It is over. All this has been done without a notary, without a deed, without discussion, with a confidence and a simple honesty that are things of Toulven.

"Rat-tat-tat!" at the door. It is the contractor for the building, and he arrives in the nick of time.

But with this gentleman it is desirable to use stamped paper. He is an old rogue from Quimper, with only a smattering of French, but he seems cunning enough for all that, with his town manners.

It is given to me to explain to him a plan which we had thought out during our evenings on board, and in which a room is provided for me. I discuss the construction in the smallest details and the price of all the materials, with an air of knowledge which imposes on the old man, but which makes Yves and me laugh, when by ill-luck our eyes chance to meet.

On a sheet bearing a twelve sou stamp I write two pages of clauses and details:

"A house built of granite, cemented with sand from the seashore, limewashed, joinered in chestnut wood, with skylit attic, shutters painted green, etc., etc., the whole to be finished before the 1st May of next year and at the price fixed in advance of two thousand nine hundred and fifty francs."

This work and this concentration of mind have

made me quite tired; I am surprised at myself, and I can see that they all are amazed at my foresight and my economy.　It is unbelievable ·what these good people have made me do.

At last it is signed and sealed.　We drink cider and shake hands all round.　And Yves now is a landowner in Toulven.　They look so happy, Yves and his wife, that I regret no part of the trouble I have taken for them.

The two old ladies make their final curtsey, and all the others, even little Pierre, who has been allowed to stay up, come with me, in the fine moonlit night, as far as the inn.

TOULVEN, 1st *May*, 1881.

We are very busy, Yves and I, assisted by old Corentin Keremenen, measuring with string the land to be acquired.

First of all we had to select it, and that took us all yesterday morning.　For Yves it was a very serious matter this fixing of the site of his little house, in which he pictured, in the background of a melancholy and strange distance, his retirement, his old age and death.

After many goings and comings we had decided on this spot.　It is in the outskirts of Toulven, on the road which leads to Rosporden, on high ground, facing a little village square which is brightened this morning by a population of noisy fowls and red-cheeked children.　On one side is Toulven and its church, on the other the great woods.

At the moment it is just an oatfield very green. We have measured it carefully in all directions; reckoned by the square yard it will cost fourteen hundred and ninety francs, without counting the lawyer's fees.

How steady Yves will have to be, and how he will have to save to pay all that! He becomes very serious when he thinks of it.

CHAPTER LXXI

On board the *Sèvre, May*, 1881.

Yves, who will soon be thirty years old, begs me to bring him from the town a bound manuscript book in order that he may commence to record his impressions, after my manner. He regrets even that he can no longer recall very clearly dates and past events so that he might make his record retrospective.

His intelligence is opening to a crowd of new conceptions; he models himself on me and perhaps makes himself more " complex " than he need. But our intimacy brings in its train another and quite unexpected result, namely that I am becoming much simpler in contact with him; I also am changing, and almost as much as he.

Brest, *June*, 1881.

At six o'clock, on the evening of the feast of St. John, I was returning with Yves from the " pardon " of Plougastel on the outside of a country omnibus.

In May the *Sèvre* had been as far as Algiers, and we appreciated, by contrast, the special charm of the Breton country.

The horses were going at full gallop, beribboned, with streamers and green branches on their heads.

The folk inside were singing, and, on top, next to us, three drunken sailors were dancing, their bonnets on one side, flowers in their button-holes, with streamers and trumpets, and, in mockery of those unfortunate enough to be short-sighted, blue spectacles—three young men, smart of bearing and intelligent in face, who were taking a last French leave before their departure for China.

Any ordinary man would have broken his neck. But they, drunk as they were, kept their feet, nimble as goats, while the omnibus careered at full speed, swinging from right to left in the ruts, driven by a driver who was as drunk as they.

At Plougastel we had found the uproar of a village fête, wooden horses, a female dwarf, a female giant, a fat lady, and a boneless man, and games and drinking stalls. And, in an isolated square, the Breton bagpipes played a rapid and monotonous air of olden times, and people in old-fashioned costume danced to this age-old music; men and women, holding hands, ran, ran like the wind, like a lot of mad folk, in a long frenzied file. It was a relic of old Brittany, retaining still its note of primitiveness, even at the gates of Brest, amid the uproar of a fair.

At first we tried, Yves and I, to calm the three sailors and make them sit down.

And then it struck us as rather comical that we, of all people, should assume the rôle of preacher.

"After all," I said to Yves, "it's not the first sermon of the kind we've preached."

"To be sure, no," he replied with conviction.

And we contented ourselves with holding on to the iron rails to prevent ourselves from falling.

The roads and the villages are full of people returning from the " pardon," and all these people are amazed at seeing pass this carriage-load of madmen with the three sailors dancing on the top.

The splendour of June throws over this Brittany its charm and its life; the breeze is mild and warm beneath the grey sky; the tall grass, full of red flowers; the trees, of an emerald green, filled with cockchafers.

And the three sailors continue to dance and sing, and at each couplet, the others, inside, take up the refrain:

" Oh! He set out with the wind behind him,
He'll find it harder coming back."

The windows of our carriage rattle with it. This air, which never changes and is repeated over and over again for some six miles of our journey, is a very ancient air of France, so old and so young, of so frank a gaiety and so good a quality, that in a very few minutes we too are singing it with the rest.

How beautiful Brittany looks, beautiful and rejuvenated and green, in the June sunshine!

We poor followers of the sea, when we find spring in our path, rejoice in it more than other people, on account of the sequestered life we lead in the wooden monasteries. It was eight years since Yves had seen a Breton spring, and we both had long grown weary of the winter, and of that eternal summer which in other parts reigns resplendent over the great blue sea; and these green fields, these soft perfumes, all this charm of June which words cannot describe held us entranced.

Life still holds hours that are worth the living, hours of youth and forgetfulness. Away with all melancholy dreams, all the morbid fancies of long-faced poets! It is good to sail, in the face of the wind, in the company of the most lighthearted among the children of the earth. Health and youth comprise all there is of truth in the world, with simple and boisterous merriment and the songs of sailors!

And we continued to travel very quickly and very erratically, zigzagging over the road among these crowds of people, between very tall hawthorns forming green hedges, and under the tufted vault of the trees.

And presently Brest appeared, with its great solemn air, its great granite ramparts, its great grey walls, on which also grass and pink foxgloves were growing. It was as it were intoxicated, this mournful town, at having by chance a real summer's day, an evening clear and warm; it was full of noise and movement and people, of white head-dresses and sailors singing.

CHAPTER LXXII

5th July, 1881.

At Sea.—We are returning from the Channel. The *Sèvre* is proceeding very slowly in a thick fog, blowing every now and then its whistle which sounds like a cry of distress in this damp shroud which envelops us. The grey solitudes of the sea are all about us and we feel them without seeing them. It seems as if we were dragging with us long veils of darkness; we long to break through them; we are oppressed as it were to feel that we have been so long enclosed within them, and the impression grows that this curtain is immense, infinite, that it stretches for league on league without end, in the same dull greyness, in the same watery atmosphere. And then there is the endless roll of the waters, slow, smooth, regular, patient, exasperating. It is as if great polished and shining backs heaved and pushed us with their shoulders, raising us up and letting us fall.

Suddenly in the evening the fog lifts and there appears before us a dark thing, surprising, unexpected, like a tall phantom emerging from the sea:

" Ar Men Du (the Black Rocks)! " says our old Breton pilot.

And, at the same time, the veil is rent all round us. Ushant appears: all its dark rocks, all its reefs are outlined in dark grey, beaten by high-flung showers of white foam, under a sky which seems as heavy as a globe of lead.

Immediately we straighten our course, and taking advantage of the clearing, the *Sèvre* stands in for Brest, whistling no longer, but hastening and with every hope of reaching port. But the curtain slowly closes again and falls. We can see no longer, darkness comes, and we have to stand out for the open sea.

And for three long days we continue thus, unable to see anything. Our eyes are weary with watching.

This is my last voyage on the *Sèvre*, which I am due to leave as soon as we reach Brest. Yves, with his Breton superstition, sees something unnatural in this fog, which persists in midsummer as if to delay my departure.

It seems to him a warning and a bad omen.

CHAPTER LXXIII

BREST, 9*th July*, 1881.

WE reach port at last, however, and this is my last day of duty on board. I disembark to-morrow.

We are in the heart of the Brest docks, where the *Sèvre* comes from time to time to rest between two high walls. High gloomy-looking buildings overlook us; around us courses of native rock support the ramparts, a roundway, a whole heavy pile of granite, oozing sadness and humidity. I know all these things by heart.

And as we are now in July there are foxgloves, and tufts of silenes clinging here and there to the grey stones. These red plants growing on the walls strike a note of summer in this sunless Brest.

I have a kind of pleasure, nevertheless, in going away. This Brittany always causes me, in spite of everything, a melancholy sense of oppression; I feel it now, and when I think of the novelty and the unknown which await me, it seems to me that I am about to awaken with the passing of a kind of night. . . . Whither shall I be sent? Who knows? In what particular corner of the earth shall I have to acclimatize myself to-morrow? No doubt in

some country of the sun where I shall become
another person altogether, with different senses, and
where I shall forget, alas! the beloved things I am
now about to leave behind me.

But my poor Yves and my little Pierre, I shall
not part from either of them without a pang.

Poor Yves, who has so often himself had to be
treated like a spoilt and capricious child, it is he now,
at the hour of my departure, who surrounds me with
a thousand kind attentions, almost childlike, at a
loss to know what he can do to show sufficiently his
affection. And this attitude in him has the greater
charm, because it is not in his ordinary nature.

The time we have just passed together, in a daily
fraternal intimacy, has not been without its storms.
He still deserved in some degree, unfortunately, the
epithets " undisciplined," " uncontrollable," inscribed
long ago in his sailor's pay-book; but he had
improved very much, and, if I had been able to
keep him near me, I should have saved him.

After dinner we came up on deck for our usual
evening promenade.

I say for a last time:

" Yves, make me a cigarette."

And we begin our regular little walk up and
down the wooden deck of the *Sèvre*. We know by
heart all the little hollows where the water collects,
all the angle blocks in which one's feet may be
caught, all the rings over which one may stumble.

The sky is overcast for our last walk together,
the moon hidden, and the air damp. In the distance,
from the direction of Recouvrance, come as usual
the eternal songs of the sailors.

We speak of many things. I give Yves much

advice, and he, very submissive, makes many promises; and it is very late when he leaves me to seek his hammock.

At noon on the following day, my trunks scarcely packed and many visits unpaid, I am at the station with Yves and my friends of the wardroom who have come to see me off. I shake hands with them all, I think even that I embrace them, and then I depart.

A little before dark I reach Toulven, where I propose to stop for a couple of hours to make my adieux.

How green it is and decked with flowers, this Toulven, this fresh and shady region, the most delightful in Brittany!

There I find them waiting for me to cut little Pierre's hair. The idea that anyone would entrust me with such a task had never occurred to me. They told me "that I was the only one who could keep him quiet." The previous week, they had brought in the barber from Toulven, and little Pierre had made such a fuss that the first thing the scissors did was to cut his little ears; and it had been necessary to abandon the project. I made the attempt, however, in order to please them, hard put to it not to laugh.

Then when I had done, the notion came to me to keep one of the little brown curls which I had cut off, and I took it away with me, surprised that I should set so much store by it.

CHAPTER LXXIV

A Letter from Yves

" On board the *Sèvre*, Lisbon,
" 1*st August*, 1881.

" Dear Brother,—I am sending you this short letter in reply on the same day that I have received yours. I write in haste and am taking advantage of the luncheon hour. I am on the stand of the main mast.

" We put into Lisbon yesterday evening. Dear brother, we have had very bad weather this time; we have lost our head sails, the mizzen and the whaler. I may tell you also, that, in the heavy rolling of the ship, my kit-bag and my locker have disappeared, and all my possessions with them; I have suffered a loss of nearly a hundred francs in this way.

" You asked me what I did on the Sunday, a fortnight ago. My good brother, I remained quietly on board and finished reading ' Capitaine Fracasse.' And, since your departure, I have only been ashore once, on Sunday last; and I was very sober, for in the first place, I had sent home the whole of my month's money; I had drawn sixty-nine francs and sent sixty-five of them to my wife.

" I have had news from Toulven and it is all good. Little Pierre is very sharp and he can now run about very well. Only he is very naughty when he gets *his little sea-gull mood on him*, like me, you know; from what his mother says, he upsets every-thing he can get hold of. The walls of our house are already more than six feet above ground; I shall be very happy when it is quite finished, and especially when I see you installed in your little room.

"Dear brother, you bid me think of you often; I assure you that never an hour passes in which I do not think of you, and often many times in the hour. Besides, now, you understand, I have no longer anyone to talk to in the evening—and sometimes I have no cigarettes.

"I cannot tell you when we are leaving here, but please write to me at Oran. I hear we shall be paid at Oran, so that we may be able to go ashore and buy tobacco.

"I end, my dear brother, in embracing you with all my heart.

"Your affectionate brother who loves you. Ever yours,

"YVES KERMADEC.

"P.S.—If I have enough money at Oran, I will lay in a large supply of tobacco, and, especially for you, of that sort which is like the Turkish tobacco, wḥich you are fond of smoking.

" The Captain has given me for you a table-napkin, the last you used on board. I have washed it, and, in doing so, I have torn it a little.

"As regards the manuscript book you gave me for writing my notes, that too was spoilt by the storm and I have laid it aside.

"Dear brother, I embrace you again with all my heart,

"YVES KERMADEC.

"P.S.—On board, things are just the same and the Captain has not changed his habit of insisting on the tidiness of the deck.   There was a great dispute between him and the lieutenant, once more about the *cacatois*, you know.   But they were good friends again, afterwards.

" I have also to tell you that in seven or eight months, I think we shall have another little child. A thing, however, which does not altogether please me, for I think it is a little too soon.

" Your brother,

" Yves."

CHAPTER LXXV

I was in the Near East when these little letters of Yves reached me ; they brought me, in their simplicity, the already far-off perfume of the Breton country.

My memories of Brittany were fading fast.   Even now I seemed to see them as through a mist of dreamland ; the reefs I had known so well, the lights on the coast, Cape Finistère with its great dark rocks ; and the dangerous approaches to Ushant on winter evenings, and the west wind blowing under a mournful sky, in the fall of December nights. From where I was now, it all seemed a vision of a sunless country.

And the poor little cottage at Toulven!   How small it seemed, lost at the side of a Breton lane!

But it was the region of deep beech woods, of grey rocks, of lichens and mosses; of old granite chapels and high-growing grass speckled with red flowers. Here, sand and white minarets under a vault surpassingly blue, and sunshine, eternal, enchanting sunshine!

CHAPTER LXXVI

Another Letter from Yves

"BREST, 10*th September*, 1881.

" MY DEAR BROTHER,—I have to tell you that our *Sèvre* is being disarmed; we handed her over yesterday to the authorities at the docks; and, I can assure you, I am not very grieved about it.

" I reckon on remaining for some time on shore, in the neighbourhood; also (since our little house is not very far advanced, as you will understand) my wife has come to live with me in Brest until it is finished. I think you will agree, dear brother, that we have done the right thing. This time we have taken rooms almost in the country, at Recouvrance, on the way to Pontaniou.

" Dear brother, I have to tell you that little Pierre was taken ill with colic as a result of eating too many berries in the woods, on that last Sunday when we were at Toulven; but he got over it. He is becoming a dear little chap, and I spend hours playing with him. In the evening all three of us go for a walk together; we never go out now unless we go together, and when one returns the other two return also!

" Dear brother, if only you were back in Brest, I should have everything I want; and you would see me now as I am, and you would be very pleased with me; for never have I been so peaceful.

" I should like to go away with you again, my dear brother, and to find myself on a ship bound for the Levant where I might find you.   This is not to say that I do not want to continue the life I am now living, for I assure you I do.   But that is not possible, because I am too happy.

" I end in embracing you with all my heart. Little Pierre sends his love; my wife and all my relations at Toulven ask to be remembered to you. They look forward to seeing you and I can promise you so do I.

" Your brother,
" YVES KERMADEC."

CHAPTER LXXVII

TOULVEN, *October*, 1881.

PALE Brittany once more in autumn sunshine! Once more the old Breton lanes, the beech trees and the heather!   I thought I had said good-bye to this country for many a long day, and coming back to it I am filled with a strange melancholy.   My return has been sudden, unexpected, as the returns and the departures of sailors so often are.

A fine October day, a warm sun, a thin white mist spread like a veil over the countryside. All about is that immense peace which is peculiar to the fine days of autumn; in the air a savour of dampness and of fallen leaves, a pervading sense of the dying year. I am in the well-known woods of Trémeulé, on the height overlooking all the region of Toulven. Below me, the lake, motionless under this floating mist, and, in the distance, wooded horizons, as they must have been in the ancient days of Gaul.

And those who are with me, sitting among the thousand little flowerets of the heather, are my Breton friends, my brother Yves and little Pierre, his son.

It has become in some sort my own country, this Toulven. A few short years ago it was unknown to me, and Yves, for all that even then I called him brother, scarcely counted for me. The aspects of life change, things happen, are transformed, and pass.

The heather is so thick that, in the distance, it looks as if the ground were covered with a reddish carpet. The tardy scabious are still in flower, on the top of their long stalks; and the first of the heavy rains have already littered the earth with dead leaves.

It was true, what Yves had written to me; he had become very steady. He had just been taken on board one of the ships in the Brest roadstead, which seemed to assure for him a stay of two years in his native country. Marie, his wife, was installed near him in the suburb of Recouvrance, waiting for the little house at Toulven, which was growing slowly, with very thick and solid walls, in the manner of olden times.   She had welcomed my unexpected return as a blessing from heaven; for my presence in Brest, near them, reassured her greatly.

That Yves should have become so steady, and so suddenly, when so far as one could see there was no decisive circumstance to account for the change in him, was a thing scarcely to be believed! And Marie, in confirming her happiness to me, did so very timidly; she spoke of it as one speaks of unstable, fugitive things, with a fear lest their mere expression in words should break the spell and frighten them away.

CHAPTER LXXVIII

AND then one day the demon of alcohol crossed their path again. Yves came in with the sullen troubled look Marie had such cause to dread.

It was a Sunday in October. He arrived from his ship, where he had been ordered to irons, so he said; and he had escaped because it was unjust. He seemed very exasperated; his blue jersey was torn and his shirt open.

She spoke soothingly to him, trying to calm him. It so happened that the day was beautifully fine; it was one of those rare days of late autumn which have an exquisite and peaceful melancholy, which are as it were a last resting place of summer before the winter comes. She had on her best dress and her embroidered collarette, and had dressed little Pierre in all his finery, thinking they would all three go for a walk together in the soft sunshine. In the street, couples passed, in their Sunday clothes, making their way along the roads or into the woods as in the spring-time.

But no, it was not to be; Yves had pronounced the terrifying phrase she knew so well: " I am going to find my friends! " It was all over!

Then, almost distracted with grief, she had ventured on an extreme measure: while he was looking out of the window, she had shut and locked the door and hidden the key in her bodice. And he, who knew very well what she had done, turned round and said, hanging his head, his eyes glowering:

" Open the door! Open it! Do you hear me? I tell you to open the door."

He went and shook the door on its hinges; something restrained him yet from breaking it—which he could have done without any trouble. And then, no; he would make his wife, who had locked it, come and open it herself.

And he walked up and down the room, with the air of a wild beast, repeating:

" Open the door! Do you hear me? I tell you to open it."

The joyous sounds of the Sunday came up from the street. Women in wide head-dresses passed on the arm of their husbands or their lovers. The autumn sun illumined them with its tranquil light.

He stamped his foot and repeated again in a low voice:

"Open! I tell you to open!"

It was the first time she had attempted to retain him by force, and she saw that she was succeeding badly and she was strangely afraid. Without looking at him, she flung herself on her knees in a corner, and began to pray, out loud and very quickly, like one possessed. It seemed to her that she was approaching a terrible moment, that what was going to happen was more dreadful than anything that had happened before. And little Pierre, standing up, opened very wide his serious eyes, afraid also, but not understanding.

"You won't? You won't open it for me? . . . I will break it, then! You will see!"

There was a thud on the floor, then a heavy, horrible sound. Yves had fallen from his full height. The handle by which he had seized the door remained in his hand, broken, and he had been thrown backwards on his son, whose little head had struck against the corner of an iron fire-dog in the fireplace.

And then there was a sudden change. Marie ceased her praying. She got up, her eyes dilated and wild, and snatched her little Pierre from the hands of Yves, who was attempting to raise him. He had fallen without a cry, overcome at being hurt by his father. Blood trickled from his forehead and he uttered no word. Marie pressed him close to her breast, took the key from her bodice, unlocked the door with one hand and threw it wide open. . . . Yves watched her, frightened in his turn; she shrank away from him, crying:

"Go! Go! Go!"

Poor Yves! He hesitated now to pass out! He

was trying to understand what had happened. This door which had now been opened for him, he had no longer use for it; he had a vague notion that this threshold was going, in some way, to be a fatal one to cross. And then, this blood he saw on the face of his little son and on his little collar. . . . Yes he wanted to know what had happened, to come near to them. He passed his hand over his forehead, feeling that he was drunk, making a great effort to understand what the matter was . . . God! No, he could not; he understood nothing. Drink, the friends who were waiting for him below, that was all.

She repeated once more, her son clasped close to her heart:

" Go! Go, I tell you! "

Then turning about he went downstairs and out.

CHAPTER LXXIX

" HELLO! Is that you, Kermadec."

" Yes, Monsieur Kerjean."

" And on French leave, I bet? "

" Yes, Monsieur Kerjean."

So much indeed might have been guessed from his appearance.

" And so, I understand you are married, Yves? Someone from Paimpol, that big fellow Lisbatz, I think, told me you were a family man."

Yves shrugged his shoulders with a movement of bad-tempered carelessness, and said:

" If you are looking for men, Monsieur Kerjean
. . . it will suit me very well to join your ship."

It was not the first time that this Captain Kerjean
had enrolled a deserter. He understood. He
knew how to take them and afterwards how to
manage them. His ship, *la Belle-Rose*, which
sailed under the American flag, was leaving on the
following day for California. Yves was acceptable
to him; he was indeed an excellent acquisition to a
crew such as his.

The two moved aside and discussed, in a low
voice, their treaty of alliance.

This took place in the Mercantile docks, on the
morning of the second day after he had left his
home.

The day before he had been to Recouvrance,
skirting the walls, in an attempt to get news of his
little Pierre. From a distance, he had seen him
looking out of the window at the people passing
below, with a little bandage round his head. And
then he had returned on his tracks, sufficiently
reassured, in the half-muddled condition of drunkenness in which he still was; he had returned on his
tracks to " go and find his friends."

On this morning he had awakened at daybreak,
in a hangar on the quay where his *friends* had left
him. His drunkenness had now passed, completely
passed. The fine October weather continued, fresh
and pure; things wore their customary aspects, as if
nothing had happened, and his first thoughts were
thoughts of tenderness for his son and for Marie;
and he was on the point of rising and going back to
them and asking them to forgive him. Some
minutes passed before he realized the extent of his

misfortune, realized that all was over, that he was lost. . . .

For how could he go back to them now? It was impossible! For very shame he could not.

Besides, he had escaped from the ship after being ordered to irons and, since, had absented himself for three whole days. These were not matters easily dismissed. And then to take once more those same resolutions, taken twenty times before, to make once more those same promises, to say once more those same words of repentance. . . . It did not bear thinking on. He smiled bitterly in self-pity and disgust.

And then again his wife had bidden him to "go!" He remembered that vividly, and her look of hate, as she showed him the door. No matter that he had deserved it a thousand times, he could never forgive her that, he who was so used to being lord and master. She had driven him away. So be it then, he had gone, he was following his destiny, she would never see him again.

This backsliding was all the more repugnant to him, in that it followed upon this period of decent peace during which he had caught a glimpse of and begun to realize a higher life; and this return to misery seemed to him a thing decisive and fatal. He observed now that he was covered with dust and mud and filth of other sort, and he began to dust himself, raising his head, and gradually assuming an expression of grimness and disdain.

That he should have fallen like a senseless brute on his little son and injured his poor little forehead! He became to himself a miserable, repulsive thing at the thought of it.

He began to break with his hands the sides of a wooden box which lay near him, and under his breath, after an instinctive glance round to see that he was alone, he called himself, with a bitter, mocking smile, vile names such as sailors use.

Now he was on his feet, looking determined and dangerous.

To desert! If he could join some ship and get away at once! There should be one in the docks; in fact that day there were many. Yes, he would desert at any price and disappear for ever!

His decision had been taken with an implacable resolve. He walked towards where the ships lay, his shoulders well back, his head high, the Breton self-will in his half-closed eyes, in his frowning brows.

He said to himself: "I am worthless, I know it, I always knew it, and they had far better let me go my ways. I have done my best, but I am what I am and it is not my fault."

And he was right perhaps: *it was not his fault.* As he was now he was not responsible; he yielded to mysterious influences which had their origin in the remote past and came to him with his blood: he was a victim of the law of heredity working through a whole family, a whole race.

CHAPTER LXXX

At two o'clock on this same day on which he had
concluded his bargain with Captain Kerjean, Yves,
having bought some ordinary seaman's clothes, and
changed clandestinely in a tavern on the quay, went
on board the *Belle-Rose*.

He went all over the ship, which was badly kept
and had aspects of primitive roughness, but which
nevertheless seemed a stout and handy vessel, built
for speed and the hazards of the sea.

Compared with the ships of the navy it looked
small, short, and, above all, empty; an air of
abandonment with scarce a soul on board; even at
anchor this kind of solitude struck a chill to the
heart.   Three or four rough-looking seamen lounged
about the deck; they composed the whole crew,
and were about to become, for some years perhaps,
Yves' only companions.

They began by staring at one another before
speaking.

Throughout the day the fine weather continued,
warm and peaceful; a sort of melancholy summer
persisting into the autumn and bringing with it a
kind of tranquillity.   And on Yves, too, his decision
irrevocably taken, a calm descended.

They showed him his little locker, but he had
scarcely anything to put in it.   He washed himself
in cold water, adjusted his new clothes, with an air

of something like vanity; he wore no longer the livery of the state which he had often found so irksome; he felt at ease, freed from all the bonds of the past, almost as much as by death itself. He began to rejoice in his independence.

On the following morning, with the tide, the *Belle-Rose* was going to put off. Yves scented the ocean, the life of the sea which was about to commence in the new fashion so long desired. For years this idea of deserting had obsessed him in a strange way, and now it was a thing accomplished. The decision he had taken raised him in his own eyes; he grew bigger as he felt himself outside the law; he was no longer ashamed, now that he was a deserter, of presenting himself before his wife; he even told himself that he would have the courage to go to her that very night, before he went away, if only to take her the money he had received.

At certain moments, when the face of little Pierre passed before his eyes, his heart ached horribly; it seemed to him that this ship, silent and empty, was as it were a bier on which he was about to be carried living to his grave; he almost choked, tears welled into his eyes, but he checked them in time, with his strong will, by thinking of something else; and quickly he began to talk to his new-found friends. They discussed the method of manœuvring the ship with so small a crew, and the working of the large pulleys which had been multiplied everywhere to replace the arms of men, and which, so Yves thought, made the gear of the *Belle-Rose* unduly heavy.

In the evening, when it was dark, he went to Recouvrance and climbed noiselessly to his door.

He listened first before opening it; there was no sound. He entered softly.

A lamp was burning on the table. His son was alone, asleep. He leaned over his wicker cradle, which had the scent of a bird's nest, and placed his lips very gently on those of his child in order to feel once more his soft breathing. Then he sat down near him and remained still, so that his face might be calm again when his wife should enter.

CHAPTER LXXXI

MARIE had seen him coming, and climbed the stairs after him, trembling.

In the last two days she had had time to consider in all its aspects the misfortune which had come upon them.

She had shrunk from questioning the other sailors, as the poor wives of absentees commonly do, to ascertain from them whether Yves had returned to his ship. She knew nothing of him, and she was waiting, prepared for the worst.

Perhaps he would not come back; she was prepared for that as for everything else, and was surprised that she could think of it with so much calmness. In that case her plans were made; she would not return to Toulven, for fear of seeing their partly built house, for fear also of hearing the name of her husband execrated daily in the home of her parents, to which she would have to go. Not to Toulven; but to the country of Goëlo, where there

was an old woman who resembled Yves, and whose
features suddenly assumed for her an infinite kindli-
ness. It was at her door she would knock. She
would be indulgent to him, for she was his mother.
They would be able to speak without hatred of the
absent one; they would live there, the two deserted
women, together, and watch over little Pierre,
uniting their efforts to keep him, their last hope,
with them, so that he at least should not be a sailor.

And it seemed to her, too, that if one day, after
many years perhaps, Yves, the deserter, should
return seeking those who belonged to him it was
to that little corner of the world, to Plouherzel, that
he would come.

The night before, she had had a strange dream of
Yves' return; it seemed to her that many years had
passed and that she was already old. Yves arrived
at the cottage in Plouherzel in the evening; he
too was old, altered, wretched. He came asking
forgiveness. Behind him Goulven and Gildas
entered, and *another Yves*, taller than them all, with
hair quite white, trailing behind him long fringes
of seaweed.

The old mother received them with her stern
face. In a voice infinitely sad she asked:

"How comes it that they are all here? My
husband was lost at sea more than sixty years ago.
. . . Goulven is in America. . . . Gildas in his
grave in the cemetery. . . . How comes it that they
are all here?"

Then Marie awoke in fear, understanding that
she had been surrounded by the dead.

But this evening Yves had returned alive and
young; she had recognized in the darkness of the

street his tall figure and active step. At the thought
that she was going to see him again and to determine
her lot, all her courage and all her plans had
deserted her. She trembled more and more as she
ascended the staircase. . . . Perhaps after all he
had simply passed the last two days on board and
was now returning in the ordinary way. Perhaps
they would settle down once more. . . . She
paused on the stairs and prayed God that this might
be true, a quick, heartfelt prayer.

When she opened the door, he was indeed there,
sitting by the cradle and looking at his sleeping son.

Poor little Pierre was sleeping peacefully, the
bandage still on his forehead where the fire-iron had
cut it.

As soon as she entered, pale, her heart beating so
violently as almost to hurt her, she saw at once that
Yves had not been drinking: he raised his eyes to
her and his gaze was clear; but he lowered them
quickly again and remained bent over his son.

" Is he much hurt? " he asked in an undertone,
slowly, with a calmness that surprised and frightened
her.

" No, I have been to the doctor for the dressing.
He says that it will not leave a mark. He did not
cry at all."

They remained there, silent, one before the other,
he still sitting near the little cradle, she standing,
white-faced and trembling. There was no ill-will
between them now; perhaps they loved each other
still; but now the irreparable was accomplished and
it was too late. She looked at the clothes he wore,
which she had never seen him in before: a black
woollen jersey and a cloth cap. Why these clothes?

And this little parcel near him on the floor, out of which the end of a blue collar peeped? It seemed to contain his sailor's effects, put aside for ever, as if the real Yves was dead.

She found courage to ask:

" The other day, did you return to the ship? "

" No! "

There was silence again. She was conscious of a growing anxiety.

" During the last three days, you have not returned? "

" No! "

Then she did not dare to speak again, fearing to hear the dreadful truth; trying to prolong the minutes, even these minutes compact of uncertainty and anguish, because he was still there, before her, perhaps for the last time.

At last the poignant question fell from her lips:

" What are you going to do then? "

And he, in a low voice, simply, with the calmness of an unalterable resolve, let fall the fatal word:

" Desert! "

Desert! . . . Yes, she had divined it only too well in the last few moments, when she saw his altered clothing, and this little parcel of sailor's kit carefully folded in a handkerchief.

She recoiled under the weight of the word, supporting herself with her hands against the wall behind her, almost choking. Deserter! Yves! lost! The thought of Goulven, his brother, passed through her mind, and of distant seas from which sailors never return. And, feeling her helplessness against this fate which crushed her, she remained silent, utterly overwhelmed.

Yves began to speak to her very kindly, pointing with sorrowful calm to the little parcel which he had brought.

" I want you, my poor Marie, to-morrow, when my ship has left, to send that on board, you understand.   You never can tell! . . . If I am caught . . . It is always more serious to take away the property of the State!   And this is the advance payment they have given me. . . . You will return to Toulven. . . . Oh! I will send you money, all I earn; you know, I shall not want much myself. We shall not see each other again, but you will not be too unfortunate . . . as long as I live."

She wanted to throw her arms round him, to hold him with all her strength, to struggle, to cling to him when he was going away, if needs be to let herself be dragged down the staircase, and even into the street. . . . But no, something held her bound where she stood: first the knowledge that all that she might do could be of no avail, and then a sense of dignity, there, where their son lay asleep. . . . And she remained against the wall, without a movement.

He had placed two hundred francs in large silver pieces on the table near him.   They represented the payment that had been made to him in advance, all that remained of it, after he had paid for his clothes.   He looked at her now very thoughtfully, very kindly, and with his woollen sleeve brushed off some tears that were rolling down his cheeks.

But he had nothing more to say to her.   And now the last minute had come and all was over.

He bent again for a last time over his little son, then straightened himself and got up to go.

CHAPTER LXXXII

And the Celts mourned three barren rocks under a lowering sky, in the heart of a gulf dotted with islets.
—G. Flaubert, Salammbô.

The Coral Sea!   At the Antipodes of our old world. Nothing but blue anywhere.   Around the ship which proceeds slowly, the infinite blue spreads its perfect circle.   The surface shines and glitters under the eternal sun.

Yves is there, alone, carried high in the air in a thing which oscillates slowly; he passes, in his top.

He gazes, with unseeing eyes at the limitless circle; he is as it were dazed with space and light. His expressionless eyes come to rest at hazard, for, everywhere, all is alike.

Everywhere, all is alike. . . . It is the great blind, unconscious splendour of things which men believe have been made for them.   Over the surface of the waters pass life-giving breezes which no one breathes; warmth and light are poured out in abundance; all the sources of life are open on the silent solitudes of the sea and fill them with a strange glory.

The surface shines and glitters under the eternal sun.   The great blaze of noon falls into the blue desert in a useless and wasted magnificence.

Presently Yves thinks he can discern in the distance a trail less blue, and his attention, which

just now wandered idly over the sparkling and
tranquil monotony, is concentrated upon it: it is no
doubt the sea breaking into foam over the whiteness
of coral, breaking on isles unknown, level with the
water, which no map has yet shown.

How far away is Brittany—and the green lanes
of Toulven—and his little son!

Yves has come out of his dream, and is watching,
his hand shading his eyes, that distant trail which
still shows white.

He does not look like a deserter, for he is wearing
still the blue collar of the navy.

Now he can distinguish the breakers and the
coral quite clearly, and he leans over a little in the
air, and calls out to those below: " Reefs on the
port bow."

No, Yves has not deserted, for the ship he is on
is the warship *Primauguet.*

He has not deserted, for he is still with me, and
when he announced from aloft the approach of the
reefs it was I who climbed up to him in his top, to
reconnoitre with him.

At Brest on that unhappy day when he had
decided to leave us, I had seen him pass in common
seaman's garb, carrying his sailor's kit so neatly
folded in a handkerchief, and I had followed him
at a distance as far as Recouvrance. I had let Marie
enter and then I had entered too, after them; and
as he came out he had found me waiting outside his
door, barring his passage with my outspread arms—
as, once before, at Toulven. Only this time it was
not merely a matter of checking a childish caprice;
I was about to engage in a supreme struggle with
him,

And long and cruel the struggle was, and there
was a moment when I almost lost heart and
abandoned him to the gloomy destiny which was
carrying him away. And then, abruptly, it had
ended. Tears came to save him, tears that had been
wanting to come for the last two days—but could not,
so little used were his eyes to this form of weakness.
Then we put little Pierre, who had just awakened,
on his knee; his little Pierre bore him no ill-will at
all, but put his arms straightway round his neck.
And Yves, at last, had said to me:

"Very well, brother, I will do anything you tell
me to do. But, no matter what, you must see now
that I am done for. . . ."

His case was indeed very serious and I did not
know myself what course to take: it was a sort of
rebellion, to have escaped from the ship after having
been sentenced to irons, and then to have absented
himself for three days! I had been tempted to say
to them, after I had made them embrace: "Desert
both of you, all three of you, my dear friends; for
it is too late now to do anything better. Let Yves
go away on the *Belle-Rose* and do you go and join
him in America."

But no, that was too desperate a remedy, to
abandon for ever their Breton land, and the little
house at Toulven, and their old parents!

So, trembling a little at my responsibility, I had
taken the contrary decision: to return that very
evening the advance already received, to free Yves
from the hands of this Captain Kerjean, and, when
morning came, as soon as the port should open, to
hand him over to the naval authorities. Anxious
days had followed, days of applications and of

waiting, and at last, with much leniency and kindness, the matter had been settled in this way: a month in irons and six months' suspension from the rating of petty officer, with return to the pay of a simple sailor.

That is how my poor Yves, embarked once more with me on this *Primauguet*, finds himself back in the crow's nest, again a topman as before, and performing the rough work he knew of old.

Standing, both of us, on the yard of the foresail, our bodies swung out into the void, with one hand shading our eyes, with the other holding on to the cordage, we watched together, in the distance of the resplendent blue solitudes, the white line of breakers growing ever more distinct; the continuous noise they made was like the distant sound of a church organ in the midst of the silence of the sea.

It was in fact a large coral island which no navigator had hitherto discovered; it had risen slowly from the depths below; century after century it had put forth patiently its branches of stone; even now it was only an immense crown of white foam, making, amid the infinite calm of the sea, the noise of a living thing, a kind of mysterious and eternal murmuring.

Everywhere else the blue expanse was uniform, safe, deep, infinite; we could proceed on our way without misgiving.

"You have won *the double*, brother," I said to Yves.

I meant: the double ration of wine at dinner. On board, this *double* is the usual recompense for a sailor who has been the first to sight land or to announce a danger—or for him who catches a rat without the help of a trap—or even for him who has turned himself out more smartly than the others for the Sunday inspection.

Yves smiled, but with the air of one who suddenly has a sombre thought.

" You know very well that now wine and I . . . But that's no matter, I can give it to the topmen at my table.   They will drink it willingly enough."

It was the fact that since the day when he had pushed little Pierre against the fire-irons in the grate, far away, in Brest, he had drunk only water. He had sworn this on the poor little wounded head, and it was the first solemn oath of his life.

We were talking together, in the pure virgin air, among the loosely hanging sails, which looked very white in the sun, when the sound of a whistle came from below, a quite distinctive whistle which meant in nautical language: " The leader of the foresail top is wanted below.   Let him come down quickly ! "

It was Yves who was leader of the foresail top ; he descended in great haste to see what was wanted of him.   The second-in-command had asked to see him in his room ; and I knew very well why.

In the remote and tranquil seas in which we were cruising the sailors became rather hazy about the seasons, the months and the days ; they lost the sense of the passage of time in the monotony of the days.

And in fact summer and winter had lost their qualities ; they were no longer recognizable, for the climate was different.   Nor did the things of nature serve now to mark them out.   There was always this infinity of water, always this wooden house in which we dwelt, and, in the spring, there came no touch of green.

Yves had resumed without difficulty his former occupation, his habits of topman, his life in the crow's nest, well-nigh naked, exposed to wind and sun, with his knife and his "mooring." He had ceased to count the days because they were all alike, merged one into another by the regularity of the watches, by the alternation of a sun that was always hot with nights that were always clear. He had accepted this time of exile without measuring it.

But to-day was the day when his six months of punishment expired; and the captain had to tell him to take back his stripes, his silver whistle and his authority as petty officer. He did so with much cordiality and shook him by the hand; for Yves, while his punishment had lasted, had shown himself exemplary in conduct and courage and no top had ever been kept like his.

Yves came back to me with a broad smile of happiness:

"Why didn't you tell me it was to-day?"

He had been promised that, if he went on as he was going, his punishment would soon be quite forgotten. Clearly, the oath he had taken on the wounded head of his little Pierre, at the end of that dreadful evening, was succeeding beyond his hope.

CHAPTER LXXXIII

THE afternoon of the same day.   Yves is in my
room, busy putting his stripes on his sleeves, in
haste to finish before darkness falls, looking comical
as always, with his big air of sea-rover, when he is
engaged in sewing.

They are not very elegant, his poor clothes; they
show signs of hard wear.   For he was not rich when
he left Brest with his reduced pay; and, so as not
to break into his allowance, he had refrained from
drawing too many things from the store.   But they
are so clean, the little woollen stripes are so neatly
placed one above the other, on each forearm and on
the bottom of each sleeve, that he will pass muster
very well.   These new stripes give them even a
certain lustre of youth.   Besides, Yves looks well in
anything; and then, too, one wears very little clothing on board, and as he will put them on but rarely,
they will certainly serve him until the end of the
voyage.   As for money, Yves has none; he has
forgotten even the use and value of it, as often
happens to sailors—for he allots to his wife, at Brest,
his pay and his stripe-money, all that he earns.

By the time it is dark, his work is finished.   He
carefully folds his coat and then sweeps away the
little ends of thread which he has let fall on the
floor.   Then he informs himself very exactly of

the month and the date, lights a candle, and begins
to write.

"At sea, on board the *Primauguet,*
"*23rd April,* 1882.

"My Dear Wife,—I am writing these few words
in advance to-day in M. Pierre's room. I will post
them next month when we touch at the Hawaii
Islands (a country . . . but I don't suppose you
will know where it is).

"I want to tell you that I have recovered my
stripes to-day and that you may set your mind at
rest, I shall not lose them again; I have sewn them
on *very tight* this time.

"Dear wife, this reminds me that it is only six
months since we parted, and that it will be a long
time yet before we see each other again. But I
assure you that I should dearly love to be back for
a time at Toulven, to give you a hand in getting
our house ready; and yet, it is not simply for that,
you know, but above all, to spend some time with
you, and to see our little Pierre running about.
They will have to give me a long leave when we
return, at least fifteen or twenty days; indeed I do
not think twenty will be enough and I shall ask for
as many as thirty.

"Dear Marie, I can tell you, however, that I am
very happy on board, especially because I have been
able to embark with M. Pierre. It is what I had
hoped for for a very long time. It has been a very
fine voyage and a very economical one for me who
have need to save a lot of money as you know.
Perhaps I may get another promotion before we

disembark, seeing that I am on very good terms with all the officers.

" I have also to tell you that the flying fish . . ."

Crack! On deck someone whistles: "Aloft everyone!" Yves hurries away; and no one has ever heard the end of the story of the flying fish.

He has preserved with his wife his childlike manner of being and writing. With me, he is changed, he has become a new Yves, more complex, more sophisticated than the Yves of old.

CHAPTER LXXXIV

THE night which follows is clear and exquisite. We are moving very slowly, in the Coral sea, before a light, warm breeze, advancing with precaution, in fear of encountering white islands, listening to the silence, in fear of hearing the murmur of reefs.

From midnight to four o'clock in the morning, the time of the watch has passed in vigil, amid the great, strange peace of the southern waters.

Everything is of a blue-green, of a blue of night, of a colour of infinite depth; the moon, which at first sails high in the heaven, throws little flickering reflections on the sea, as if everywhere, on the immense empty plain, mysterious hands were agitating silently thousands of little mirrors.

The half-hours pass one after another, undisturbed, the breeze steady, the sails very lightly stretched. The sailors of the watch, in their linen clothes, are asleep on the bare deck, in rows, all on the same side, fitted in one with another, like rows of white mummies.

At each half-hour a bell rings, startlingly; and two voices come from the bow of the ship, singing out one after the other, in a kind of slow rhythm: " Keep a look out on the port bow! " says one. " Keep a look out on the starboard bow! " replies the other.   The noise is surprising, producing the impression of a formidable clamour in all this silence; and then the vibrations of the voices and of the bell die away and there is no longer a sound.

Meanwhile the moon is slowly sinking and its blue light grows wan; it is much nearer the water now and its reflection in it makes a long trail of light.

It becomes yellower, scarcely giving any light, like a dying lamp.

Slowly, it begins to get larger, disproportionately larger; then it becomes red, loses its shape, and is swallowed up, strange, terrifying.   And then what one sees has no longer a name: on the horizon is a great dull fire, blood-red.   It is too large to be the moon, and, besides, distant things now mass in front of it in large dark shadows; colossal towers, toppling mountains, palaces, Babels!

One feels as it were a veil of darkness weighing upon the senses.   There comes to you an impression of apocalyptic cities, of clouds heavy with blood, of suspended maledictions; a conception of gigantic horrors, of chaotic destructions, of the end of the world. . . .

For a moment the mind has slept, involuntarily;

and a waking dream has come and gone, very quickly.

Mirage! And now it is over and the moon has set. There was nothing beyond save the infinite sea and floating mists announcing the approach of dawn; now that the moon is no longer behind them, they are not even discernible. All has vanished and the darkness has returned, the real darkness of night, clear and calm as ever.

They are far away from us, those countries of the Apocalypse: for we are in the Coral Sea, on the other side of the world, and there is nothing here but the immense circle, the limitless mirror of the waters. . . .

A signalman has gone to see the time by the chronometer. Out of deference to the moon, he is going to note in the large register, always open, which is the ship's log, the precise moment at which it set.

Then he comes to me and says:

"Captain, it is time to call the watch." My four hours of the night watch are already finished, then, and the officer to relieve me will shortly make his appearance.

I give the order:

"Master-gunners and loaders, call the watch!"[1]

Then, some of those who were sleeping on the deck, like white mummies, get up and awaken some of the others; they move off in a group and go

---

[1] The regulation order. On board the crew is divided into a number of groups, each forming a gun's crew. The master-gunner and the loaders escort the men of their group and awaken those who replace them for the watch.

below. And then, from the spar-deck, comes the
sound of twenty voices, singing one after the other
—in the manner of glee-singing—a very ancient air,
at once joyous and mocking.

They sing:

" Have you heard, you larboard men, get up for
the watch, get up, get up, get up! . . . Have you
heard, you larboard men, get up for the watch, get
up, get up, get up! . . ."

They move hither and thither, stooping under the
suspended hammocks, and, as they pass, shake the
sleepers with thrusts of their powerful shoulders.

And presently, inexorable, I give the order:

" Fall in on deck, the larboard watch!"

And they come up half-naked; there are some
who yawn, others who stretch themselves, who
stumble. They line up in groups, while a man, with
a lantern, peers into their faces and counts them.
The others who were sleeping on deck go below and
sleep in their place.

Yves has come up with the men of the larboard
watch who have just been awakened. I recognize
at once his way of whistling which I had not heard
now for a year. And presently I recognize his
voice which rings out in command for the first time
on the deck of the *Primauguet*.

Then I call him very officially by the title which
has just been restored to him: " Master of the
Watch."

It was only to shake him by the hand, to wish him
good luck and good night before I went to bed.

CHAPTER LXXXV

" HAUL away there, Goulven! "

It was a difficult boarding. I had come, in a cutter from the *Primauguet*, to examine a suspicious-looking whaling ship, which showed no flag.

In the southern ocean, still; near the Isle of Tonga, and to windward of it. The *Primauguet* itself was anchored in a bay of the island, within the line of reefs, in the shelter of a coral bank. The whaler lay off-shore almost in the open sea, as if in readiness for flight, and the swell was heavy about her.

I had been sent with a party to reconnoitre her, to " speak " to her as we say in the navy.

" Haul away there, Goulven! Haul! "

I looked up at the man who was called Goulven; he was the one, who, on the deck of the equivocal craft, held the rope which had just been thrown to me. And I was struck by his face, by his familiar look: he was another Yves, not so young, more sunburnt and more athletic perhaps—harsher in feature, as one who had suffered more—but he was so like him in the eyes, in the expression, that he looked to me like his double.

I had sometimes thought that we might come across this brother Goulven, on one of these whaling boats which we found, now and then, in the anchorages of the southern seas, and which we " spoke " to when we did not like their look.

I went straight to him, without worrying about the captain, who was a huge American, headed like a pirate, with a long, thick, seaweed-like beard. I entered there as on conquered territory and etiquette mattered little to me.

"So it's you, Goulven Kermadec?"

And I advanced towards him holding out my hand, so sure was I of his identity.

But he, for his part, paled under his tan, and shrank back. He was afraid.

And I saw him, in an instinct of uncivilized man, clenching his fists, stiffening his muscles, as if prepared to resist to the utmost, in a desperate struggle.

Poor Goulven! The surprise of hearing me call him by his name—and then my uniform—and the sixteen armed sailors who accompanied me, had been too much for him. He thought that I had come in the name of the law of France, to seize him, and, like Yves, he became exasperated under the threat of force.

It took a minute or two to reassure him; and then when he was persuaded that his *little brother* had become mine, and that he was hard by, on the warship from which I had come, he asked my pardon for his fear with the same frank smile I knew so well in Yves.

It was a singular looking crew. The boat itself had the movements and the appearance of a pirate-ship. Licked and fretted by the sea, during the three years in which it had wandered in the swell of the great ocean without having once touched any civilized country, but solid still, and built for the seas' highways. In its shrouds, from bottom to top, on each ratline, hung whale's fins, looking like long dark fringes. One would have said that it had passed under the water and become covered with seaweed.

Within, it was laden with the fats and oils from the bodies of all the great beasts which they had slain. There was enough there to make a small fortune, and the captain was reckoning on returning shortly to America, to California where his home was.

A mixed crew: two Frenchmen, two Americans, three Spaniards, a German, an Indian "boy," and a Chinese cook. In addition a Peruvian *chola*— half-naked like the men—who was the wife of the captain and was suckling a baby two months old conceived and born at sea.

The living quarters of this family, in the stern, had oak walls as thick as ramparts, and doors barred with iron. Within was a veritable arsenal of revolvers, knuckle-dusters, and life-preservers. Precautions had been taken; if occasion arose one would be able there to stand a siege by the whole crew.

For the rest, her papers were in order. She had not hoisted a flag for the simple reason that she had not got one; beetles had eaten the last, of which they showed me the rags to substantiate their excuse; it had the American colours right enough, red and white stripes, with the starred Jack. There was nothing to be said; everything was, in fact, correct.

. . . Goulven asked me if I knew Plouherzel; and I told him how I had slept one night under his mother's roof.

"And you," I said, "are you never going to return."

I could see that he was much moved.

"It is too late now. I should have my punishment to do for the State, and I am married in California. I have two children in Sacramento."

"Will you come with me to see Yves?"

"Come with you?" he repeated darkly, in a low voice. He seemed astonished at what I proposed to him. "Come with you? But you know . . . I am a deserter?"

At this moment he was so like Yves, he said this so exactly as Yves might have said it, that I felt a pang.

After all, I understood his fears of a man free and jealous of his liberty; I respected his terrors of French territory—for the deck of a warship is French territory—on board the *Primauguet*. We should have the right to arrest him; that was the law.

"At any rate you would like to see him?"

"Like to see him! . . . My poor little Yves!"

"Very well, then, I will bring him to you. When he comes, all I ask of you is that you will advise him to be steady. You understand . . . Goulven?"

It was he then who took my hand and pressed it in his.

CHAPTER LXXXVI

I HAD accepted an invitation to dinner on the
following day with the captain of the whaler. We
had got on famously together. His manners were
not those of polite society, but there was nothing
vulgar or commonplace about him. And besides
it was the only way in which I could get Yves on
board his ship.

I half expected on the following morning, at daybreak, to find that the whaler had disappeared, flown
during the night like a wild bird. But no; there it
was in its position off-shore, with all its black fringes
in its shrouds, standing out against the great circular
mirror of the waters; which, on that morning, were
motionless, and heavy, and gleaming, like coulées
of silver.

The invitation was seriously meant, therefore,
and they were waiting for me. As a precaution,
the captain had decided that the crew of the cutter
which took me should be armed and should remain
with me throughout. This fitted in admirably so
far as Yves was concerned, and I took him with me
as coxswain.

CHAPTER LXXXVII

The captain received me on his quarter-deck, dressed in reasonably correct American fashion; the *chola*, transformed, wore a red silk dress with a magnificent collar of pearls collected on the Pomoto islands; I was struck by her good looks and her perfect figure.

We repair together to the room of the formidable iron-barred walls. It is dark and gloomy there; but, through the little deep-set windows, we see the splendour of what look like enchanted things: a sea of a milky blue, and with the polish of a turquoise, a distant island, of a purple iris colour, and a multitude of little orange-tinted clouds floating in a golden green sky.

Afterwards when we turn our eyes from these little open windows, from the contemplation of all this light, the low-pitched cabin seems stranger than before, with its irregular shape and its massive beams, its arsenal of revolvers, of knuckle-dusters, leather thongs and whips.

The dinner consists of tinned foods from San Francisco, exquisite fruits from the Isle of Tonga-Taboo, needle-fish, slim little inhabitants of the warm seas; and we drink French wines, Peruvian *pisco* and English liqueurs.

The Chinaman who waits upon us wears a silk robe of episcopal violet and slippers with thick paper soles. The *chola* sings a *zamacuéca* of Chile, playing, on a *diguhela*, a sort of accompaniment which sounds like the monotonous little clatter of a trotting mule. The doors of the fortress are wide open. Thanks to the presence of my sixteen armed men, a sense of security reigns, a peaceful intimacy, which are really very touching.

In the bow the men from the *Primauguet* are drinking and singing with the crew of the whaler. It is a general holiday on board. And, from the distance, I see Yves and Goulven, who, for their part, are not drinking, walking up and down in conversation. Goulven, the taller of the two, has passed his arm round the shoulders of his brother, who holds him, in turn, round the waist. Isolated from the rest they continued their stroll, talking together in a low voice.

The glasses were emptied everywhere in strange toasts. The captain, who at first resembled the impassive statue of a marine or river god, woke up, and began to laugh a powerful laugh which shook his whole body; his mouth opened like that of a cetacean, and he started to talk of strange things in English, forgetting himself so far in his confidences as to tell me things for which he might well have been hanged; his conversation turns into a pretty tale of unmitigated piracy. . . .

The *chola* retires to her cabin, and a tattooed sailor is brought in and undressed during the dessert. The object of this is to show me the tattooing which represents a fox hunt.

It begins at the neck: horsemen, hounds, in full cry, wind in a spiral round his body.

"You haven't yet seen the fox?" the captain asks me with a boisterous laugh.

The discovery of the fox, it seems, is going to be a very funny business, for he is ready to die with laughter at the thought of it. And he makes the man, who is already tipsy, turn round and round several times so that we may follow the hunt which continues its downward course. In the neighbourhood of his loins, the hunt thickens and one foresees the end is near.

"See! there he is!" cries the captain with the head of a river god, at the height of his savage merriment, throwing himself back, transported with satisfaction and laughter.

The hunted beast has gone to earth; only half of it can be seen. And that is the great culminating surprise. The sailor is invited to drink with us, as a reward for letting us see him.

It was time to go on deck and get a little pure air, the fresh and delicious air of the evening. The sea, which still was motionless and heavy, gleamed in the distance, reflecting the last lights that came from the west. And now the men began to dance to a jig-like air played on a flute.

As they danced the men cast sidelong glances at us, half in shy curiosity, half in scornful disdain. They had some of those tricks of physiognomy which sea-going men have preserved from our primitive ancestors; and comical gestures at every turn, an excessive mimicry, like animals in the wild state. Sometimes they threw themselves back, cambering their bodies; sometimes, by virtue of natural suppleness and their habits of stratagem, they crouched down, arching their backs, in the manner of wild beasts when they walk in the light of day. Round and round they went, to the sound

of the fluted music, of the little jigging, infantine
tol-de-rol-lol; very serious, dancing very well, with
graceful poses of arms and circular movements of
legs.

But Yves and Goulven continued to walk up and
down together. They had many things still to say
to each other, and they were making the most of
these last final minutes, for they knew that I was
about to leave. They had seen each other once,
fifteen years before, while Yves was still quite a
little fellow, on that day which Goulven had
spent at Plouherzel, in hiding like a fugitive, and,
as far as could be seen, they would never meet
again.

Suddenly, we saw two of the dancers seize each
other round the waist, throw themselves to the
ground, still close grappled one with the other, and
then begin to fight, to throttle one another, taken
with a sudden rage; they tried to use their knives
and already there were red marks of blood on the
deck.

The captain with the river god head separated
them by lashing them both with a whip of hippo-
potamus hide.

"No matter," he said in English; "they are
drunk!"

It was time to go. Goulven and Yves embraced
each other, and I saw tears in Goulven's eyes.

As we were returning over the tranquil sea, the
first southern stars enkindling on high, Yves spoke
to me of his brother:

"He is not very happy. Although he earns a
good deal of money and has a little house in California, to which he hopes to return. But there it

is; it is the longing for his home country which is killing him."

This captain promised to bring his *chola* to have dinner with me on the following day on my ship. But, during the night, the whaler put to sea, vanished into the empty immensity; we never saw her again.

CHAPTER LXXXVIII

"AND so you have come to get your allowance, too Madame Quéméneur?"

"And you, too, Madame Kerdoncuff?."

"And where is your husband now, Madame Quéméneur?"

"In China, Madame Kerdoncuff, on the *Kerguelen*."

"And mine, too, you know, Madame Quéméneur; he is there, too, on the *Vénus*."

It is in the Rue des Voutes, in Brest, with a fine rain falling, that this dialogue of strangely shrill, falsetto voices takes place.

The street is full of women who have been waiting there since the morning, outside an ugly granite building: the sailors' pay office. Women of Brest, deterred in no wise by the cold rain, they are talking querulously, their feet in water, hugging the walls of the mournful little street, in the grey mist.

It is the first day of the quarter. They form a queue to get their money and none too soon, for

money is wanting in all the dark dwellings of the
town.

Wives of sailors far away at sea, they are waiting
to draw their allowances, the pay which those sailors
have allotted them.

And when they have drawn it they will spend it
on drink. There is, opposite, a tavern which has
been established specially for their convenience.
It is called À *la mère de famille* and the pro-
prietress is one Madame Pétavin. It is known in
Brest as *le cabaret de la délégue* (the tavern of the
allowance).

Madame Quéméneur, pug-faced, square-jawed,
big-bellied, wears a waterproof and a bonnet of black
tulle trimmed with blue shells.

Madame Kerdoncuff, sickly, greenish, with a look
of a blue-bottle, shows a mean, sly-looking face
under a hat trimmed with two roses with their
foliage.

As the hour approaches the crowd of inebriates
increases. The paying office is besieged; there are
disputes at the doors. The cashier's desk is about
to open.

And Marie, the wife of Yves, is there too, in this
unclean promiscuousness, holding little Pierre by
the hand. Timid, depressed, filled with a vague
fear of all these women, she allows the more
impatient to pass and waits against the wall on the
side sheltered from the rain.

"Come in, my good woman, instead of letting the
dear little fellow get wet like this."

It is Madame Pétavin who speaks. She has just
appeared at her door, her face wreathed in smiles.

"Can I get you anything? A little of the best?"

"No, thank you; I do not drink," replies Marie, who, however, seeing that the tavern is empty, enters for fear lest her little Pierre should catch cold. "But if I am in your way. . . ."

Surely not, she was not in Madame Pétavin's way at all. Madame Pétavin had a kind heart and made her sit down.

Presently Madame Quéméneur and Madame Kerdoncuff, among the first to be paid, enter, shut up their umbrellas, and sit down.

"Madame! Madame! Bring us half a pint in two glasses."

No need to ask half a pint of what. Brandy, and raw brandy at that, is what they crave.

These good ladies begin to talk:

"What did you say your husband was, on the *Kerguelen*, Madame Quéméneur?"

"He's a leading seaman, Madame Kerdoncuff."

"And mine, too, you know, is a leading seaman, Madame Quéméneur! Wives of leading seamen ought to be friends! Here's to you, Victoire-Yvonne!"

The women were already addressing each other by their Christian names. The glasses were emptied.

Marie turned upon them big, serious eyes, examining them suddenly with much curiosity, as one might animals in a menagerie. And she had an impulse to leave, to get away. But, outside, it was raining heavily, and there was a crowd still at the door of the paying office.

"Your health, Victoire-Yvonne!"

"Your health, Françoise!"

Glasses are replenished again.

The women now begin to talk of their domestic affairs: it is difficult enough to make ends meet! But it can't be helped! The baker, this time, will have to wait until next quarter day. The butcher will have to be satisfied with something on account. To-day, pay day, may not one have a little enjoyment?

"But I, you know," says Madame Kerdoncuff, with a coquettish smile full of suggestion, "I am not too badly off, because, you see, I let a furnished room to an old sailor, who is a petty officer in the port."

There is no need to be more explicit. The face of Madame Quéméneur wears a smile of comprehension.

"And I, too, I have a quartermaster. . . . Here's to you, Françoise! . . ." (The women whisper to each other.) "He's a gay dog, my quartermaster, I can tell you! . . ."

And the chapter of intimate confidences begins.

Marie Kermadec gets up. Has she heard aright? Many of the words used are unknown to her, it is true, but the meaning of them is transparent and gestures make it doubly clear. Are there really women who can bring themselves to say such things? And she goes out, without looking back, without a word of thanks, red, conscious of her burning cheeks.

"Did you see her? We have shocked her!"

"Oh well, you know, she's from the country; she still wears the coif of Bannalec; she's green yet."

"Here's to you, Victoire-Yvonne!"

The tavern is filling. At the door, umbrellas are

closed, old waterproofs are shaken; many more
women come in, liquor flows.

And, at home, are little mites puling with the
voices of jackals in distress; emaciated children
whimpering from cold and hunger. So much the
worse, here's to you, for is it not pay day!

When Marie got outside, she saw a group of
women in large coifs who were standing aside to
make way for the press of the brazen ones; and she
went quickly and took her place amongst them so
that she might once more be in honest company.
Amongst them were dear old women from the
villages who had come to draw the allowance of their
sons, and who were waiting under their cotton
umbrellas, with the dignified, prim faces, which
peasant women assume in the town.

As she was waiting her turn, she entered into
conversation with an old woman from Kermézeau,
who told her the history of her son, a gunner on the
Astrée. It appeared that in his early youth he had
had bouts similar to those of Yves, but afterwards,
as he got older, he had quite settled down; one need
never despair of a sailor. . . .

Nevertheless in her indignation against these
women of Brest, Marie had come to a momentous
decision: to return to Toulven at whatever cost,
and to-morrow if possible.

As soon as she got back to her room, she began to
write a long letter to Yves giving the reasons for
her decision. It was true, their tenancy of the
lodgings at Recouvrance had still three months to
run and that the little house at Toulven would not
be finished for a long time yet; but she would make
up for all that by working and strict economy; she

would take in mending for the neighbours, and would goffer the large native collarettes, work of some difficulty, which she knew how to do very perfectly by the skilful use of very fine reeds.

And she went on to tell him all the new things which little Pierre had learnt to say and do; in very naïve terms, she told of her great love for the absent one; she enclosed a curl, cut from a certain little brown and very restless head; and put the whole in an envelope of thin paper which she superscribed thus:

" To Monsieur Kermadec, Yves, Leading Seaman on board the *Primauguet*, in the southern seas, c/o the French Consul at Panama, to be forwarded."

Poor little letter! Will it ever be delivered? Who can tell? It is not impossible, more unlikely things have happened. In five months, six months, travel-stained and covered with American postmarks, it will be delivered, perhaps, faithfully to Yves, and bring him the deep love of his wife and the brown curl of his son.

CHAPTER LXXXIX

May, 1882.

IN the evening, in the southern solitudes. The wind was rising. Over all this moving immensity in which the *Primauguet* dwelt long dark blue waves were chasing one another. It was a damp wind and struck chill.

R

Below on the spar-deck, Le Hir the idiot was hastening, before darkness fell, to sew up a corpse in pieces of grey canvas which were the remains of sails.

Yves and Barrada, standing, were watching him with a kind of horror. They had perforce to remain close to him, in a very small mortuary chamber, which had been made by suspending other sails and which was guarded by a gunner, cutlass in hand.

It was Barazère who was being sewn up in these grey remnants. He had died of a disease contracted long before in Algiers—on a night of pleasure. . . . Many times he had believed himself cured; but the deadly poison remained in his blood, reappeared from time to time, and at last had killed him. Towards the end he had been covered with hideous sores and his friends had avoided him.

It fell to Le Hir to sew him up, for all the others had refused, out of fear of his malady. Le Hir had accepted on the strength of a promise of a pint of wine.

The rolling of the ship worried him, hampered him in his work, kept shifting the corpse out of position; and he was eager to be done and to get the wine that was waiting for him.

First, the feet; he had been told to bind them tight on account of the cannon-ball which is attached to the dead body to make it sink. Then the legs; and presently the body was entirely hidden, enveloped in many thicknesses of coarse canvas; only the pale face was now visible, tranquil in death, and looking strangely handsome with a peaceful smile. 'And then roughly, with a brutal indifference, Le Hir drew over it an end of the grey canvas and the face was veiled for ever.

In a French village the old parents of this Barazère were looking forward to the day of his return.

When the job was done Yves and Barrada came out of the mortuary chamber pushing Le Hir before them by the shoulders, to see that he washed his hands before he drank his wine.

They had been exchanging ideas about death apparently, for Barrada, as he came out, said in his Bordeaux accent:

"Ah! Nonsense! It is with men as with beasts; others will come, but those who die . . ."

And he finished by laughing that curious laugh of his, which sounded deep and hollow like a roar.

From his lips, there was nothing impious in the phrase; it was simply that he knew nothing better to say.

They were both, as a matter of fact, much moved; they grieved for Barazère. Now, the malady which had caused them fear was covered up, forgotten; in their memory, the dead man had emerged from that final impurity and become suddenly ennobled; they saw him again as in the time of his strength, and in thinking of him they were moved to pity.

CHAPTER XC

" THERE'S no foppery in a sailor who has washed his skin in the waters of five or six oceans."

On the following morning, when the sun rose, the wind was still fresh. The *Primauguet* was moving very quickly, rocking in its course with the supple and vigorous movement of a mighty runner. In the bow the men released from the watch were singing as they made their morning toilet, stripped, resembling, with their muscular arms and shoulders, the statues of ancient Greece; they were washing themselves liberally in cold water; they plunged their head and shoulders into tubs, covered their chests with a white foam of soap and then, turn and turn about, rubbed one another down.

Suddenly they remembered the dead man and their blythe song subsided. For they had just seen the men of the other watch assembling at the order of their officer and lining up in the stern, as if for an inspection. They guessed why and drew near.

A long new plank had been placed crosswise on the nettings, overhanging, making a kind of see-saw over the water, and a sinister thing which seemed very heavy, a sheath of grey canvas which betrayed a human form, had just been brought up from below.

When Barazère was laid on the long new plank, suspended in mid air over the foaming waves, the bonnets of the sailors were all removed in a last salute; a signalman recited a prayer, hands made the sign of the cross—and then, at my command, the plank was tilted and there came the dull sound of a heavy thing plunging into the water.

The *Primauguet* passed on its way, and the body of Barazère sank into the abyss, immense in depth and extent, of the great ocean.

Then, very softly, as a reproach, I repeated to Yves who was near me, the phrase of the night before:

" It is with men as with beasts: more will come, but . . ."

" Oh! " he replied; " it was not I who said that; it was he." (*He*—that is to say, Barrada—heard him and turned his head towards us. There were tears in his eyes.)

We looked behind us with uneasiness, at the wake; for it happens sometimes, when the following shark is there, that a stain of blood appears on the surface of the sea.

But no, there was nothing; he had descended in peace into the depths below.

An infinite descent, first rapid as in a fall; then slow, slow, petering out little by little in the ever-increasing density of the deeper waters. A mysterious journey of many leagues into unplumbed abysms; during which the darkened sun shows first like a pale moon, then turns green, then trembles, and finally is effaced. And then the eternal darkness begins; the waters rise, rise, gathering over the head of the dead traveller like the waters of a deluge which should reach up to the stars.

But, below, the dead body has lost its loathsomeness; matter is never unclean in an absolute sense. In the darkness the invisible animals of the deep

waters will come and encompass it; the mysterious
madrepores will put forth upon it their branches,
eating it very slowly with the thousand little mouths
of their living flowers.

This grave of sailors cannot be violated by any
human hand. He who has descended to sleep
below is more dead than any other dead man;
nothing of him will ever appear again; never will he
mingle with that old dust of men which, on the
surface of the earth, is for ever seeking to recombine
in an eternal effort to live again. He belongs to
the life of the world below; he is going to pass into
plants of colourless stone, into sluggish animals
which are without shape and without eyes. . . .

CHAPTER XCI

ON the evening of the burial of Barazère, Yves had
brought his friend Jean Barrada with him to my
room. They were now the only survivors of the
old band: Kerboul, Le Hello, had been sleeping
for many a long day at the bottom of the sea, to
which they too had descended in the fullness of
youth; the others had left to join the merchant
service, or had returned to their villages: all were
scattered.

Yves and Barrada were very old friends. On
shore, when they were together, it was not good to
cross them in their whims.

I can still see the two of them sitting there before

me, sharing the same chair on account of the limited space of the room, holding on with one hand in the habit learnt from the rolling of the ship, and looking at me with attentive eyes. For I was endeavouring to prove to them on this evening that *it was not with men as with beasts*, and to speak to them of the mysterious *beyond*. . . . And they, with Barazère's death fresh in their memory, were listening to me surprised, fascinated, in the midst of that very special peacefulness of calm evenings at sea, a peacefulness which predisposes to the comprehension of the incomprehensible.

Old arguments repeated over and over again at school which I developed to them and which it seemed to me might still make an impression on their young minds. . . . It was perhaps very stupid, this discourse on immortality; but it did them no harm; on the contrary.

CHAPTER XCII

THESE seas in which the *Primauguet* was were almost always of the same lapis blue; it was the region of the trade winds and of fine weather without an end.

Sometimes, in our passage from one group of islands to another, we had to cross the Equator, to pass through the motionless immensities and mournful splendours.

And afterwards, when, in one hemisphere or the other, we ran into the life-giving trade wind again,

when the awakened *Primauguet* began once more to
gather speed, then one realized better, by contrast,
the charm of moving quickly, the charm of being on
this great, inclined, quivering thing which seemed
to be alive, and which obeyed you, alert and supple,
as it sped onwards.

When we sailed eastward in these regions of the
trade winds, we sailed close to the wind; and then
the *Primauguet* rushed upon the regular, crisped
waves of the tropics for whole days, without ever
getting tired, with little joyous flutterings such as
sportive fishes might have.

Afterwards, when we returned on our course, with
the wind behind us, fully rigged, every inch of our
white canvas spread, our progress, rapid as it was,
became so easy, so effortless, that we no longer felt
that we were moving; we were lifted up as it were
in a kind of flight and our movement was like the
soaring of a bird.

As far as the sailors were concerned one day was
very much like another.

Every morning there was first of all a kind of
frenzy of cleaning which began with the réveillé.
One saw them, half-awake, jump up and start
running to commence as quickly as might be the
great diurnal washing. Naked, in their pompomed
bonnets, or maybe wearing a " tricot de combat "
(a little knitted thing for the neck, not unlike a
baby's bib) they set to work to swill the deck.
Water spurted from hosepipes; water was flung by
hand from buckets. Wasting no time they threw
it over legs and over backs until they were all
besplashed, all streaming; they overturned everything in order to wash everything; afterwards,

scouring the deck, already clean and white, with mops and scrapers to make it cleaner and whiter still.

Sometimes they would be ordered to break off and go aloft to make some alteration in the rigging, to shake out a reef or trim the sails; then they would dress themselves hastily, for decency's sake, before climbing, and quickly carry out the manœuvre ordered, eager to get down again and amuse themselves in the water.

This is the work which makes arms strong and chests round; and the feet, too, from being used to climbing bare, become in some measure prehensile, like those of monkeys.

At about eight o'clock, at the roll of a drum, the washing would be done. Then, while the hot sun was quickly drying all these things which they had made wet, they would begin to furbish; the copper-work, the iron-work, even the ordinary rings were made to shine like mirrors. Each one would address himself to the little pulley, the little object, the toilet of which had been specially entrusted to him and would polish it with solicitude, stepping back every now and then with a critical air to see how it looked, to see whether it did him credit. And, around these great children, was still and always the blue circle, the inexorable blue circle, the resplendent solitude, profound, having no end, where nothing ever changed and nothing ever passed.

Nothing passed save the madcap bands of flying fish, moving like arrows, so rapidly that one had time only to see the glistening of their wings and they were gone. They were of several kinds; some large, which were steel-blue in colour; some smaller and rarer which seemed to have colours of mauve and peony; they surprised you by their rosy flight, and, when you tried to distinguish them, it was too late; a little patch of water eddied still and sparkled in the sunshine as if under a hail of bullets; it was there they had made their plunge, but they were no longer there.

Sometimes a frigate bird—a great mysterious bird which is always alone—crossed, at a great height, the regions of the air, flying straight with its narrow wings and scissor-like tail, hastening as if it had a goal. Then the sailors pointed out to one another the strange traveller, following it with their eyes as long as it remained in sight, and its passage was recorded in the ship's log.

But a ship, never; they are too large, these southern seas; there are no meetings there.

Once, however, we came across a little oceanic island surrounded by a white belt of coral. Some women who dwelt there approached in canoes, and the captain allowed them to clamber on board, guessing why they had come. They all had admirable figures, eyes of true savages, scarcely opened and fringed with very heavy lashes, and teeth of wonderful whiteness which their laugh revealed to their whole extent. On their skin, which was of the colour of reddish copper, were very complicated tattooings resembling a network of blue lace.

Their passage had broken for a day the continence which the sailors preserved. And then the island, barely seen, had vanished with its white beach and its green palms, a very little thing amid the immense desert of the waters, and we thought of it no more.

But there was no boredom on board. The days were quite adequately filled with duties and amusements.

At certain hours, on certain days fixed in advance, the sailors were allowed to open the canvas sacks in which their treasures were stored (it was known as "getting out the sacks "). Then they spread out all their little belongings, which had been folded inside with a comical care, and the deck of the *Primauguet* took on all at once the appearance of a bazaar. They opened their needle-work boxes, and sewed little patches very neatly on holes in their clothes, which the continual play of strong muscles soon wore out. There were some of them who stripped to the skin and sat gravely mending their shirts; others, who pressed their big collars in a rather extraordinary way (by sitting on them for a long time); others who took from their writing cases poor little faded yellow papers, bearing the postmarks of remote little corners of Brittany or of the Basque country, and settled down to read: they were letters from mothers, sisters, sweethearts, who dwelt in villages at the other side of the earth.

And, later on, at the sound of a particular whistle, which signified: " Pack up the sacks! " all this disappeared as by enchantment, folded, packed and re-consigned once more to the bottom of the hold, in the numbered lockers which the terrible sergeants-at-arms came and locked with little iron chains.

Looking at them, one might have been deceived by their wise and patient airs, if one had not known them better; seeing them so absorbed in these occupations of little girls, in these unpackings of dolls, it was impossible to imagine what these same young men might become capable of once they were allowed on shore.

There was only one hour of inevitable melancholy; it was when the evening prayer had been said, when the Bretons had finished making the sign of the cross and the sun had set: at that hour, assuredly, many of them thought of home.

Even in the regions of wonderful light, there is still that vague hour between day and night, which brings always and everywhere a touch of sadness; then one might see sailors' heads turned involuntarily in the direction of that last band of light which persisted in the west, very low, touching the line of the waters.

A variegated band always; on the horizon there was first a dull red, above, a little orange, above again, a little pale green, a trail of phosphorescence, and then it merged with the dull greys above, with the shades of darkness and obscurity. Some last reflections of a mournful yellow lingered on the sea, which glistened still here and there before taking on the neutral colours of night; this last oblique glance of day, cast on the deserted depths, had something a little sinister, and, in spite of oneself, there came a sense of desolation in the immensity of the waters. It was the hour of secret revolts and wringing of hearts. It was the hour when the sailors had the vague notion that their life was strange and against nature, when they thought of their sequestrated and wasted youth. Some far-off image of a woman passed before their eyes, wreathed in a languishing charm, in a delectable sweetness. Or perhaps there came to them, with a sudden trouble of the senses, a dream of some senseless orgy of lust and alcohol, in which they would seek compensation and appeasement when next they were let loose on shore. . . .

But, afterwards, came night itself, warm, full of stars, and the fleeting impression was forgotten; and the sailors gathered in the bow of the ship and, sitting or lying there, began to sing.

There were some among the topmen who knew long and very pleasing songs, the choruses of which were readily learnt by heart. And in the sonorous silence of the night the voices sounded fine and vibrant.

There was, too, an old petty officer who never tired of telling to a certain attentive little circle interminable stories; stories of adventures which had really happened once upon a time to some handsome topmen whom amorous princesses had carried away to their castles.

And still the *Primauguet* sped on, tracing behind her, in the darkness, a vague white trail which gradually disappeared like the trail of a meteor. All night long she sped, without resting or sleeping; only, her large wings lost at night their sea-gull whiteness and outlined then, in fantastic shadow against the diffused light of the sky, the points and scallops of a bat's wing.

But speed on as she might, she was always in the middle of the same great circle, which seemed eternally to reform, to widen and to follow her.

Sometimes this circle was dark and traced all round its clean-cut inexorable line which stopped at the first stars in the sky. Sometimes the immense contour was softened by mists which mingled sea and sky together; and then it seemed as if we were sailing in a kind of grey-blue globe, spangled with stars, and the wonder was that we never encountered its fugitive walls.

The expanse was full of the soft sounds of water; it rustled continuously and to infinity, but in a restrained and almost silent manner; it gave out a powerful, unseizable sound, such as might be made by an orchestra of thousands of strings touched by bows very, very lightly and with great mystery.

At times, the southern stars shone out with surprising brilliancy; the great nebulæ sparkled like a dust of mother-of-pearl, all the colours of the night seemed to be illumined, in transparency, by strange lights.   One might have imagined oneself, at these moments, in a fairyland where everything was lit up for some immense apotheosis; and one asked oneself: " What is the meaning of all this splendour, what is going to happen, what is the matter? " . . . But no, there was nothing, ever; it was simply the region of the tropics and this was its way.   There was nothing but the deserted seas, and everlastingly the circular expanse, absolutely empty. . . .

These nights were indeed exquisite summer nights, mild, infinitely mild, milder than the mildest of our nights of June.   And they troubled a little all these men, the eldest of whom was not yet thirty years of age.

The warm darkness brought thoughts of love which were not of their seeking.   There were moments when they came near to weakening again in a troubling dream; they felt the need of opening their arms to some desired human form, of clasping it with a strong and forceful infinite tenderness.

But no, no one, nothing. . . . It was necessary to pull themselves together, to remain alone, to turn over on the hard planks of the wooden deck, and to think of something else, to begin to sing again. . . . And then the songs, merry or sad, rang out more strongly than before, in the emptiness of the sea.

Nevertheless it was very pleasant on this forecastle during these evenings at sea. The fresh wind of the night blew in our faces, the virgin breezes which had never passed over land, which bore no living effluvium, which were without odour. Lying there, one lost little by little all notion of time and place, all notion of everything but speed, which is always a pleasing thing, even when you are without a goal and know not whither you are going.

They had no goal, these sailors, and they knew not whither they were going. What did it matter anyhow since nowhere were they allowed to set foot on shore? They were ignorant of the direction of this rapid course and of the infinite extent of the solitudes in which they were; but it amused them, nevertheless, to be going full speed ahead in the bluish darkness, to feel that they were moving very rapidly. As they sang their evening songs, their eyes were on the bowsprit, ever thrusting forward, with its two little horns and shape of drawn cross bow, which leapt over the sea, skimming the noisy waters in the lightsome fashion of a flying fish.

CHAPTER XCIII

ON the *Primauguet*, my dear Yves was above reproach, as he had promised us. The officers treated him with a rather special consideration on account of his general bearing and manner which were no longer those of the others. But he remained, nevertheless, in the first rank of that hardy band of which the chief boatswain said with pride:

" It is half shark; it knows no fear."

He had resumed his old-time habit of coming, silent-footed, to my room in the evening, in the hours when I abandoned it to him. He would settle down to read my letters and my papers, knowing well that he was at liberty to look at them all; he learnt to understand the marine charts, and amused himself by marking points on them and measuring distances. Very often he used to write to his wife, and it happened that his little letters, interrupted by a call aloft, remained mixed with my papers. I found one one day which was intended no doubt to be placed in a second envelope and on which he had put this quaint address:

" To Madame Marie Kermadec, c/o her parents, at Trémeulé in Toulven, Country of Brittany, Commune of Wolves, Parish of Squirrels, on the right, under the largest oak."

It was hard to imagine my great big Yves writing these childish things.

This was his first long absence since his marriage. Half a world away, he fell to thinking much of his young wife who already had suffered so sorely on his account and who had loved him so well; she appeared to him now, at this great distance, under a new aspect.

CHAPTER XCIV

In July—the worst month of the southern winter— we left the region of the trade winds and made our way to Valparaiso.

There, I was due to leave the *Primauguet* and to embark on a large sailing ship which was returning to Brest after a tour round the world.

It was called the *Navarin*; all the men of our ship who had finished their term of service were embarking on it also: among others, Barrada, who was going to Bordeaux, with his belt lined with gold, to marry his little Spanish sweetheart.

Very abruptly, as always, I said good-bye to Yves, recommending him once more to all, and left for France by way of Cape Horn.

CHAPTER XCV

20th October, 1882.

I REMEMBER very well this day passed in Brittany. We three, under the grey sky, roaming the woods of Toulven, Marie, Anne and I.

My eyes still dazzled by sun and blue sea, and this Brittany, seen again so quickly and so suddenly for a few brief hours, absolutely as in the dreams we had of it at sea. . . . It seemed to me that I understood its charm for the first time.

And Yves was at the other side of the world, in the great ocean. How strange it was to feel that he was so far away and that I was here without him in these Toulven lanes!

We rushed about, all three, like people possessed, in the green lanes, under the grey sky, the large coifs of Marie and Anne blown back by the wind. For night was closing in and we wanted during this last hour to gather the harvest of ferns and heather, which, on the following morning, I was going to carry off to Paris. Oh! these departures, always coming too soon, changing everything, casting a sadness over the things you are about to leave, and plunging you afterwards into the unknown!

This time again, there was the pervading melancholy of the late autumn: the air was still mild, the verdure admirable, with almost the intense green of the tropics, but the Breton sky was there, grey and sombre, and already the savour of dead leaves and of winter. . . .

We had left little Pierre in the house so that we might walk more quickly. On our way we picked the last foxgloves, the last red silenes, the last scabious.

In the sunken lanes, in the green darkness, we passed long-haired old men, and women in cloth bodices embroidered with rows of eyes.

There were mysterious crossways in the woods. In the distance one could see the wooded hills ranged in monotonous lines, the unchanging ageless horizon of the country of Toulven, the same horizon as the Celts must have seen, the farthest planes losing themselves in the grey obscurities, in bluish tones tending to black.

And with what pleasure I had greeted my little Pierre, as I came along this road of Toulven! I had seen the little fellow in the distance and failed to recognize him; and he had run to meet me, skipping like a young goat. They had told him: "That is your godfather coming yonder," and he had rushed off at once. He had grown and improved in looks and had a more enterprising not to say boisterous air.

It was at this visit I saw for the first and last time little Yvonne, Yves' little daughter who was born after our departure, and who made on this earth only a brief appearance of a few months. She was very like him; the same eyes, the same expression. It was strange to see this resemblance of a small girl-baby to a man.

One day she returned to the mysterious regions whence she had come, called away suddenly by a childish malady, which neither the old nurse nor the learned woman brought in from Toulven had understood. And they laid her in the churchyard, the eyes that were so like Yves' closed for ever.

We had spent in the woods our two hours of daylight. It was not until after supper that Marie and I went to see, in the moonlight, what was to be their new home.

On the site of the oat field which we had measured in June of the preceding year stood now the four walls of Yves' house; it had yet no shutters, no floor, no roof, and, in the moonlight, looked like a ruin.

We sat down on some stones inside, alone together for the first time.

It was of Yves we talked, needless to say. She asked me anxiously about him, about his future, imagining that I knew better than she this husband whom she adored with a kind of fear, without understanding him. And I reassured her, for I was very hopeful: the sea-rover had a good and honest heart; and if we could touch him there, we ought in the end to succeed.

Anne appeared suddenly, having approached noiselessly in order to startle us:

"Oh, Marie!" she said, "move away quickly! See what an ugly shadow you are making behind you!"

We had not noticed it, but in the moonlight her head, with the wings of her coif moving in the wind, cast behind her, on the new wall, a shadow in the form of a very large and very ugly bat. It was enough to bring us misfortune.

In Toulven there was a music of bagpipes. To

reach the inn, to which they were both escorting me, we had to pass through an unexpected fête, going on in the moonlight. It was the wedding of a well-to-do couple and there was dancing in the open, on the square. I stopped, with Anne and Marie, to watch the long chain of the gavotte whirl and pass, led by the shrill voice of the pipes. The full moon made whiter the coifs of the women which flitted past us as if carried away by wind and speed; on the breasts of the men we caught the fleeting glitter of embroidered gorgets and silver spangles.

At the farther end of Toulven we came upon another concourse. It did not seem natural, this animation in the village, at night; more coifs again, hurrying, pressing forward in order to get a better view; for a band of pilgrims was returning from Lourdes. They entered the village singing hymns.

"There have been two miracles, sir; we heard so this morning by telegraph."

I turned round and saw that it was Pierre Kerbras, Anne's sweetheart, who vouchsafed us this information.

The pilgrims passed, their large rosaries about their necks; behind came two infirm old women, who, for their part, had not been cured, and who were being carried in men's arms.

The following morning old Corentin, Anne and little Pierre, in their Sunday clothes, accompanied me in Pierre Kerbras' wagonette to the station at Bannalec.

In the compartment I entered two English women were already installed.

Little Pierre, his happy face the colour of a ripe peach, was lifted up to the carriage window to kiss me good-bye, and he burst out laughing at the sight of a little bulldog which the women carried in their blazoned travelling-bag. He was sorry enough that I was going away; but this little dog in the bag seemed to him so comical that he could not get over it. And the old ladies smiled also, and said that little Pierre was " a very beautiful baby."

And this was the last of Brittany for a long time; I had spent some twenty hours there, and, on the following morning, it was already far away from me.

CHAPTER XCVI

A Letter from Yves

" MELBOURNE, *September*, 1882.

" DEAR BROTHER,—I write to let you know we have reached Australia; we have had a very fine voyage and to-morrow we are to leave for Japan; for, you know, we have had instructions to pay a visit to that country.

" I found here two letters from you and two also from my wife; but I am looking forward to the one you will write me when you have been to Toulven.

" Dear brother, your successor on board is just like you; he is very considerate with the sailors. As regards Mr. Plunkett's successor, he is rather severe, but not with me; on the contrary. Mr. Plunkett told me he would recommend me to him when he left and I think he must have done so. The others and the second-in-command are still the same; they often speak to me of you and ask me for news of you.

"The captain has called upon me to act as boatswain since we buried poor Marsano, of Nice, who was found dead one morning in his hammock at the réveillé. And I like the work very much.

"Dear brother, the men have twice been allowed to go ashore, at San Francisco, and you will be glad to know that, with you away, I have not even given in my name to go with them. As a matter of fact, on the second night, the topmen had a great row with some Germans, and knives were used.

"I have also to tell you, dear brother, that your name has not yet been removed from above the door of your room, and I think it must have been quite forgotten. And in the evening I make my way along the spar-deck for the pleasure of seeing it.

"Next year, when we return, I hope I may have a long leave to go and see my wife and my little Pierre and my little daughter; but it will be all too short in any case, and I shall never have any real leisure until I get my pension. On the other hand, when I am old enough to put aside the blue collar, my little Pierre will be thinking of going to sea himself in his turn; or perhaps there will be a place for me a little farther away, in the direction of the pond, near the church; you know what place I mean.

"Dear brother, you think I am taking my note from you? But no, I think as I have always thought.

"As for the 'coco-nut heads'[1] I fear I must give

[1] Very ugly human heads made by the convicts in Caledonia out of coco-nuts, in which they fix eyes and

up all idea of them, for we shall not touch Caledonia; but perhaps, later on, I may be able to return and buy some. If you should pass by the Gulf of Juan, you would give me great pleasure if you would go to Vallauris and obtain for me two of those candlesticks which they make there, and which have owls' heads on them (the *parrots of France*, you know). I should like very much to have some in my home. I am very eager, brother, to furnish my little house.

"Among the many things which make me sad when I awaken in the morning, that which grieves me most is the thought that my mother cannot be persuaded to come and live at Toulven. It seems to me that if I could get leave and go to see her, I should certainly be able to induce her to come. But, against this, I should then have no one belonging to me at Plouherzel; and that again is a thing I cannot bear to contemplate; for after all Plouherzel is our home, you know. If I could believe what you have often told me on the subject of a life after death, then, assuredly, I could still be contented enough. But it seems to me that you yourself do not believe very much in it. Funnily enough, though, I am afraid of ghosts, and I rather think, brother, that you are afraid of them, too.

"I ask you to forgive these dirty sheets I am sending you, but it is not altogether my fault that they are in this condition. As you know I no longer have your desk now to write my letters on like an officer. I was writing to you peacefully enough at the end of my night watch on the lockers in the

teeth and hair. Yves wanted them for his staircase at Toulven.

bow, when the idiot Le Hir came and knocked over my candle. I have not time to copy out my letter neatly as sometimes I do, in the way you have praised. I am writing hurriedly and I ask you to forgive the hasty scrawl.

"We are leaving at daybreak to-morrow for Japan; but I will send my letter by the pilot who is coming to take us out.

" Your affectionate brother,
" YVES KERMADEC.

"Dear brother, I cannot tell you how much I love you."

CHAPTER XCVII

December, 1882.

I WAS walking on the quay at Bordeaux. A very smart person came up to me, hat doffed, holding out his hand: Barrada! A Barrada transformed, having shed his beard and his one-and-thirty years at the same time, no doubt, as he laid aside his blue collar: with cheeks carefully shaved, a budding moustache, and the air of a young lover of twenty.

The old distinction and beauty of line were still there, but his face now was happier and kinder, as if brightened by a deep joy.

He had married at last his little Spanish sweetheart. The gold he used to carry in his belt had furnished their home; and he had found occupation as a stevedore, a very lucrative calling, it seems, in which he could use to perfection his great strength and instinctive "handiness." He made me promise solemnly that on the return of the *Primauguet* I would call at Bordeaux with Yves and come and see him.

He, at any rate, was happy!

And the end of this wanderer over the sea made me think. I asked myself whether my poor Yves, who, with a heart as good, had offended far less against the laws of decent society, might not also find one day a little happiness. . . .

CHAPTER XCVIII

Telegram: " Toulon, 3rd April, 1883.—To Yves Kermadec, on board the *Primauguet*, Brest. You have been appointed mate. All good wishes.

" PIERRE."

It was his joyous welcome, his home-coming feast, for, only twenty-four hours before, the *Primauguet*, returned from its distant cruise in the Pacific, had come to anchor in the waters of France.

And these golden stripes which I sent to Yves by telegraph, he did not water them, as he had watered formerly his stripes of wool. No, times had changed; he took refuge in the spar-deck, in the corner where his sack and locker were, which he regarded as his little home; he hurried down to this quiet spot in order that he might be alone to contemplate this happiness which had come to him, to read and read again this blessed little blue paper which had opened before him an entirely new era.

It was so wonderful, so unexpected, after his past bad conduct!

I had been to Paris to ask this favour, intriguing hard for my adopted brother, and making myself answerable for his future conduct.   A woman friend had been good enough to exert in my cause her very powerful influence, and, with her help, the promotion of Yves was carried by assault, difficult though it was.

And Yves could not cease from contemplating his good fortune in all its aspects. . . . First, instead of asking for a short leave which might perhaps have been given to him very grudgingly, now, with his gold stripes he could depart straightway for Toulven; he would be put on the reserve list for three months at least, perhaps for four; he would have the whole summer to spend with his wife and son, in the little house which was now completed, and where they were only waiting for him to enter into occupation. . . . And secondly, they were quite rich, which was by no means a drawback. . . .

Never in the life of this poor wandering toiler had there come an hour so happy, a joy so deep as that which his brother Pierre had just sent him by telegraph. . . .

CHAPTER XCIX

When the winds brought me back to Brittany again, it was in the last days of May, when the Breton spring was at its fairest.

Yves had already been six weeks in his little house at Toulven, arranging my room, and preparing everything for my arrival.

The ship on which I had embarked had left the Mediterranean and was going north in the Atlantic, bound for the northern ports and Brest where it was to be laid up.

18*th May, at sea*. Already one feels that Brittany is near. It is fine still, but the day is one of those fine Breton days which are calm and melancholy. The smooth sea is of a pale blue, the salt air is fresh and smells of seaweed; over everything there is a veil of bluish mist, very transparent and very tenuous.

At eight o'clock in the morning we round the point of Penmarc'h. The Celtic rocks, the tall sad cliffs become visible little by little and draw nearer.

Now there are real banks of mist—but very light still, summer mists—which rest everywhere on the distances of the horizon.

At one o'clock, the channel of the Toulinguets, and then we enter Brest.

19*th May*. Eight days' leave. At midday I am in the train, on my way to Toulven.

Rain all the way over the Breton countryside. The meadows, the shady valleys are full of water.

From Bannalec to Toulven is an hour's drive through the woods.   With my eyes fixed in front of me I watch for the granite steeple of the church in the distance of the green horizon.

And now it appears reflected deep below in the mournful pool.   The weather has cleared and the sky is blue again, a pale blue.

Toulven! . . . The diligence stops.   Yves is there waiting for me, holding little Pierre by the hand.

We look at each other—and our first impulse is to laugh, on account of our moustaches.   Our faces are altered, and we seem odd to each other.   We had not seen each other since permission had been given to sailors to leave the upper lip unshaved. Yves expressed the opinion that it made us look much more knowing.

Then we shook hands.

And what a fine little fellow Pierre has become! So tall, so strong!   We set off together, going through Toulven, where the good folk know me and come to their doors to watch us pass.   We make our way through the narrow grey street, between the ancient houses, between the walls of massive granite. I recognize the old woman with the owl-like profile who presided at the birth of my godson; she nods to me from an open window.   The large coifs, the collarettes, the spangles on the bodices, stand out, in the deep embrasures against the dark backgrounds, and the impression I receive as I pass by is one peculiar to Brittany, of olden times, of days remote and dead.

Little Pierre, whose hands we hold, walks now like a man. He had said nothing at first, a little overcome at seeing me again, but presently he begins to talk; upturning towards me his round face he looks at me as at a friend with whom he may share his thoughts, and a sweet small voice with which I am not yet very familiar pipes out with a strong Breton accent:

" Godfather, have you brought me my sheep? "

Fortunately I had remembered my promise of a year ago; this sheep on wheels for little Pierre is in my trunk. And I have brought also some candlesticks with owls' heads on them (heads of the *parrots of France*) which I had promised to my other baby —Yves.

And here is the house, gay and white and new, with its Breton window frames, its green shutters, its attic store-room, and, behind, the horizon of the woods.

We enter. Below in the open-hearthed kitchen, Marie and little Corentine are waiting for us.

But, immediately, Yves hurries me away, impatient that I should see their handsome white room upstairs, with its muslin curtains and its cherry wood furniture.

And then he opens another door.

" And now, brother, you are in your own room? "

And he looks at me, anxious to see the effect produced, after all the pains his wife and he have taken to ensure that I should find everything to my taste.

I enter, touched, moved. It is all white, my room, and filled with a delicious fragrance. There are flowers everywhere, flowers which they have gone

very far to find for me; in vases on the mantelpiece,
bunches of mignonette and large bouquets of sweetpeas; in the fireplace, a mass of heather.

But they could not bring themselves to put in my
room the old furniture, the old Breton odds and
ends, and they excused themselves saying they had
found nothing that seemed to them nice enough and
suitable enough; and so they had gone to Quimper
and bought me a bed like their own, in cherry wood,
a light wood, bright and slightly reddish in colour.
The tables and chairs are of the same wood. The
smallest details have been arranged with tender
thought; on the walls, in gilt frames, are drawings
which I had made in earlier days and a large
photograph of the tower of Saint Pol-de-Léon,
which I had given Yves at the time when we were
together in the misty waters of the North.

The boards of the floor are as clean as newly-sawn
wood.

"You see, brother, everything is as spotless as on
board," says Yves, who himself has taken the
greatest pains to make it so, and who removes his
shoes whenever he goes up so that he may not dirty
the stairs.

And I must see everything, go everywhere, even
into the store-room where the potatoes are laid by,
and the logs of wood for the winter; even into the
little vestibule of the staircase where is suspended,
like the *ex-voto* of a sailor in a chapel of the Virgin,
a miniature ship which Yves had made during his
spare time in the crow's nest of the *Primauguet;*
and finally into the garden where the strawberries
and various green things are beginning to push up
their fresh shoots in long neat rows.

Now we sit down at the table, Yves, Marie, little Corentine, little Pierre and I, round the spotless white cloth on which the dinner has been placed. And Yves, my brother Yves, becomes self-conscious and nervous all at once in his rôle of master of the house. And so it is I who have to carve, and, as it is the first time in my life, I get a little confused too.

At this dinner, I eat to please them; but this great happiness which I feel here near me and of which in some small measure I am the cause, this deep gratitude which surrounds me, all this moves me very strangely. To be in the midst of these rare things brings me the surprise of a new, delightful experience.

"You know," Yves says to me, low as if in confidence, " I go with her to mass now every Sunday."

And he makes in the direction of his wife a little grimace of childlike submission, very comical to see in one so serious. But his manner with Marie has quite changed, and I saw as soon as I entered that love had come at last to make its home for good and all in the new house. And my dear friends, therefore, have attained all that is best on earth. As Yves said " All that was wanted now was that the pendulum of time should stop so that this great happiness of their fulfilled dreams might never leave them."

They also are silent in their happiness, as if they feared they might frighten it away if they spoke too loud or too lightheartedly about it.

Besides we have to speak of the dead, of that little Yvonne who departed last autumn without waiting

for the return of the *Primauguet* and whom Yves
never saw; of old Corentin, her grandfather, who
had found the cold weather of December too much
for him.

It is Marie who speaks:

"He became very difficult towards the end, he
who had always been so considerate. He said we
did not know how to look after him, and he asked
continually for his son Yves: 'Oh! if Yves were
here he would help me; he would lift me in his
strong arms and turn me over in my bed.' On the
last night he called him without ceasing."

And Yves replied:

"What grieves me most when I think of our
father, is that we were a little angry with each other
on the day I went away, in connection with the
settlement, you know. You cannot believe how
often the recollection of that dispute with him comes
into my mind."

Dinner is finished. It is evening, the long mild
evening of May. We are walking, Yves and I,
towards the church, to pay a visit to a white cross
which stands there on a little flower-decked mound:

Yvonne Kermadec, thirteen months.

"They say that she was very like me," says Yves.

And this resemblance of the dead infant to him
makes him very thoughtful.

As we look at the cross, the mound and the
flowers, we both think of this mystery: a little baby
girl who was of his blood, his issue, who had his
eyes, and . . . probably, too, his nature, and who
was given back so soon to the Breton earth. It is
as if something of himself had already gone from

T

him to mingle with the dust; it was like an earnest-money which he had already given to eternal nothingness. . . .

In four years, this little cross which may be seen now from the distance, will exist no longer; Yvonne and her mound and her flowers will be swept away. Even her little bones will be gathered up and mixed with the others, the bones of those long dead, under the church, in the ossuary.

For four years still the cross will remain, and those who pass may read this name of a little child. . . .

It stands on the edge of the pond.   It is reflected in the deep, stagnant water, by the side of the tall grey steeple.   On the mound the blooming carnations make white tufts, already indistinct in the oncoming darkness.   The pond is like a mirror, pale yellow, of the colour of the dying daylight, of the sunset sky; and, all round, is the line, already dark, of the woods.

The flowers of the tombs give out their soft perfumes of the evening.   A mild stillness surrounds us and seems to close in upon us. . . .

In the distance we hear the hooting of the owls, and we cannot distinguish now little Yvonne's white carnations. . . . The summer night has come.

Suddenly a loud noise startles us, amid this silence in which we were thinking of the dead.   It is the Angelus sounding, very close, above us, in the steeple; and the air is filled with the deep vibrations of the bell.

Yet we had seen no one enter the church which is shut and dark.

" Who is ringing? " asks Yves anxiously.   " Who

can be ringing? I would not do it, ever. . . . I would not enter the church at this hour, not even for all the gold in the world! "

. . . We leave the cemetery; there is too much noise and the Angelus sounds strange there; it awakens unexpected echoes, in the waters of the pond, in the enclosure of the dead, in the darkness. Not that we are afraid of the poor little tomb with the white carnations; but there are the others, these mounds of turf which are all about us, these graves of men and women unknown. . . .

Ten o'clock. I am going to sleep for the first time under the roof of my brother Yves.

Later. We have already said good night, but he returns and opens my door.

" The flowers. They may not be good for you; it has just occurred to us. . . ."

And he takes them all away, the mignonette, the sweetpeas, even the bunches of heather.

CHAPTER C

THE " pendulum of time " has continued its swing. It even seems that it has moved more quickly than usual, for the week's leave which had been given me is almost over.

Every day we spend in the woods. The weather is splendid. The heather, the foxgloves, the red silenes, all are in flower.

There had been a great " pardon " on Sunday, one of the most famous of this region of Brittany:

it was held near the chapel of *Our Lady of Good Tidings*—which stands alone in the heart of the woods as if it had been sleeping there, forgotten, since the middle ages.

It happened that the day before, the Saturday, we had sat down in the shade, Yves, little Pierre and I, near the church, in the hour of the great calm of noon. A very silent spot, above which the ancient oaks and beeches linked, as if they had been arms, their great moss-grown branches.

Two women had come, one young, the other old and decrepit; they wore the costume of Rosporden and seemed to have travelled far. They carried large keys.

And they opened the old sanctuary, which remains closed throughout the year, and began to prepare the altar for the feast of the following day.

In the green half-light of the windows and the trees, we saw them busying themselves about the statues of the old saints, dusting them, wiping them; and then sweeping the flagstones covered with dust and saltpetre.

At the foot of Our Lady someone, out of piety, had placed a skull, found, no doubt, in the earth of the wood. Greenish-looking, the cranium staved in, it gazed at us from the bottom of the chapel, with its two black eye sockets.

" Tell me, godfather, what is that? . . . Did someone find that face in the earth? . . ."

Little Pierre is vaguely disturbed by this thing, the like of which he had never seen; as if it was for him the first revelation of an order of sinister objects dwelling under the earth. . . .

The weather, for this day of pardon, was a little dull, but delightful nevertheless.

For ten hours, the bagpipes played in front of the chapel, under the great oaks, and gavottes were danced on the mossy turf.

That indescribable quality of Breton summers, which is somehow melancholy, is, if one may so express it, a compound of many things: the charm of the long, warm days, rarer here than elsewhere and sooner over; the tall-growing herbage fresh and green, with the extreme profusion of red flowers; and then the sentiment of olden times, which seems to slumber here, to permeate everything.

Old land of Toulven, great woods where the black fir trees, trees of the north, mingle already with the oaks and beeches; Breton countrysides, which seem to be wrapt still in the past. . . .

Great rocks covered with grey lichen, as fine as an old man's beard; plains in which the granite crops out of the ancient soil, plains of purple heather. . . .

They are impressions of tranquillity, of appeasement, which this country brings me; and also an aspiration towards a more complete repose under the mossy turf, at the foot of the chapels which are in the woods. And, with Yves, all this is vaguer, more inexpressible, but more intense also, as with me when I was a child.

To see us sitting together in the woods in the calm of these fine summer days, one would never imagine what our youth had been, what life we had lived, nor what terrible scenes there had been between us formerly, when first our two natures, very different and very alike, had come in conflict one with the other.

Every evening before we go to bed, we play with little Pierre a Toulven game, amusing enough, which consists in holding one another by the chin and reciting, without laughing, a long rigmarole: " By the beard of Minette I hold you. The first of us two who shall laugh . . . etc." At this game little Pierre is always caught.

After that come the gymnastics. Yves goes through the performance with his son, turning him over, making him " go about," head down, legs in the air, at arm's length, then raising him very high. " Tell me, little Pierre, when will you have arms like mine? Tell me!" "Oh, never; never arms like yours, father; I shall not suffer hardship enough for that, I am sure."

And when Yves, dishevelled, tired from having romped so much, says, as he readjusts his clothes, in his most serious way: "Now then, little Pierre has finished his gymnastics for the present," little Pierre comes to me with that smile which always gets for him what he wants: " It is your turn, god-father; come!" And the gymnastics begin again.

CHAPTER CI

THE pendulum of time, inexorable, swings on.   In
a few hours I shall have to leave, and soon my
brother Yves will depart also, both of us for distant
parts, for the unknown.

It is the last day, the last evening.   Yves, little
Pierre and I are on our way to the cottage of the
old Keremenens, where I am to say good-bye to
grandmother Marianne.

She lives alone, now, under her moss-grown roof,
under the spreading vault of the great oaks.   Pierre
Kerbras and Anne, who were married in the spring,
are building in the village a proper house in granite,
like that of Yves.   All the children have departed.

Poor little cottage in which the white coifs and
collarettes moved about so joyously on the day of
the baptism!   All that is over; now, the cottage is
empty and silent.   We sit down on the old oak
benches, resting our elbows on the table on which
the great baptismal feast was served.   The old
grandmother is on a stool, spinning at her distaff,
her head bowed, looking already decrepit and
forlorn.

Although the sun is not yet very low, inside the
cottage it is dark.

Around us, none but old-fashioned things, poor
and primitive.   Large rosaries are hung on the
rough granite of the walls; in corners, lost in
shadow, one sees the oak logs amassed for the

winter, and old household utensils, blackened and dusty, in ancient and simple forms.

Never had we realized so clearly that all this is of the past and far from us.

It is the old Brittany of an earlier time, almost dead.

Through the chimney filters the light of the sky, green tones fall from above on the stones of the hearth, and through the open door appears the Breton lane, with a ray of the setting sun on the honeysuckle and the ferns.

We become dreamers, Yves and I, on this visit we have come to pay to the dwelling of the grand-parents.

Besides, grandmother Marianne speaks only Breton. From time to time Yves addresses her in this language of the past; she replies, smiles, seems pleased to see us; but the conversation quickly flags and silence returns.

Vague melancholy of the evening, dreams of far-off days in this old dwelling which soon will collapse by the roadside, which will fall into ruin like its old inmates, and which no one will ever rebuild.

Little Pierre is with us. He is very fond of this little cottage and of this old grandmother, who spoils him with adoration. He loves especially the little oaken cradle, a work of another century, in which he was put when he was born. He is longer than his cradle now and uses it, sitting within, as a see-saw, looking about him with his wide-open dark eyes. And now his grandmother, stooping near him, her back bent under her frilled collarette, begins to rock him herself to amuse him. And as she rocks she sings, and he, every now and then, interrupts the quavering notes with a burst of his child's laughter.

Boudoul galaïchen! boudoul galaïch du!

Sing, poor old woman, with your broken, trembling voice, sing the ancient lullaby, the air which comes from the distant night of dead generations, and which your grandchildren will no longer know!

Boudoul, boudoul! Galaïchen, galaïch du!

One expects to see gnomes and fairies descend by the wide chimney, with the light that comes from above.

Outside, the sun gilds stills the branches of the oaks, the honeysuckle and the ferns.

Inside, in the lonely cottage, all is mysterious and dark.

Boudoul, boudoul! Galaïchen, galaïch du!

Rock your little grandson, rock him still, old woman in white frilled collar! Soon the Breton songs, and the old Bretons who sing them, will be no more!

And little Pierre joins his hands to say his evening prayer.

Word for word, in a very sweet voice which has a strong Toulven accent, he repeats, watching us the while, all that his grandmother knows of French:

"Oh God, and blessed Virgin Mary, and good Saint Anne, I pray to you for my father, for my mother, for my godfather, for my grandparents, for my little sister Yvonne. . . ."

"For my Uncle Goulven who is far away at sea," adds Yves in a grave voice.

And still more solemnly:

"For my grandmother at Plouherzel."

"For my grandmother at Plouherzel," repeats little Pierre.

And then he waits for something more to repeat, keeping his hands joined.

But Yves is almost in tears at the poignant recollection which has suddenly come to him of his mother, of the cottage in which he was born, of his village of Plouherzel, which his son scarcely knows and which he himself will perhaps never see again. Life is like that for the children of the coast, for sailors; they go away, the exigencies of their calling separate them from beloved parents who scarcely know how to write to them and whom afterwards they never see.

I look at Yves, and, as we understand each other without speaking, I can imagine very well what is passing in his mind.

To-day he is happy beyond his dream, many sombre things have been distanced and conquered, and yet, and yet . . . and afterwards? Here he is now plunged suddenly into I know not what dream of past and future, into a strange and unexpected melancholy! And afterwards?

Boudoul galaïchen! boudoul galaïch du!

sings the old woman, her back bent under her white frilled collar.

And afterwards? . . . Only little Pierre is inclined to laugh. He turns from one side to the other his vivacious head, bronzed and vigorous; merriment, the flame of a life quite new are still in his large dark eyes.

And afterwards? . . . All is dark in the abandoned cottage; it seems as if the objects there are talking mysteriously among themselves of the past; night is closing in around us on the great woods.

And afterwards? . . . Little Pierre will grow up and sail the seas, and we, my brother, we shall pass away and all that we have loved with us—our old mothers first—then everything and we ourselves, the old mothers of the Breton cottages as those of the towns, and old Brittany also, and everything, all the things of this world!

Boudoul galaïchen! boudoul galaïch du!

Night falls and a sadness unexpected, profound, weighs upon our hearts. . . . And yet, to-day we are happy.

CHAPTER CII

And the Celts mourned three barren rocks, under a lowering sky, in the heart of a gulf dotted with islets.
GUSTAVE FLAUBERT, SALAMMBÔ.

Yves and I take our departure, leaving little Pierre with his grandmother. We follow the green lane, under the vault of oaks and beeches, hearing in the distance, in the sonorousness of the evening, the noise of the rocking of the ancient cradle and the old lullaby and the outburst of child's laughter.

Outside, there is still daylight; the sun, very low, gilds the tranquil countryside.

"Let us go as far as the chapel of Saint Eloi," says Yves.

The chapel is on the top of the hill; very old it is, and corroded with moss, bearded with lichen, alone always, closed and mysterious in the midst of the woods.

It opens but once in the year, for the "pardon" of the horses, which are brought hither in great numbers, at the hour of a low mass which is said here for them.   This "pardon" was held quite recently and the grass is still trodden down by the hoofs of the beasts which came.

This evening there is a strange tranquillity round the chapel.   The wooded horizons, stretching out into the distance, are very peaceful, as if they were about to fall asleep.   It seems also that it might be the evening of our own life, and that all that we had to do now was to rest here for ever, watching the night descend on the Breton countrysides, to let ourselves sink gently into this sleep of nature.

"All the same," says Yves, very thoughtful, " I feel sure that it will be to somewhere over there (*over there* means Plouherzel) that I shall return when I get old, so that they may lay me near Kergrist Chapel; you know, where I showed you? Yes, I am sure I shall find my way there to die."

Kergrist Chapel, in the district of Goëlo, under a lowering sky; the sea-water lake, and, in the middle, the granite islets, the great squatting beast asleep on the grey plain. . . . I can see the place now, as it appeared to me, many years ago already, on a winter's day.   And I remember that there is Yves' native land, there is the earth which awaits him.   When he is far away at sea, at night, in hours of danger, there is the grave of which he dreams.

"Yves, my dear brother, we are two great

children, I assure you. Often very merry when there is no cause, here now we are sad and talking nonsense at a moment when peace and happiness by rare good fortune have come to us. I doubt very much if the newness of the experience is sufficient excuse.

" For who to look at us would imagine we were capable of dreaming these foolish things in our waking hours, simply because the night is falling and there is stillness in the woods?

" Think of it! We are neither of us more than thirty-two years old. Before us yet there should be many more years of life, years that will be filled with travel, with danger, with suffering. To each of us will come sunshine, and beauty, and love . . . and, perhaps, who knows?—between us there may be again scenes, rebellions, struggles! "

In many fewer words than there are above all this crossed his dream.

And he answered me with an air of sad reproach:
" But you know well, brother, that I am altered now, and that there is *one thing* which is finished for ever. There is no need to speak to me of that."

And I grip the hand of my brother Yves trying to smile as one who had completest confidence.

The stories of real life ought to be able to be finished at will like the stories in books. . . .

THE END

T - #0018 - 270225 - C0 - 234/156/16 [18] - CB - 9780710308634 - Gloss Lamination